Deadly
Stroke

Philip Hayward

Cover design by Jeanne Clemente Kelly
www.PhilipHaywardBooks.com

For Polly

PROLOGUE

All was right in Anders Martin's world.

Atop his stiletto-narrow racing shell, Martin sliced through the glassy water of the Potomac with long and easy strokes. That it was 5:15 in the morning meant little to accomplished rowers like Martin. Even though the sun would not rise above the Maryland shoreline for another two hours, he could discern objects drifting by – plastic water bottles, children's toys, sections of trees, and enough fast-food packaging to open a franchise.

He had no worries about colliding with other rowers, since their boats sported clamp-on running lights on their bows and sterns. Besides, Martin always headed south, under Wilson Bridge, away from most other rowers and toward the beautiful expanses where the Potomac widened dramatically.

The dark, instead, brought out the most in his other senses. Hearing served him particularly well. The gentle *ker-klunk* of the two oars working back and forth in their locks with each stroke spoke to time-polished form and technique. With each drive of the boat, water bubbled and gurgled along its hull. Martin inhaled the aromas wafting from a commercial bakery as it readied bread and rolls for the city's restaurants and delis. Any other day, with wind from the south and east, that aroma could as easily have been the daily gift from Blue Plains, where the sewage of half a million Washingtonians underwent an altogether different process. He chuckled at the notion that many people could not tell the difference.

Pulsing through the water at twenty-two strokes a minute, brisk but not so fast as to be an all-consuming effort, Martin indulged himself. Overhead, nature's planetarium was wrapping up its starry feature presentation. To the north, the distant Washington skyline offered in miniature detail the landmarks by which rowers steered: the Library of Congress, the Washington Monument, Old Post Office Building, and the U.S. Capitol. Northeast of Port City, the runways of Reagan National Airport flashed and blinked with brilliant blues, reds, yellows, and whites. Soon, dawn would introduce its slow, multi-colored magic show.

Preoccupied with rowing and marveling at nature's majesty, Martin never heard the boat with no running lights hurtling at him. Instead, he felt only the wave smash into his shell, flipping it.

Even with his layers of carefully selected clothing, Martin was shocked by the water more than he'd ever remembered from his occasional spills on the river. Surfacing and wrapping his arms around the hull, he assessed his situation. Had it only been July – hot and joyously light – instead of late February with its inky darkness and killing forty-five degree water, he could have laughed off the whole incident.

One thought mattered most at this point. Hypothermia would do its job in a matter of minutes if he didn't get out of the water immediately. But experienced rowers know how to re-right their boats, get in, and return to shore as fast as possible. He had practice-flipped his boat numerous times and each time the maneuver prepared him for when he would need it.

This looked to be different and easier: The boat that had swamped his was one of the recreational varieties found on lakes and rivers everywhere. Martin could discern the figure waving to him to swim the fifteen feet to the ramp on the boat's stern. Grateful, he concluded the owner didn't want to risk butting the overturned shell. With swift, bold strokes, he came within an arm's length of the boat, only to see it drift a foot or two out of his reach. As he labored to make up the lost distance, the boat receded farther away. Concern turned to horror as the vessel circled behind him to the shell. Extending a boat hook, the figure snagged the shell's oar rigger and quietly idled in front of the rower.

Yelling would only further drain his remaining strength, so

Martin concentrated on staying afloat. Treading in place, he could make out the lights of the opposite shorelines: Maryland to the east and Port City to the west, where home, comfort, family, friends, and a fine career in archaeology were slipping away. Hypothermia's brutal confusion and shivering were setting in. The rattling of his 190-pound body's natural defenses against the cold was so severe, he initially thought the river was shaking him. Such was hypothermia. But why the ear-splitting roar, growing louder by the second? And why the searchlight racing across the water toward them?

For an instant, the landing lights of the FedEx jet on its daily descent to Reagan National illuminated the phantom boat, answering Martin's first question, who, as well as his second, why.

To remove his watch, he had to kick harder than he ever thought possible, just to keep his head above water and his hands free. Unlatching the timepiece from his right hand became the most consuming and difficult undertaking in the 52 years of his all too short life. As his shaking worsened, confusion set in. Feeling had all but left his fingers. Finding the connection where the watchband latched took lifetimes. The effort to remove the timepiece without sending it to the river bottom made Martin cautious to the point of wasting crucial moments. With the heavy, multi-faceted watch now in his right hand, Martin began methodically tearing at the skin of his left forearm. Pain meant nothing at this point. Back and forth he worked at his arm until certain of a triangle's shape.

Maybe it was the wake of a passing boat, hundreds of yards away, or perhaps a sudden gust of wind. But the wave that would have been pleasant in the swelter of a Washington summer had the effect on this winter morning of a small tsunami, slapping Martin in the face and robbing him of his last breath. Too weak to cough away the grimy water filling his lungs, he began to sink.

Maybe in another life, in another death, Anders Martin could have experienced the time-honored ritual of last thoughts − a lifetime flashing by, frame-by-frame, rendering the faces of families, lovers, workers, friends. Not this time.

ONE

Rounding the corner of King Street onto St. Edmunds Street, Kip Alexander approached the office of the Port City *Beacon* with the same mix of emotions he had felt every morning since he had taken over publishing his family's 247-year-old weekly newspaper. Over those three years he'd never fully articulated the thought to himself, much less to his fractious, extended family; but publishing the paper was not how he wanted to spend his life.

Journalism on the world stage had been his dream, and he'd achieved it. Then, after a meteoric rise on the investigative team of the *Washington Post*, it all came to an end with a phone call. His twin sister Cass delivered the news of his parents' crash on the notorious Washington Beltway. The mayhem wrought by the 18-wheeler snatched the husband-wife team that had nurtured the weekly over a lifetime. How different life might have been had he only said No to the summons home.

By habit and preference, he arrived before his staff. The times he came in late guaranteed too much, too fast. If it wasn't Carrie Brant waving a sheaf of advertising contracts to be signed, it would be Willie Carter chiding him for not ordering enough newsprint for a special supplement. The last time Kip arrived at the ripe hour of 9:30, an Old Town matron with her three leashed terriers lunging at him in the foyer had demanded a correction to an article about her late husband. It was Mrs. Hauser's third visit that year, and Kip ached for the doddering woman in her quest to right the wrong of having her husband's rose-growing prowess having been demeaned in the *Beacon* with a second-place finish. "That was thirty-seven years ago and way

4

before my time," Kip had told her. "Let's drop it, Mrs. Hauser, and move on." He'd been relieved to see her receding through the doorway when she murmured about his lack of manners and how it would have shocked his parents. Flinching, he knew the sting would prompt an unwanted round of family memories lasting well into the day. Yes, it was saner to preempt each day with an early start – if he could make it through the door.

With a backpack of sweaty workout clothes slung over his shoulder and a paper cup of coffee in his left hand, Kip ascended stone steps to a heavy oak door to do battle with its ancient lock. *Just once, please, open on the first try,* he pleaded. Denied such good fortune, he set his coffee and backpack on the stoop and spent the next minute cajoling the lock, like a leaking toilet.

Contemplating being locked out of the Twenty-first Century, Kip wondered if his predecessor only three generations back, Thomas Kilpatrick Alexander, had comparable complaints about the dawn of the twentieth. Maybe his family board of directors had been too tight to allow indoor plumbing and electricity. As Kip snickered at the difficulty of old Tom landing a new-fangled typewriter, the lock relented and he entered the hallway of the three-story townhouse.

Treading creaky pine floorboards to his office at the end of the hallway, he passed what the staff dubbed Alexander Row – nine portraits of his predecessors dating to the late 1740s. The subjects appeared stern and disapproving of the current incarnation. On his second day in command, Kip returned the favor by hanging on the opposite wall contemporary scenes of Port City taken by the *Beacon*'s photographer. His sister liked the touch but his cousins howled at the breach of heritage. Argue as they might, his was the only decision that mattered in operational affairs.

The advertising department occupied space immediately to the left, followed by the editorial office and then production and administration offices. A conference room doubling as a staff gathering room took up most of the second floor. Pigeons and bats had the run of the third-floor attic. Pre-press production and printing occurred in a modern annex built in the 1870s. The office positioning was no accident: revenue first, news second, production and administration third. He didn't disapprove of the arrangement.

Two framed items hanging on the wall next to his desk hinted at the mind of the 38-year-old publisher and editor. The color photograph of a college rower had been taken on a dock along the Charles River in Boston on a brilliantly blue afternoon in late October. It depicted good health and accomplishment in its subject. Six-foot two-inches tall with broad shoulders and thin waist, he was clad in a rower's spandex uni-suit. With an angled grin, he held an oar in one hand and in the other a gold medal at the end of thick ribbon. He had won a sculling event at the Head of the Charles, America's premiere rowing event. The other artifact on the wall consisted of the front page of the *Washington Post*. Below it was the certificate for journalism's grandest award, the Pulitzer. Whether he agreed or not, the glamor and excitement that went with the two citations contradicted his return to small town living and its patient rhythm and predictability. Three years of this life had convinced him that much more of the same might drive him crazy.

Kip was well into a pile of invoices when his phone rang. The voice on the other end of the line was agitated.

"Kip, you need to come to the boathouse."

"Not really. I just left it."

"Now. Anders Martin's boat was found drifting in the middle of the river and nobody can find him."

"What do you mean, nobody can find him? Didn't he sign out? Didn't . . ."

He cut himself short, once he realized what Ann Norton, the volunteer head of Port City Rowing Club, was trying to tell him.

"Sorry. I'll be right there."

Kip scribbled a note explaining his whereabouts, deposited it on Della Simpson's desk, and dashed out of the building, slamming the door, which cruelly latched a whole lot easier than it had opened. Cutting through alleys behind shops and restaurants shaved minutes from his route back to the boathouse on Monroe Street.

He was glad he'd walked. Police cars, EMS trucks, harbor patrol SUVs, and other emergency vehicles crammed the small lot. Soon, a flotilla of saucer-domed TV trucks would be setting up shop.

The only way to the dock was through the main bay past dozens of rowing shells resting on their racks. Congestion awaited him on the other side. The din of crackling two-way radios of responders and the loud speakers of two harbor patrol boats made hearing nearly impossible. Kip found Norton and other club leaders huddled at one end of the dock.

He nearly had to shout. "Ann, sorry, your call didn't register at first. It's not quite what I was expecting."

"Tell me about it," she said. "None of us could absorb the news at first. And look around. This place isn't even ours."

"What do you know at this point?" Kip asked.

"Mostly what I told you on the phone. A couple of people saw him warming up upstairs. The logbook indicates he signed out at 5:15. Steve Jones saw him launch his boat. That was the last anyone saw of him."

"Who found the boat?"

"A guy in a cabin cruiser found it drifting upside down near Heron Marsh," Deanna Miller said. "He called 911, the police called the boathouse. So, that guy saved us a lot of time."

"What's happening now?" Kip asked.

"Those two harbor patrol boats are leaving in a few minutes to search the area where his boat was found," she said. "A helicopter should arrive by the time the boats get there. The police are sending people to check the shoreline. The problem is, if the current pulled him under, it could be days before anyone finds him."

Kip knew this part all too well from articles in the *Beacon* on search-and-rescue missions on the river, and they seldom ended well. Typically, boaters too stupid or drunk for their own good failed to heed weather reports and when their boats swamped in rough waters, they tried to swim to shore. They realized too late that life preservers have more important uses than as seat cushions. Then there were even more tragic cases, when a child waded into the river and a desperate non-swimming relative jumped in to save the child, only to fall victim as well. Usually, the body washed ashore, where a fisherman or hiker found it. Kip suspected Anders Martin would end up the same way.

On Norton's suggestion, the group moved to a quieter area in the boathouse to resume the conversation. She sat on a storage chest while the others pulled up a ratty collection of cast-off chairs. Paul Schultz, the club's equipment magician, and Miles Tennyson, its treasurer and chief bill payer, nursed cups of coffee. Owen Draper, the racing coordinator, chose to stand, leaning on a support girder. Kip sat with his elbows on his knees and waited for the conversation to resume.

Norton broke the silence.

"At least we will be able to say our sign-out system works," she said. "If Anders had been too lazy to fill in the logbook before he went out, who knows how long it would have been before we'd known he was missing."

Paul Schultz frowned, as though Norton had uttered the dumbest thing possible.

"It's always the bozos who don't sign out who cause the most grief," he said. "At least that clown spared us that headache."

The group had heard worse from Schultz, which was not to say they ever got used to his mouth.

In Schultz, the rowing club had a gifted facilities manager and even better acquirer and maintainer of boats and equipment. So prescient was his knack for researching winning boat and oar brands, no one ever blamed a second-place finish on his choice of equipment. The club needed Paul Schultz. Still, Kip wished Norton would this one time tell the man to wash out his mouth or clear out. The shock would have been entertaining, even if it cost them his services.

"Yeah, I'd rather an annoying false alarm to this," she stammered. "I've heard of other clubs expelling members for not signing out. I don't think we'll need to be issuing reminders to the members about this for a while."

"So, how do we proceed?" Kip asked. As communications coordinator for the boat club, he had a good idea of what needed to be done, and he wanted out of it. "This place is going to be crawling with the media any minute, and I don't want to be the one to feed those beasts."

"Conflict of interest?" Schultz asked.

Tensing, Kip said nothing. When Norton didn't respond, either, Tennyson intervened.

"Paul," he said sharply before switching to disarming blandness, "Do you think you could ease up, at least until we get through this situation."

For his diplomacy Tennyson got a cold scowl, but at least no further comment.

Kip used the time to recalibrate his response. "It's that I'm not looking forward to dealing with them while I pull together our own reporting." He left his comment hanging in air for effect before adding, "Besides, I've got two days until my deadline. So, no, Paul, I have no conflict of interest."

"Okay, let me handle it," Norton said. "I'll work with the police department to set up a press conference, probably later today if they don't already have one in mind. I don't know what there will be to say, though I wish it could be that Anders managed to swim ashore and thaw out and that we're mad as hell and love him all the more."

With nothing more to say, they agreed to disperse for the day. But before they could leave, a dozen two-way radios crackled simultaneously. One of the harbor patrol boats was calling in.

Two minutes of eternity ensued, and Port City Police Chief Jake Johnson approached the group. The stony look on the burly man's usually expressive face said everything they needed to know.

"I'm sorry. Really sorry," Johnson said. His delivery, while flat, was also quick and clipped. Kip had heard Johnson's announcements many times, and he figured the chief must have learned over the years to make the difficult at least appear to be smooth. "Our guys found Mr. Martin near Heron Bay Marina. They're bringing him here now. We'll be transporting him to the medical examiner at the hospital."

No sooner had Johnson spoken than the small black-and-red trimmed white patrol boat approached the dock. Kip was glad this had happened so quickly – nobody needed to see this part of the tragedy in high definition on the 6 o'clock news. With brisk efficiency, the boat eased to a stop and two crew members secured it.

Johnson looked the group over and continued. "We need to make an informal identification," he said. "He had no I.D. on him. So, can one of you help out?"

Nobody made a move to volunteer and moments ticked by. Then Kip volunteered.

"I will. Let's go," was all he said.

"Are you sure you want to do that?" Draper asked.

As much as he appreciated Draper's concern for confronting the sight of his long-time friend, Kip knew he had no choice. Martin would have done the same for him. "Yeah, I'm sure," he said.

Johnson nodded and led Kip down the ramp to the waiting gurney.

The closer they approached, the more thoughts washed over Kip. Martin had been a close but complicated friend. Theirs was the kind of friendship formed at the many intersections of community life – professional, civic, play and, most of all, personal. Kip never really knew whether it was in spite of or because of their scrapes and tiffs that theirs was such a solid friendship. He knew, however, the moment the sheeting was lifted, only a painful void would remain. God help Helen Martin when she learned about her husband's death.

Kip recoiled at the sight of the inert form. A skillfully prepared body in a fabric-lined coffin at a funeral was far different from what lay in front of him. Martin was disheveled and his face had a bluish gray cast about it. With his arms at his side, he stared skyward into infinity.

When the officer laid a hand on his shoulder, Kip whispered, "Yes, that is Anders Martin."

He was about to turn and leave when he noticed the wrist on

Martin's arm. Even in winter the white stripe where the sun had never managed to assert itself was clearly visible.

"For what it's worth," Kip told them, "he's missing his watch."

TWO

Not so very long ago, the building Jake Johnson oversaw would have been called a police station, not a public safety center, as the soaring postmodern brick Oz was officially termed. Kip recalled the police chief's objections to the design and construction of a structure so large and stark that it seemed to intentionally isolate itself in an era that begged for closer relations with the community it served. Every agency and branch in Port City law enforcement, from the SWAT team to school crossing-guards, called the building their "office." Still, even that failed to soften its sterile image.

Johnson and Kip sat on opposite sides of a conference table in the chief's office – not at his desk, which was off-limits, thanks to rolling dunes of paper. Kip's summons after the press conference with law enforcement, boathouse officials, and the medical examiner had come with no explanation. The media session, routine and brief, generated only modest interest on the part of the larger news outlets. A few questions bordered on the snotty, betraying boredom and, in a few cases, a bias against the sport of rowing. But Kip knew the chief hadn't asked him back to his office to discuss the lack of decorum among the scribe tribe.

Johnson wasted no time getting to the point. "Let me give you some advice," he said.

"And if I don't want it?" Kip said.

Johnson stared at him until he relented. Kip nonetheless worried that the day would come when he snapped, severing his benevolent ties with Johnson. For now, though, they needed each other.

"Let's hear it," Kip said.

"This was not a good day for your boat club," Johnson said. "It must not happen again."

"Why would it?" Kip could not imagine such a statement coming from, say, the local office of the F.B.I.

"I'm saying your group doesn't need the attention another incident would rain down on it. Did you notice that most of the questions in the press conference dealt with safety issues and lawsuits?"

Staring out the windows behind Johnson, Kip could see across train tracks and the Beltway to the far-off Potomac where it widened into Heron Bay. At this distance, the river seemed more of an aesthetic abstraction than a concrete giver and taker of life.

"Hell, Chief, we all know the risks every time we go out on the water," he said. "We sign liability waivers and watch safety videos until we're dizzy. We can't walk twenty feet in the boathouse without smacking into a safety poster. We provide more health and medical information than an astronaut. We can't help it if the entire world doesn't know that."

"You made that abundantly clear to that reporter from the *Mirror*. Nice rivalry you've got going with Ralston's paper. But you might have gone easier on the woman. She was only doing her job."

"You're probably right," Kip said. "I'll make it up to her some way that doesn't help out that pay-for-play piss pot of a paper. But, Chief, you of all people should know how seriously we take safety. Your daughter rows for the high school, which makes us look like brazen risk-takers."

Then it clicked, and he didn't wait for Johnson to spell it out for him. "I'll contact the other boat clubs to tighten up their messaging," he said, realizing that the media would be calling on the other four rowing clubs on the Potomac and its in-town tributary, the Anacostia. "They ought to be contacted anyway in case they get challenged."

"There you go," Johnson said. "Let's stay in front of this."

"By the way, Chief, did it bother anybody that Anders's watch was missing this morning," Kip asked.

Johnson's withering stare and follow-up told Kip how little he cared for the question. "Why should it?"

Kip missed the shift from avuncular to annoying, and instead of holding off for another time with an "Oh, nothing," he ignited the dry tinder of the man who had never accepted Kip's constant challenging. "Because it's something people need to know," he said.

Without rising from his chair, Johnson leaned toward Kip and palmed his desk. "What you need to know, goddammit, is to leave police work to me," he snapped. "Stick to newspapering. We've got people for such things, in case you didn't know." He never shifted his hands from the table when he delivered the next broadside, "And for fuck's sake, don't go making a caper of this."

Kip half flinched, half nodded, though less in agreement and more to buy time. As trips to the woodshed with Johnson went, he'd seen worse. Yet, the sharp turn in the conversation with the man whom he always respected and relied on jolted him. In the past, and for more concrete transgressions, Johnson had confronted Kip with far worse than this short exchange. He wondered how the chief dealt with people he actually disliked, and he then recalled hearing of the fury the man could unleash. His was clearly not an elected position.

"How's your family these days?" Johnson asked. "You getting along any better with that crusty bunch?"

"It depends on your definition of getting along," Kip replied, relieved that Johnson had changed the subject. "If you mean we haven't killed each other yet or sued one another, sure, we're getting along. But, on the other hand, nothing has changed. They all want the same thing in any number of ways. Sell the paper, outsource it, but mostly milk it for all they can without putting any money into it."

"I suppose it's small consolation," Johnson said, "but the paper is better than it's ever been. I hope you can hang in there."

THREE

Rest did not come for Kip. Monday night had been bad enough but Tuesday was worse. And Wednesday morning he awoke more tired than when he'd turned in. He'd gone to bed saturated with thoughts of Anders Martin and all the work he and the *Beacon* staff had put into the upcoming coverage of his death. Now, an introspective stew of sorrow, guilt, and loss had quickly set in. Flickering, menacing dreams made for an interminable night of tossing and turning.

Dark sockets had replaced Martin's once penetrating blue eyes and his strong angular face was grotesquely gaunt. His neat blond beard was scruffy and dirty white and so speckled with river mud and debris that he looked like a feral creature.

No matter how much Kip tried to back off, the apparition stayed in his face, all the while hissing a string of challenges. "When are you going to grow up, Man?" "You're no friend of mine if you can't commit to something, anything!" "Can't you say anything? Spit it out!"

The dream repeated itself, but with few differences. Where he would normally bark back when confronted by anyone, Kip could only sputter inanities. "You don't understand . . ." "What I meant . . ." Each time he failed at a coherent reply, shame sank in deeper. In his last dream, they faced off on a tiny version of the club's rowing dock, where the younger man had no room to retreat but into the river. The most Kip could work up was a cry of anguish that was mercifully interrupted at 4:30 by the gentle chiming of the alarm on his cell phone.

The presence of his hungry old hound, Ike, and stout tabby, Samantha, at his bedside reminded him that life must go on regardless of phantasmagorical upheaval. With only minutes to get to the boathouse for rowing practice, he postponed dream analysis. The ten-minute walk usually took long enough to shake loose sleep's cobwebs and to consider the workout ahead. With the aftermath of his recent dream fest rattling around below his subconscious, however, this day felt different.

Bo Hansen, coach of the men's competitive sweep program, didn't know about Kip's night of lost sleep, but he smartly anticipated how his charges would be dealing with the loss of a fellow rower.

"Let's keep it simple today," Hansen said, "and only do two twenty-minute pieces, with five minutes rest in between. Coxswains, start out at 18 strokes per minute and take it up two beats every two minutes to 26 and work your way back down to 18 until we're done. On the way back, let's do a steady-state twenty minutes at 22. We're working on form and timing today, so keep the power down to 75 to 80 percent."

And, with that, the two boats took off into the darkness, with only the thunking of oars turning in their locks and the splash of the blades breaking the stillness.

Even at three-quarters power, Kip typically found forty minutes of relentless rowing a physical feat. What appeared graceful and effortless to bystanders on the shoreline was in reality rougher and more physical. Once he and his teammates began a practice piece or a race, every stroke of their oars counted. Cough, sneeze, or itch, their row had to go on, stroke after stroke with no pause until the coxswain's command to "let it run" – or stop paddling.

For Kip, the drill was the right medicine. With each pull of his oar, the outside world faded a bit more. Afterwards, he would feel drained until breakfast and coffee kicked in. Still, he wondered, how was he supposed to weather a meeting with the *Beacon*'s board of directors in the afternoon and the funeral viewing for Martin later in the evening, on only five miserable hours of sleep?

FOUR

"Hey, check this out!"

The staff of the *Beacon* had barely begun its ritual of dissecting the week's news when the conversation veered off course. It was 23-year-old assistant pressman Calvin Perkins who had this time derailed the orderly train of thought when he noticed an article in a part of the paper not being discussed. Here we go again, Kip thought.

"Check what out?" asked Willie Carter, the *Beacon*'s head pressman. "I thought we were talking about real estate sales."

"We were. But the new nightclub on King Street opens this week, and our band is playing," Calvin said. A gangly totem pole of tattoos and piercings, he had the ability to both charm and irk Willie with eager non-linear comments. "Look, the *Beacon* has it right here," he said, pointing to an article far from the real estate section. "'Local band to open Stone Lizard.'"

"What band?" From atop her perch on a pallet of freshly minted *Beacon*s Della Simpson did her best to keep pace with Calvin and other younger staff members. After forty-three years as office administrator and business manager her pursuit of relevancy at times felt like a lost cause.

"The Dizzy Gillespies, Della," Calvin answered. "It's our band. We'll be on our way with this gig."

He was unfailingly polite with everyone, Willie and Della most of all. That alone endeared him to Willie, who knew enough of the wretched home life Calvin escaped when he found the *Beacon*. A fast and enthusiastic learner, Calvin made it possible for Willie to take time off, knowing the presses would reliably roll on. Willie didn't have to be an expert on the local indie music scene to know that opening the Stone Lizard was no small accomplishment for the kid and his bandmates. His announcement was one more reason why Wednesday afternoons in the back of the building were so special.

That's when the staff pitched in to help as copies of the newspaper shot out of the press. Calvin stacked them on carts. Della distributed them to three people stationed at a long, chest-high table where the first would insert advertising supplements into the B section (sports, entertainment, obituaries, real estate news, classifieds). She would pass the B section to the person on her right who would insert B into A (front page news, more news, editorials, letters to the editor, and columns). A third person gathered the completed newspapers and stacked them on pallets where some would be distributed around town while others would be rolled and stuffed into plastic bags for home delivery.

It was slow, old-fashioned newspaper work that could have easily been outsourced to printing companies in the Washington area. But no one complained.

When the last copy was dealt with, the staff retreated to stools, pallets of papers, and wherever else they could sit and peruse the week's news before anyone else in town. For fifteen minutes of each week the pressure of deadlines and revenue goals evaporated in the camaraderie that came with discussion of the town's doings.

Not much about the printing bay shouted tradition to the first-time visitor at the *Beacon*. With its high, fluorescent-lit ceiling and flaking faded white brick walls and bare concrete floor, the room could as easily have been in any other warehouse throughout the city. But the *Beacon* was located in the heart of Port City's historic district where galleries, boutiques, and restaurants dominated the streetscape. When the bay was added to the main building more than a century ago, little thought was given to such considerations as appropriate commercial and residential mix. Time and taste might sort that out over the next century.

Just as Della kept the front of house neat and orderly, Willie insisted on precise systems and order in the print bay. The waist-high rolls of newsprint were stacked in the rear in easy proximity of the ancient King press. Desks and tables were situated to form passable aisles. Padded matting in front of the tables eased the ache of standing so much. The one aspect Willie couldn't completely subdue was the aroma of ink and solvents common to every printing plant. The new vents and fans Kip had installed immediately upon taking over the Beacon went a long way in making the environment healthier. What was left in the air, depending on one's outlook, gave the *Beacon* either a patina of working-class romance and old world values or Twenty-first Century grounds for an OSHA complaint. The staff never gave it a thought. To acknowledge their special corner of the world would be tantamount to jinxing a good thing.

From a high-top stool, Kip took in the sight of everyone digging into the week's news. No group of people is ever perfect, and when it came close, it never lasted. People came and went, and there would always be someone to mess with the chemistry of any all-star team. It was one of his biggest worries at the *Beacon*. Nearly any combination of characters could push a newspaper out the door. Very few could do it with the style of his staff.

As his gaze settled on Willie Carter, he once again appreciated the prickly stability he brought to the operation. The *Beacon* was as much Willie's home as anybody's. Still, in the three years since he'd taken over as publisher, Kip could never avoid Willie's impeccably timed in loco parentis lectures.

From their conversations, he knew Willie felt like a dinosaur living on borrowed time. Given the trends of print newspapers across the country, Willie was right. Both were witness to the upheaval of print publishing. The *Beacon* teetered on that threshold, and Willie never let him forget it.

Not that Kip needed reminding. Having so reluctantly taken over the paper, he recognized the prize-winning chip growing on his shoulder. It provoked Willie bitterly.

"You damned fool, Kip," Willie had snapped in their most recent exchange. "You're sitting on one of the best things in this town, yet you act like you couldn't care less."

From his repertoire of responses Kip usually chose the least assailable.

"The deck is stacked against us – why can't you see that, Willie. Sooner or later Port City will get its news a whole lot better than with a rolled-up piece of paper tossed on to their driveways. Hell, they all already have tablets and smart phones.

"It's bad enough that real journalism is dying," he would continue. "Everybody seems to be regurgitating someone else's work and calling it aggregation. So, you try to break through that with a Neanderthal board of directors more interested in money than principles."

Willie was never put off. "I could give a rat's ass how people get their news," he countered. "I don't want to see a Starbuck's sign hanging from the front of our building because . . ."

"Now, wait a minute, Willie." The anger in Kip's voice rose quickly, right on schedule. "I . . ."

But Willie always found a way to drive his point home. ". . . just because the current publisher won't defend himself better," he interrupted. "Hell's bells, Kip, we go back a long way, you and me. I remember you in high school – pushing, always pushing on some cause. Whatever you wanted, you got, because you went after it. And, you know what? You were usually right. You stood up, even when everyone considered your causes goners. What happened to the Kip I knew?"

Kip would be pacing by this point. "For once, remember that I did not ask for this gig," he said. "Alf fled to Australia rather than deal with family matters. Cass never had an interest in publishing, only education."

He and his sister had been appalled at the number of times their parents bailed out their younger brother for transgressions ranging from speeding tickets to pub brawls. Yet Willie never seemed to take him to task like he did with Kip. Cass got a free pass from Willie for pursuing the teaching of special education in the city's public school system. Kip's fierce work ethic and steadfast principles, however, must have raised the bar of people's expectations, beginning with Willie.

And so it went between the two men. Both knew the center on that one would not hold forever.

"Hey, here's a good one." Calvin had returned to the business section. "It says here the government is looking at Port City for a new installation."

"Brace yourself," Della said. "It's not exactly news." She knew, because on Monday she'd taken the space reservation for the standard legal notice announcing a public hearing. Most people in the business community already knew something about the federal government's plan to build an annex to the Pentagon. The project had even garnered a moniker: P2.

Port City, more than most municipalities inside the Washington Beltway, had enough land to accommodate the buildings, parking, and infrastructure needed for 6,000 workers. Outside the Beltway, the requisite space multiplied greatly, but proximity to the Washington power hub declined proportionately. Access, after all, trumped other considerations. With P2 would come the myriad private contractors who had serviced the Department of Defense since the 1950s. The legal announcement merely met the bureaucratic requirements to proceed with preliminary work. Paul Schultz, as the contracted development agent for the Defense Department, had probably placed the ad. Kip, however, had no idea how much hell and aggravation the project would bring to the city – and to him personally – before its fate was resolved.

"You all can debate it," Kip said, shifting his thoughts to more immediate warfare. "I've got to get ready for today's board meeting."

FIVE

Four times a year, whether they needed to or not, the board of directors of the Port City Publishing Inc. met to assess the newspaper's fortunes. When most boards meet, the directors follow scripted agendas, beginning with approval of minutes, then discussion of old business, fiscal reports, and, lastly, new business. Well-oiled board meetings run on time, with trivialities and digressions snuffed out by firm leadership and conflict smoothed over by ageless rules of civility. Presumably, the time of a board member is valuable, making brevity and efficiency an inviolable virtue. But such was not the case of Port City Publishing Inc.

Where a normal board likes nothing better than to get in and out of a meeting with a minimum of distractions, the *Beacon* board saw the quarterly gatherings a chance to get together. Dissecting the merits of the closing of a shop on King Street or the inclusion of a new home to the garden week tour could derail the best-laid plans of Kip and Colbert Jenkins, the *Beacon*'s long-time attorney, to accomplish the one item of importance slated for a given meeting.

On this day, Kip sorely wanted approval for an upgrade to the phone system so that each staff member need not function as a switchboard operator when calls came in. It wasn't much of a capital expenditure, but it still required the board's approval. If the struggle that went with the recent installation of a fire suppression system in the print bay was any indication, then he was in for a long afternoon.

Kip and Cass each had a vote. Had Alf been on hand, they might have been a bloc of three to offset the lopsided votes of their three cousins, Melvin, Dorothy, and Stephen.

Kip had yet to understand the adversarial dynamic that emerged when he had taken on the publisher's role, though he suspected petty jealousies lay behind his cousins' curmudgeonly ways. He and Cass would always be perceived as privileged insiders, no matter how hard Kip worked and how much the paper prospered. In their eyes, Cass would always side with her brother. Yes and no to that assessment, Kip thought: After all, it was their parents who ran the paper for a generation, instilling in their children their values for the often conflicting needs of sustainability and improvement. He and Cass usually conducted post-game analyses of each board meeting's contretemps, and today's would probably include another.

Maybe Kip didn't seem to notice that he was sitting on top of one of the best things in Port City, as Willie Carter had told him so pointedly, but his cousins knew it in their own convoluted ways. With their ties to the *Beacon* came an easy cachet that required little work while entitling them to bragging rights around town. As a lawyer (Stephen), real estate agent (Melvin), and a gallery owner (Dorothy), the cousins Alexander projected a respectability that papered over livelihoods bolstered by nearly exhausted family trust funds and the small perks that came their ways by virtue of dividends from the *Beacon*.

After the print bay, the venue for the quarterly board meetings was the second largest space in the building. The conference room did multiple duty, hosting meetings, serving as the staff lunchroom, and the go-to place for celebrating birthdays, retirements, and other milestones. Its high ceiling, plaster walls, and ornate wainscoting created a formal atmosphere that suggested the debating of weighty matters. Legend had it that British Gen. Edward Braddock presented young George Washington with his marching orders in the French and Indian War in the room. If true, then the Colonial bigwigs would have been aghast at the bathetic lack of decorum on St. Edmunds Street in the early Twenty-first Century.

Della had managed to transform the chamber from glorified lunchroom to workmanlike boardroom by stashing the implements of everyday life into closets and empty cubicles.

Flowers in vases lent a touch of class and taste. A place in the office administration hall of fame awaited her if she could take the board minutes with similar efficiency. But Kip knew from hard experience that was asking too much.

Today, they were half-discussing, half-arguing the commercial merits of the Defense Department's consideration of Strawberry Flats as an expansion site for the Pentagon. That this neighborhood was long thought to be a pre-Civil War settlement for freed slaves meant little to the board; nor did its status as having the most affordable housing in the city impress them. In their eyes, Strawberry Flats represented the future. Every office worker locating to Port City to work in the mini-Pentagon would come with housing, legal, mercantile, and myriad other needs. And there happened to be a lawyer, real estate agent, and gallery owner to see to their every need. Kip had accurately anticipated the board would use the prospect of advertising as leverage in their arguments in support of P2.

"Think of the real estate ads to be had," Melvin said.

"Our title business could use the boost," Stephen added.

"My gallery can see to their cultural needs," Dorothy said.

"And my school cannot accommodate one more student," Cass said. "Who do you think is going to pay for the police, teachers, fire fighters, and social workers needed to deal with the problems when your herd of cash cows stampedes into the city?"

"Cass, clearly neither of you understand economic development," Melvin answered. As the sole principal of a sleepy, dusty real estate office, Melvin had never sold anything more lucrative than distressed row houses. It never occurred to him that national real estate developers and their sophisticated sales offices would suck the oxygen right out of his grand vision.

Kip glared at Melvin. The man never changed. He was as tall as Kip, but there the similarities ended. Gangly, with an elevator of an Adam's apple, Melvin could pass for a 45-year-old Ichabod Crane in casual business attire. Kip swore to himself that if he were to start balding, he'd shoot himself before attempting Melvin's comb over.

But it was Melvin's inexhaustible energy that most amazed Kip. He never tired in any pursuit, especially when it came to debates over the *Beacon*. If only his cousin would put his voltage to better use, like spending more time at his yacht club and less time trying to be a real estate agent with publishing expertise. Kip knew his sister felt the same way and he easily related to the way her fury bounced off Melvin.

Dorothy cut her short before she could reply to Melvin's assessment.

The figure sitting across from them would have amused Kip, if she hadn't been so formidable in appearance and behavior. Trying to understand or, at least appreciate, his cousin never panned out.

In Dorothy, excessive vanity got in the way of what should have been an attractive if not beautiful woman.

She herself wasn't particularly large, though everything about her encouraged that perception. Her hair was large, enough so that Kip wondered if small animals vacationed there in winter. She had a wide mouth – nothing wrong there, Kip thought; but the lipstick she layered on in thick, electric red hues over-accentuated gleaming white teeth to the point a horse would have been envious. Her expensive dresses billowed as she walked and her jewelry could have easily been subdivided among several people. Bangles pulled on each wrist and a multi-pendant necklace would have attracted gawkers had it not been obscured by a scarf the size of small throw rug. The only thing that was not large on her body was her chest, which Kip considered her saving grace. Had she been big-bosomed, Dorothy would have been a poster girl of a fat society dame. If only she could tone it down, Dorothy would be attractive. But once she opened her mouth, he knew that would never happen. Even her voice was large, the kind you could hear from the far side of a crowded restaurant. What was it about volume? Kip wondered, noting that the stronger Dorothy's opinion, the louder its delivery.

"Melvin's right, you know." Dorothy smoothly pronounced those four words, but with enough force that Kip wondered if the staff one floor below was listening. "People spend money on houses, restaurants, entertainment. You can't tell me that my gallery wouldn't benefit from them. Of all people, I thought you two might realize those are ads the *Beacon* could use."

"Your ads, too, which you do not pay for," Kip said, immediately regretting the arguments that ensued when he tried to get them to pay for their ads in the *Beacon*. But this time, the board was frenzied over the prospect of economic gain and Kip's lament went unchallenged. So, he plunged on. "You would do well to remember that the federal government does not pay local property taxes."

"And you all talk as though it's a done deal," Cass added. "There are such things as public hearings and review boards needed for approval. Not everybody will be as fond of this Pentagon as you think."

"Anders Martin certainly wasn't for it," Dorothy sniffed. "That man single handedly ruined a lot of other projects in the city and he sure was trying with Strawberry Flats."

"Especially Strawberry Flats," Kip said. "There's too much we don't know about it. All he wanted was for the city to go slow there."

"Well, I for one won't miss that human road block," Melvin said. "Besides, there is nothing but slums in Strawberry Flats. You can't preserve every last bit of history. Certainly not those houses."

"I think you are confusing affordable working-class housing with slums," Cass said. "Don't forget, most of hallowed Old Town used to be the same – until townhouses became chic."

"You're missing the point and we're running out of time," Melvin said, glancing at the clock in the far corner of the room. "What we need is for the *Beacon* to take a stand in favor of the benefits of good old red, white, and blue progress."

How many times such heavy-handed scenarios had played out in the *Beacon* boardroom Kip had lost count. Stalemates invariably ensued. This time he knew it would be either pro-development editorials and fawning features and the ensuing ads that ought to help with the upgrading of the phone system the staff needed so badly or he could stick to his guns and make do with tin-cans and string. As the managing partner, he held the upper hand – at least as far as a veto in editorial matters would go.

"Sorry, but that's not going to happen," Kip said. "The *Beacon* will be doing plenty, soon enough, but it won't be self-serving puff pieces begging the federal government to steamroll this town."

Until this point, Stephen had been silent, which worried Kip. Where Melvin and Dorothy excelled in vocal warfare, Stephen quietly gravitated to action, and no meeting was complete without one of his bombshells – whether it was proposed changes to the paper's organizational structure, calling for editorial stances, or merely formalizing the process of shooting down Kip's capital requests.

Of his three cousins, Stephen most perplexed Kip. At 47, he was the oldest of the Alexanders gathered around the table. He stood several inches shorter than Kip and Melvin and had a full head of silver hair. In his dark gray suit and crisp, white shirt, he had the lawyer look down fine. Kip knew his cousin dutifully worked out at the Port City Y and had the hard body to show for it.

He came off as more reasonable than Dorothy and Melvin. Where those two could be counted on to blurt out every thought and opinion, Stephen practiced a more studied approach to group aggression. Kip never considered him an original thinker or generator of ideas, but more of a person who straddled the gray area between opportunism and scavenging. If all three cousins agreed on something, Kip knew Stephen would let the other two do the dirty work of softening up the barrier to their goal. Then, when the time was right, he'd step in with a pompous knock-out punch. It matched the kind of person who thought all he had to do was hang out his attorney-at-law shingle and wait for clients to show up.

Reflecting later, Kip realized Stephen had let the ideological tiff over Strawberry Flats ferment long enough to break his news to Kip and Cass in a more dramatic fashion.

"You know, Kip, it's your intransigence that forces us to do things we'd rather not," Stephen said. His delivery had the whiff of parental disappointment with a child's mediocre report card – This will hurt us more than you. "We're genuinely concerned with the *Beacon*'s performance and we therefore have decided action needs to be taken."

Kip was not about to give Stephen the satisfaction of being asked what action was needed. He stared his cousin into moving along.

"We've come to feel that as long as you're in charge, we're not being adequately informed," Stephen said. "When this meeting is over, we're asking Miles Tennyson to assess the paper for its strengths and weaknesses. We need to know what our options are for dealing with the paper's prospects for the future."

It was the thought of Miles Tennyson, a Port City financier with a knack for gravitating to ailing businesses, as much as the action proposed by Stephen, that triggered Kip's explosion. Jumping to his feet, he bellowed, something he'd never done in all his dealings with the board.

"God almighty! You get P&Ls from me without fail every month that tell you every last damned thing you need to know about the paper – if you would lower yourselves to reading them." He slammed his hand on the table so hard pens, notebooks, and cups rattled while pain shot up his arm. "You go ahead and commission some expensive study, but all you will learn is what you already know. That is, unless you are trying to engineer your own results, which I strongly advise against."

Kip was fairly sure the staff and half the offices along St. Edmunds Street now knew where he stood with Stephen's proposal. The outburst stunned him even more than the people at the table.

"Well, Kip, thank you for your frankness," Stephen said. "Perhaps when you settle down, you'll begin to see our point of view. Or perhaps not; you never have so far."

A good fuck-you was in order. Instead, he looked to Cass in a time-honored signal and gathered up his notes and water bottle. Cass rose, doing the same, and Kip looked one last time at the remaining group.

"Take your vote. Knock yourselves out," he said. "I'm through for the day."

On his way back to his office on the first floor, Kip's mind wandered to thoughts of Anders Martin. *How would you have handled those grubby vipers, Anders?* Maybe his friend couldn't convert the unconvertible, but Kip knew his fiery gravitas would have topped his and Cass's efforts at rational discourse. Today, however, had been a bit different. No dream demon could challenge Kip for how he stood up to the board.

SIX

Strawberry Flats enjoyed the rare historical feat of having been left alone for the last 200 years. The affluence that shaped the rest of Port City spared the neighborhood.

The downtown waterfront district had developed first, by accommodating the tall-masted packets that hauled away locally grown tobacco. The city grew out from there. Old Town, as modern day residents called it, thrived commercially and residentially into the first part of the Twentieth Century. Then the rise of rail and truck transport eclipsed its usefulness as a port, and the city slipped into the shadow of Washington, D.C., as one of its many bedroom communities. Neighborhoods of varying degrees of affluence increasingly ringed the waterfront, beginning in the 1940s. But it would be decades before Old Town would catch up.

It didn't hurt its prospects for unhindered longevity that Strawberry Flats occupied an unwanted swath of dried-up river creek bed. The dredging of the Potomac that made Port City's waterfront so viable for shipping into the Eighteenth and Nineteenth centuries diverted and ultimately dried up Queen's Creek. Fear of malaria and yellow fever kept away all but the most desperate and intrepid settlers, and freed slaves found sanctuary in Strawberry Flats. Eventually, it evolved into a patchwork area large enough to achieve the status of a neighborhood.

Home ownership in the Flats came with property handed down from generation to generation. Each improved on the work of its predecessor, adding on and remodeling houses.

Nearly every residence with a yard sported meticulously

tended vegetable gardens in summer, thanks to the lush soil left when Queen's Creek dried up. Fruits and vegetables practically grew themselves. Long-time residents recalled how their ancestors cultivated blueberries, raspberries and, especially, strawberries. It was said their strawberries found eager markets in restaurants and residences throughout Port City and as far as into the District of Columbia. No one knew when the area became known as Strawberry Flats, but the name stuck.

With the exception of an occasional corner store and filling station, Strawberry Flats was residential. Stop signs, not lights, punctuated narrow streets that had yet to see sidewalks. Children rode standard-fare yellow buses to school and bikes and skateboards the rest of the time.

As he eased his bike on to Morning Lane less than an hour after the *Beacon* board meeting, Kip mused on the one certainty facing Strawberry Flats: Its long run of benign anonymity would soon be sorely challenged. The plans for the Defense Department annex would see to that. Maybe it was to be expected in a time of budget battles and sequestration that shrinking and consolidating the vast American military would bring much of it home to Washington. The colossus across the Potomac from Washington known as the Pentagon nonetheless couldn't possibly contain all the myriad agencies coming to roost there. P2 was meant to solve that.

But if such disparate personalities as his relatives on the *Beacon* board of directors felt a strong sense of manifest destiny, then much of Port City's establishment surely would feel the same pull. How would the residents of Strawberry Flats handle the threat of displacement? Would the city's sense of pride and heritage stand up to the gobs of money sure to be thrown into a land acquisition program? Having grown up in Port City, Kip knew this would be more than a story or two in the *Beacon*.

By far, the largest tract in Strawberry Flats was an automobile junkyard, J.D. Bushrod & Son. Thirty acres in all, the family enterprise was an aesthetic abomination in the eyes of storybook urban purists and a paradise for car and truck restorers. Rows of neatly sorted vehicles and racks of parts and spares existed to give new life to 1970s era Dodge Furies and three-quarter ton Chevy trucks alongside totaled late-model BMWs and soccer-mom vans. J.D. Bushrod & Son had it all. What couldn't be salvaged and sold got crushed into neat cubes for scrap recyclers to haul away. Restorers from throughout the Mid-Atlantic favored the Bushrod enterprise for its meticulously tended and catalogued inventory.

For close to fifty years, J.D. "Mouse" Bushrod and then briefly into the 2000s, his son, Jimmy, had made the junkyard a regional institution. Kip reflected on the anomaly of the small, neatly crafted sign. There was no "Son" anymore: A roadside bomb in Iraq took Jimmy's life in 2004.

As he looked around, Kip recalled the pain behind the headlines in the *Beacon*. Distraught with loss, Mouse wanted to sell the whole deal to whoever would take it off his hands. At his age, retirement – whatever that was – surely would be better than what he was experiencing with the death of his only child. But then, Jimmy's widow, Liza, announced her desire to pitch in. What the Hell? Why Not? Mouse had thought at the time. Maybe that fancy college education of hers could bring J.D. Bushrod & Son out of its slump. Only, no way would he change out the sign to J.D. Bushrod & Daughter-in-Law.

Kip never questioned how such a stunningly attractive Ivy League economics major with the entire world at her disposal connected with the son of a junk dealer. Jimmy was a find in his own right. He had not only been an outstanding rower with Port City High School's team, he also excelled in his studies. That he was an African-American in a predominantly white sport made him all the more attractive to university rowing programs. Jimmy and Alf Alexander had been hard-partying friends throughout high school, though their drifting apart after graduation had more to do with circumstances of college, jobs, and geography.

The same idealism that drove Jimmy to choose a Southern school for college also compelled him to enlist in the Army following the terrorist attacks of September 11, 2001. But 1st Lt. James Bushrod was no match for the bomb. War came home hard in Port City, and nobody suffered more than Mouse and Liza. Alf hid his grief amid binges and benders that further accumulated family disapproval.

In the ensuing years since taking over, Liza performed extraordinary feats. Where Mouse kept inventory in his head and on scraps of paper, Liza computerized the entire operation. Having written complex software programs for the World Bank, she found computerizing auto parts inventory a snap. Listing the inventory on their website made their product not only easily accessible, but it also made J.D. Bushrod & Son the preferred resting place for people's vehicles.

She also had the foresight to gradually upgrade the facility to make it environmentally responsible. Toxic run-off had never been a problem, but she preempted safety inspections with special grading and a rainwater containment pond. For her efforts, *Waste Age* magazine had featured Liza and Mouse on the cover of a recent issue.

Kip found Liza not at her desk but in a grassy field of cars and trucks that would never go anywhere again on their own power. In her jeans, boots, and fleece pull-over with clipboard and RFID scanner in hand, she could have easily been an organic farmer.

Liza confronted Kip even before he could get off his bike.

"I suppose you are going to write about now being the time to close down this eyesore," she said with no preambles of hospitality. "Go ahead and tell me how fitting a place J.D. Bushrod & Son would make for a new Pentagon."

"And, good morning to you, too, Liza," Kip said.

"Spare me, Kip," she interrupted. "Mouse and I have had a steady stream of every kind of developer and government official come knocking every day and at all hours. They phone, they email, leave messages on our website. Hell, your rowing buddy Paul Schultz even cornered me at the grocery store this week. They all want the same thing."

Taking a deep breath, she continued.

"Anders Martin was one of the few people in town who cared

about Strawberry Flats and now he's gone. Once the government starts gobbling up land in Strawberry Flats, this place is as good gone."

So much for pastoral relief from the long, psychic reach of Anders Martin. Even Liza felt the loss, and from the correct side of the fence, Kip thought. Too bad their conversation might not make it far today. If she would let up for even a moment, he could make a stab at conciliation.

Nope, she was still very much on message.

"And when the Port City *Beacon* comes visiting on a bike, I'd be nuts not to expect more of the same," she continued. "And, Jesus, even your family is giving me crap for standing in the way of so-called progress."

"That would have been Melvin," Kip said. "He's got the manners of a gorilla."

"You're damned right it was Melvin, and a gorilla would be insulted by the comparison," Liza said. "Tell your damned family to stay the hell out of my life."

"I suspect you are doing that well enough all on your own," Kip said. "But, yes, I did come here to see things firsthand. I also want to tell you that next week's *Beacon* will be publishing an editorial against the annex. Once that happens, my damned family, as you so graciously call them, will probably vote me out of job at next month's board meeting. Sooner, if they could pull it off."

Her hands came off her hips, and in one tick-like motion she adjusted her ball cap and zipped her jacket tighter. Her arms found a more secure resting place folded across her chest. Geez, she's still wearing her wedding ring, Kip thought when he saw her left hand.

"And why would that happen?" she asked in a decidedly more subdued tone.

"Why?" Kip said. "Because P2 is the last thing we need here or anywhere in Port City. The Defense Department will get a new palace that it may or may not need, but all we will get is more traffic and no tax revenue for the trouble. And, still, my board is in favor of P2."

Kip could see Liza digesting these last two statements and he brightened at the change in her tenor, especially when she said, "Let's go to the office where we can talk better."

The small warehouse hadn't changed on the outside since Kip was last there. When he saw the office, however, he did a mild double-take. The interior used to have an industrial feel that was accentuated by the stained concrete floor, cinderblock walls, bare girders and flickering fluorescent lighting.

Gone was the ratty chest-high retail counter. The volume of their traffic never warranted a retail-style barrier between customer and seller anyway, and now transactions could be conducted as easily from a desk. The walls and ceiling had been spray painted in a hue of white that an art gallery owner would envy. Wood flooring, lamps, and track lighting completed the makeover of J.D. Bushrod & Son. Pottery Barn meets *Road & Track*, Kip thought. Maybe he should bring Willie Carter for a tour – the print bay at the *Beacon* could do with a bit of a make-over.

With mugs in hand, Kip and Liza continued their conversation.

"I'm curious," Kip said, "Why did you bring up Anders Martin."

"No reason, really."

Huh? Kip mentally flipped through the pages of his professional playbook, instantly landing on the verbal evasion he'd heard in dozens of interviews. "Really?" he asked.

"Well, yeah. Anders knew our property would be in the Pentagon's cross hairs."

Who didn't, after all? Liza's comment could only have come out of conversation with Anders, and if it was none of his business, she would tell him, bluntly, which would still be mild by his standards.

"Hmmm, Liza, I could swear you know something I don't," Kip said.

She sighed.

"Back off, Woodward. All I can tell you is that he was working the hillside on the far end of the property."

No story there, Kip thought. But what the heck, in for a penny. . .

"Anders? I always thought of him more as an administrator kind of archaeologist than a digger and sifter," Kip said.

"What do you mean, digger and sifter?" Liza asked.

From conversations with Martin and from news articles in the *Beacon*, Kip knew public relations and museum exhibits were as important in the success of the city archaeology program as the tools and shards of pottery gleaned by graduate students and volunteers. Besides, he only had funds enough to finance digs at the Eighteenth Century Cameron House and the site of a shipbuilding enterprise on the waterfront. Those projects captured media attention and generated a nice flow of field trips from the local schools. For Martin to set up a dig at the Bushrod enterprise was an outlier.

"I wouldn't describe his dig here as something major," Liza explained. "Only a tarp covering up dried-up riverbank."

"How big?"

"Twenty feet long, at the most, and a couple of feet up the hillside.

"Why so secretive?" Kip asked. "Did he say what he was looking for?"

"No. He did spend a lot of time late last fall walking all over Strawberry Flats, not only our property. Then one day Anders asked if I'd mind if he did a small personal project on the south side of our lot. He said it wouldn't be disruptive and it would help keep his hand in the game. I assume he meant his digging and sifting skills – as you call it. Anders did ask me to keep it to myself, as though I had anybody to tell."

"I see now," Kip said. "That's why the reluctance to tell me?"

"I'd say it was none of your business, but then everything is your business," Liza replied.

Why is it that everybody is okay with me doing my job – until it involves them? Kip asked himself. Liza's rebuke had plenty of sting to it and Kip's flinch betrayed it.

"Oh, come on, Kip – you've got to be able to take what you dish out," Liza laughed. "Right?"

"I suppose so," he answered. "Though I don't feel like I've done much dishing out lately. But, since we've established everything is my business . . ."

"And?"

"And I'm still curious about all this," he said. "Did anybody ever come with Anders out here?"

"Not that I know of."

"And then it was all gone?"

"Yeah, it's like he pulled up camp and left in the night. You'd have to know what you were looking for to find the place."

The abruptness of Martin's departure now fully intrigued Kip. These things usually explained themselves when you asked enough questions. But not this time.

"Would you mind if I walked over for a look?"

"Go for it," Liza replied. "I'd be surprised if you didn't ask. I'd join you, but I'm expecting a buyer from Pennsylvania to pick up that Suburban over on Row 2. A few more sales like that one and we'll be free and clear of our loan."

"I wondered how you managed to do so much with this place so quickly," Kip said.

"Yep, and we did it the old fashioned way – we borrowed the money," Liza said. "We're so close to paying it off that even Mouse is starting to breathe a little easier. And nobody dislikes bankers more than Mouse, even if it is Miles Tennyson."

Kip thought it interesting that he had to pry Anders's hillside venture out of Liza, yet here she was freely discussing her financial situation. Honor and pride – in that order.

"I'm happy for you, Liza, really," Kip said. "As for Miles, he may have his hooks into half the deeds in town, but he's a good guy. Mouse needn't worry."

Kip, on the other hand, would soon have Tennyson prowling through the *Beacon*'s books. The paper's balance sheet, while rickety, was still in the black. And as long as its daffy board of directors was involved in any audit, he would be worried.

"By the way, what do you hear from Alf these days," Liza asked. "It's like he dropped off the planet. I miss the scoundrel."

"Nothing. Zilch. Nada," Kip said. "He clearly has no use for us."

"I know it's not easy, but you shouldn't be so hard on him," Liza said. "He meant the world to Jimmy. I don't think Jimmy would have been the person he was if Alf hadn't been there."

"How ironic," Kip said. "Too bad more of Jimmy hadn't rubbed off on Alf."

"You never know," she said.

"And I doubt we ever will."

Clearly un-attuned to the unique features of crumpled and rusting vehicles, Kip nodded at Liza's quirky set of directions to Martin's project. She pointed him to a far corner of the property, citing arcane landmarks – take a left at the white Honda at the end of Row 16, go thirty yards, turn left at the Dodge Charger, and then look for the hillside.

Even with Liza's precise but funky directions, Martin's worksite was nearly impossible to find. Kip had to concentrate hard to visualize the dull, matted grass of late winter as a dried-up creek bed. Looking for even a hillside wasn't easy.

But, there, under a grove of poplars, the land rose gently for about fifteen feet before leveling into a continuation of the field. If that was any kind of embankment, then it was a good thing Kip chose journalism as a profession instead of archaeology.

There was indeed, a twenty-foot long stretch of bare dirt. Only now, it was partially hidden by leaves and branches positioned so that the site blended with the rest of the terrain. Martin was as neat as he was thorough. It must have been a trek for him to lug all his implements and framing boxes and other gear needed to establish even a modest dig – and then haul it away.

Surveying the setting, he could see how the embankment formed a subtle wrinkle in the early March landscape. Three months from now, high grass and wildflowers would fully obscure it.

So, this is all that remains of Queen's Creek, Kip whispered. How different it might have looked today had the Colonial version of the Army Corps of Engineers not messed with the local waterways.

Not for the first time, though, did Kip consider the similarities between how he and Martin had put food on their tables. Both were researchers and investigators who relied on a specific set of technical skills to find and then tell a story. The difference, Kip knew, came down to temperament. Kip could only annoy people up to a point, whereas Martin began to thrive only when he'd crossed that threshold. His funeral service later that evening would temporarily unite people, physically if not ideologically.

Taking one last glance at the site, Kip began the walk back to Liza's office, hungrily soaking in the incongruous oasis so far removed from the larger world a mile away.

SEVEN

The place was too perfect. Out on Randolph Road, Hampton Funeral Home resembled most other brick colonial-style commercial buildings in Port City. Inside was another story.

Sitting in the back of its chapel, Kip took stock of the room and pronounced it a work of psychological genius. He had arrived at the funeral home half an hour ahead of the others who would be paying their respects to Anders Martin. Jeff Benson, Hampton's funeral director agreed to allow Kip some solitude. Benson knew Kip was one of the few people in Martin's small circle of friends.

Kip and Benson's friendship had begun in high school and continued through college and into their everyday lives in Port City. Kip was an usher in Benson's wedding and became godfather to one of his three children. For his part, Benson had suffered through Kip's long-ago short-lived marriage and assorted romances. He had been a great help with the death of Kip's parents – there when he had been needed. Kip, Benson, and two other buddies still met in the basement of the funeral home each month for a ritual game of low-stakes poker. If Kip had to put his relationship with Benson on a balance scale, he knew he would be greatly in debt to him.

The thirty steps between the front doors and the viewing area felt like a walk through an emotional airlock that prepared visitors for what awaited them. The long, lushly carpeted entrance hall set the right tone. No matter the economic or social status of the deceased, they always got a well-appointed and comfortable send-off.

Even though it could seat 200 people, the chapel felt much

smaller and more intimate. From his seat in the rear of the room, Kip began to divine the thinking behind Hampton. The soft, indirect lighting eliminated contrast, both visual and emotional, and it appeared to be coming from no particular direction.

Once he tallied the reams of fabric covering every available square inch of surface area, he realized how such a large room could be so hushed. The merlot red carpeting was thick enough to absorb the sounds of any boot, shoe, or high heel, yet thin enough for easy passage. It was the opposite of a high-decibel restaurant.

No need for any olfactory strategy here. So many floral arrangements ringed the room that Hampton's HVAC system probably had to work overtime. Classic, if not classical, the art work ran no risk of garnering more than the quickest glance from visitors – generic plants, landscapes, and grazing farm animals.

"Am I imagining this?" Kip asked Benson, when the proprietor came by to check on him.

"Not really, although you're not supposed to see through it so easily," Benson replied. "I always feel I'm doing my job better if I can take off the edge of the sadness people feel when they arrive. Sure, it's smaltzy on some level, but the people who come here have enough grief already. If we can suspend it even momentarily, all the better."

"Fair enough," Kip said.

"We'll see in fifteen minutes or so. I'm estimating between 600 and a thousand people passing through tonight."

"Well, it is a community event, though I don't expect they will all be adoring friends."

"Our buddy did annoy a lot of people in his crusades," Benson agreed. "Let's hope that part is in the past."

And come, they did.

Jake Johnson's officers had their hands full directing traffic on Randolph Road. Hampton staff steered the long, snaking procession through the front and out a side door as respects had been paid. Most came from work, dressed in suits, uniforms, khakis, jeans, sweaters. Children, the few who came, looked ready for Sunday school. Because Anders Martin was a city employee, a large contingent of city workers and politicians arrived first and hung around the longest.

The rowers arrived nearly at the same time, close to sixty of them, including spouses and significant others. By this point, every seat was taken and standing was allowed for only as long as it took to visit the closed casket. With a line starting in the parking lot, Hampton's attendants did their best to keep people moving.

Kip joined the rowers, where the conversation was light and banal which made Paul Schultz's comment all the more stark and pronounced.

"What did you say?" Kip verbalized the incredulity of the group.

"I said, good riddance. Now maybe this city can move forward a little more easily with him gone."

Schultz delivered his reply in such a nonchalant manner that even the second time he said it, people blinked.

"Maybe you should have stayed home," Beth Stevens finally said. An older rower in the sculling group, Beth had lost none of the fire that made her such a respected competitor. "What's in it for you to even be here?"

"Why? That's easy. I wanted to see him off."

"You asshole," Kip hissed. "Why don't you get out of here?"

All the fabric in the Hampton establishment failed to muffle the anger rising in that section of the visitors queue, and conversation within twenty feet stopped as heads turned in curiosity.

"Whoa, now, let's hear it from the man who thinks he can have it both ways – take the high road when it comes to news stories but who really makes his living off the Port City business community. At least I'm not afraid to say what I stand for."

Realizing that arguing the nuances of commerce with the city's maverick developer in this funeral parlor had about as much chance of success as a drunk directing traffic in the middle of the Washington Beltway, Kip opted for a more direct retort.

"What you stand for," Kip began, "is cramming buildings into any available space and when you can't do that, you bulldoze anything in the way for your high-rises. Hell, even other developers draw the line at you. It's too bad there aren't more Anders Martins to keep you from raping Port City. So, spare us your greedy credo."

Only in a barroom could matters have deteriorated any faster. Kip should have seen it coming, by the way Schultz leaned his ruddy face toward him, planting his powerful legs in the go position. At six feet two inches, Kip could look down on the taut and seething Schultz who had nonetheless become an intimidating sight.

From the corner of his mouth, Schultz said, "My greedy what?"

"Credo. You know that belief of yours that you deserve everything you can get."

Kip never saw the fist that landed below his right eye. While proverbial stars never materialized, he did feel in infinite detail the blow and then tumbling backwards where Owen Draper and Bo Hansen broke his fall. After that, he didn't remember anything until being the first person to ever awake on one of Hampton's stainless steel cadaver tables.

"What happened? Where am I?" The oldest line in the book of the newly conscious.

"Your face got in the way of Paul Schultz's right hook," Benson told him. "We brought you down here for safe keeping. It would have been swell if you two could have held off your philosophical love affair for another time."

"Please, please tell me we didn't ruin the viewing," Kip said.

"You're lucky there. Once we got you out of there, things quickly settled down. I must say, though, your encounter with Schultz was highly on the cowboy side."

Kip could barely focus on his immediate surroundings – institutional fluorescent lighting, floor-to-ceiling refrigerators, cabinets, tanks, and canisters. Even though this was where they played poker each month, Kip felt like he had awoken in a veterinarian's examining room. With Benson were several rowers,

Jake Johnson, and a pretty woman he'd never seen before but made him think there were worse ways to wake up.

"We all saw it, Kip," Johnson said. "I can charge him if you want. Though I doubt you will."

"Nope. He's an asshole, not a criminal," Kip said. "Let him be."

"Whatever, I suggest you exit by the service door here," Benson said. "You look awful and I don't need you scaring our guests."

Someone had brought his backpack over, so it was easy for Kip to slip out unnoticed. He was glad, though, that Benson was smiling when he suggested his exit route. His life had gotten messy enough without more people angry with him.

EIGHT

It never took much to derail the work routine at the *Beacon*. The cause didn't matter. It had more to do with the break from the everyday than the significance of the actual event. Mrs. Hauser and her hysterical dogs were an automatic summons to the common area as were visiting political candidates and Mormon missionaries in their neat white shirts, ties, and black trousers. It was a small-town newspaper, after all, a crossroads of all walks of life, so what was wrong with a low-grade klatch every now and then?

Still, Kip wasn't prepared for the flash mob that invaded his office the morning after the funeral to inspect his now fully developed black-and-blue shiner.

"It's 9:30 in the morning – how did you guys even hear about Schultz?" Kip asked.

"Boss, last we checked, this is a newspaper office and you conveniently got decked in front of half of Port City," Willie Carter said. "Who doesn't know?"

He easily sloughed off their questions, with the exception of Della's. "What was your rowing practice like?" she asked. "Did Schultz show up?"

"Bo Hansen put us in different boats, so we never had to deal with each other," Kip said.

"Then no brawls? Carrie asked.

"None to speak of. It was too early for that kind of stuff," Kip said.

That wasn't quite the truth. During warm-ups on the second-floor erg machines spaced out two feet apart, Schultz chose the erg next to Kip. Kip got up, went to another, only to be joined by Schultz again. Even a lamppost would have found it menacing. With hostility that intense, any rower who had arrived for practice half asleep was now fully awake. But nobody was going to let a fight erupt. The previous night's episode had crossed well over the line. Led by Miles Tennyson and Owen Draper, four other rowers stepped in between Kip and Schultz, making it clear nothing would be happening,

By that point, Hansen had arrived and further diffused the situation in his blunt but effective manner.

"This isn't high school and it's not basic training or whatever test of manhood you want to call it," Hansen growled. "Until you two settle things, you will alternate rowing each day in the *Madison* and the *Jefferson*. Right or wrong, you both will be out of the club for the season, if not longer, if there is one more incident.

"In the meantime, I've worked out details for next Saturday's scrimmage with Algonquian," he continued. "We'll be rowing two 8s and then four 4s. Each 8 team will split into two to race in the 4s, based on your seating assignment. We'll draw straws for our love birds to see which boats they race in."

Scrimmages with other boat clubs were unusual, but welcomed by rowers. Without the logistical pageantry of a full-blown regatta – judges in motor launches, dock supervisors, blaring loudspeakers, spectators, volunteers, and scores of boats and their crews – a scrimmage had a casual feel. While they didn't lessen competitive intensity, scrimmages did eliminate extraneous distractions.

How Hansen got the Algonquian Boat Club to agree to scrimmage with the mutts of Port City was impressive. Port City had many fine rowers, but Algonquian was in a league of its own. Olympians trained at its 1908 green- and white-shingled boathouse on the Georgetown waterfront. Each August, Algonquian boats could be considered contenders in the Masters Nationals. But Hansen's rowers knew that on any given day, eight men or women could find that elusive "zone" and turn in the races of their lives. Often enough, they did, which is why Port City accepted the challenge so eagerly.

"So, let's not screw it up with any playground squabbles. You hear?" Hansen looked long and hard at Schultz and Kip.

Kip nodded assent. Schultz stared coldly ahead. The man operates on anger, Kip concluded, grateful not to be rowing in the same boat.

Back at the office two hours later, Della added to his assessment.

"Schultz Development Corporation canceled its advertising half an hour ago," she said. "We've now got a hole in the real estate section where he would have been advertising his new condo project."

"So what," Kip almost spat. "We do not need that jerk's business."

"Easy there," Carrie said. "We're on the same side, if you haven't noticed."

Kip issued a long and weary sigh. "Right. Sorry. Really," he said. "So, let's short-rate him – charge him for the frequency discounts he got upfront for the rest of the ads in his contract. Though I doubt he will ever pay. Let's be done with him."

"Not entirely," Della said. "His subsidiaries and partners may pull out, you know. Real estate agents, bankers, ad agencies, building subcontractors. If they see things Schultz's way, we stand to lose a lot of money."

Damned good point, Kip thought. But short of begging and cutting rates to keep their business, little could be done.

Fresh out of other ideas, Kip said, "Well, let's take it one day at a time. That should be hard enough."

At his desk, Kip was glad for the lack of mirrors in his office. He didn't need a grisly visual reminder of his latest crisis. But he did understand why publishers and editors once kept bottles of rye within easy reach.

NINE

The line between curiosity and obsession in Kip's pursuit of a news story seldom ceased to blur. He never knew where the former left off and the latter began. Curiosity was an itch that Kip had to scratch, and quite often he enlisted his reluctant staff to help him with the process. Ben Bailey, the *Beacon*'s young managing editor, had yet to forgive Kip for any number of awkward assignments, from dumpster diving to monitoring the comings and goings of politicians.

When an offbeat tip did pan out, the reporter working that particular beat got first crack at it. If he or she demurred, which didn't happen often, Kip took it on.

Tracking down the true rationale behind a seemingly innocuous line item in a proposed city budget could consume him for weeks at a time. When Kip resurfaced, an embarrassed politician would end up rescinding a request that would have benefited one of his or her favored constituents.

It didn't happen often; but enough that *Beacon* readers had come to expect such diligent reporting, though they were unaware of the sweat and angst that went into it. Della and Willie had learned to live with Kip's obsessive quirks.

Kip's visit to J.D. Bushrod & Son the week before had left him with unanswered questions, and once again curiosity exerted its inexorable pull. Why had Anders Martin chosen Strawberry Flats for his secret dig? What was he looking for? Did he find it? Why did he drop it so suddenly and carefully hide his tracks? Was it tied in with P2? There must be an explanation, and probably Martin's office could provide it.

Getting an appointment with Erin Powers, the acting director of Port City's Office of Archaeology took only a phone call. The voice on the other end of the line gave little away about its speaker. No discernible accent or mannerisms hinted at her age. Then, again, she had lost a close colleague less than a week ago. Effervescence was not expected.

Like many of the city's smaller agencies, the Office of Archaeology was housed in an unconventional setting. While its municipal cousins called warehouses, historic houses, even Quonset huts home, the work of archaeology in Port City got done in an adapted Nineteenth Century stone and wood library on Carlyle Lane. With its nooks, crannies, and ample common area, Library House served multiple functions – office, research facility, museum, and classroom space.

With some amusement Kip compared the hip interior design of the office with the *Beacon*. While the *Beacon* looked like old money handsomely gone to seed, the archaeology office was equal parts art gallery and movie set. Stark white walls contrasted with crisp, gray carpeting. Overhead, track lighting focused on select areas. Tastefully framed exhibition posters, hand-drawn maps of city streets, and old sepia-toned photographs depicted Port City in bygone eras. Chipped and broken bowls, vases, pipes, and tools of obsolete trades filled glass display cases carefully positioned throughout the common area. The place not only told visitors that Serious Work got done there, but that the staff had fun doing it.

A woman in an ankle-length one-piece denim dress and calf-high leather boots emerged from her office. Late 20s, maybe early 30s, Kip guessed, while struggling to remember where he had seen her before. You didn't easily forget a sight like that, especially the explosion of dark red hair that a pony tail had failed to subdue. The slender hand extended to him sported a silver and turquoise ring and a just-right grip.

"Nice digs," Kip said, shaking hands.

She didn't exactly groan, but Kip detected from her half-response that pun had made the rounds plenty of times in her office.

"You are the first person to say that," she said.

"Sorry, I couldn't help myself."

"You're forgiven," she said. "You almost made me laugh. Come on in. I'll show you around, unless you've already been here. But I don't believe I've seen you at Library House before."

"It is my first visit, and I really wish it were under different circumstances," Kip said. "Anders was one of my favorite people."

"Ours, too. We feel like we've lost a family member," Powers said. "He left so much for us to carry on, we can't possibly expect to replace him. But it would be nice to continue being known for what we do and not for what happened to us."

Was that a jab?

"We do run your press releases on your tours and exhibits," Kip said. "I can't speak for the *Post* and the other big guys, but I think we've done your program justice."

"That's not what I'm talking about," she said. "Why not take an interest in what it is that we do? Why not show an interest in the city's past and not in a press release kind of way? Why not dig into our city's past? Add some dimension to your newspaper."

Maybe he should leave and come back. Another meeting with this barrel of fun could not splinter any faster than today's. Liza Bushrod had been rough enough of an encounter, but at least she didn't tell him how to run his newspaper. Professional pride and dedication was commendable. He saw it in his sister's passionate efforts in the turning of the supertanker of education in Port City. He saw it among social workers, park administrators, and others whose chosen professions did not come with glamor or fat paychecks. Kip had clearly observed it in Anders Martin, who had tilted at windmills for his entire career. But don't thrust it my face, he thought.

Seconds ticked by as Kip considered scrapping the interview.

Nah. If he let every prickly interviewee run him over, the *Beacon* would melt overnight into a pathetic freebie shopper. Besides, curiosity was getting the best of him: He wanted to know more about this woman, not to mention the story that brought him there. So, let her talk.

Kip smiled. "Where would you like to start?"

"Come on over to my office," she said, gesturing him to a room not much larger than a cubicle. For Kip, who had no window in his office, the tall, inset window to a sunny alley was the room's saving grace. He pondered the significance of why Powers had not taken over Martin's much larger and accommodating office. Humility? Respect? Mourning? A bit of everything, Kip thought, including not appearing to be in a in a rush to assume the corner office.

When they had settled in, Kip said, "Let's start by telling me what goes on here."

Powers relaxed and leaned back in her chair. "It's different in every town and county," she began. "For some, it's really basic – an extension of a town's history project. A few artifacts on display in the court house or maybe the county office building. Professional staff is part time, if there is any."

"What's wrong with that?"

"Nothing. But if you train in archaeology, intern in it, and basically live your whole life for archaeology, then that clearly is not enough. It's scratching the surface of what we do."

"I see. You live for your profession?" It was as much a statement as a question.

"I suppose you could say so. Both of my parents were archaeologists. My father is retired from William & Mary where he taught it, and my mother was dyed-in-the-wool field hound. She literally lived at digs half her life.

"They never forced it on me, which is perhaps why I was attracted so strongly to the field and not put off. That's not to say that all their contacts and knowledge of the field didn't make it easier for me. It did, and seeing how competitive this field is, I don't begrudge any advantage they afforded me."

"Competitive? How so?" Kip asked. "Isn't every field competitive? Mine certainly is."

"Maybe, maybe not. In archaeology, the usual way to get ahead and do the big stuff is to develop an expertise and reputation in a specific field."

"And you chose?"

"Pre-Industrial America. There's enough to keep me busy for

the rest of my life."

"Why that era? And why Port City?

"Port City may not look like much in that context, especially being in the shadow of Washington and other big cities, not to mention Jamestown and Williamsburg. But it's got everything," she explained. "The Potomac River was a genuine interstate highway for Native Americans well before the British arrived. The British considered the Potomac strategic for reaching the interior of the New World – no other body of water extends farther into the continent from the East Coast than the Potomac."

"What are you learning here? What's left to discover?" Kip asked.

"Maybe there are no Dead Sea Scrolls lying around in lost cellars and cisterns, but there is plenty to learn about how our ancestors lived their daily lives. Don't you think the quality of your life would be better and fuller if you knew and appreciated what people went through 300 years ago, right where you are sitting at this moment?"

"Sure, remember, I'm a journalist," Kip said. "We specialize in the writing the first drafts of history.

With the makings of a rapport established with Powers, he felt comfortable probing further. "I'm curious about what drives you within your own field," he said. "I can see how you and Anders worked together so well. That is, I assume you worked together well."

"Yes, we were a team. Anders was part mentor, part protector, and fully a friend. He took me on as an intern and then made me assistant director when the funding came through. It's a lofty title for an office of three; two people now. But it's been close to eight years now, and I've never regretted a day of it."

Running his fingers through his hair, Kip said, "I could do with a little of that devotion."

Powers laughed gently. "Really? Nobody in the outside world knows the mighty Port City media tycoon has mixed thoughts about his role of town crier."

Kip looked vacantly to his side, and ran both hands through his hair.

Powers's face softened as her emerald green eyes shone with a warmth that so far had been absent in their meeting. "I'm sorry. I wasn't looking to hit any nerves," she said. "Really, it was only conversation."

Kip shifted his weight in the chair. "Don't worry about it. I get that way if I think too much about my lot in life. I can tell you the whole sorry saga any time you've got forty-five seconds to spare. In the meantime, let's get back to Anders. He's far more interesting."

Kip recounted his visit the week before with Liza Bushrod and Martin's impromptu archaeology site. It raised more questions than it answered, Powers agreed.

"I had no inkling Anders had a project going," she said. "I'm stunned and hurt he never told me."

"From what you've told me, I'm sure he would have, had he had time," Kip trailed off, avoiding the implications of that thought.

Powers pursed her lips and took her turn at a vacant stare as she pondered Kip's news. She rose from her chair and took up a position leaning on the window sill.

"I hope you're right," she said. "The odd part is that it was so out of character for Anders."

"How so?"

"The only way I can see Anders taking on a project like that would be to find something so important that it would make Strawberry Flats off-limits to bulldozers," she said. "But it's pretty well agreed, that for all its lack of attention, the area hasn't shown much archaeological potential."

"Why not?" Kip asked. "If anybody were to find that, it would certainly be Anders. Right?"

"Perhaps. But it would take something huge, like discovering an entire plantation or Seventeenth Century village – and we know that neither existed in Strawberry Flats."

Powers's reckoning of the situation wasn't doing much for Kip. The Anders Martin he knew could browbeat a rock into submission.

"Maybe he was after something older," Kip said.

"Possibly," Powers said, "His specialty was Paleo-Indian cultures. That would qualify as older than European settlement."

"I'm not following."

"Well, archaeology works in layers – generation on top of generation. Civilization on top of civilization on top of another. When the English and Scottish settled Port City in the early Eighteenth Century, the landscape changed forever with all the building and construction, and it has ever since. Indian artifacts are few and far between, mostly stone tools and weapons. We've been able to search back only as far as the Seventeenth Century, and Paleo-Indian history goes back thousands of years."

"Then, what was Anders doing in Port City?" Kip asked.

"Port City has always been a first-class environment for pursuing archaeology. It had a decent archaeology department when Anders arrived. But he took it to new level. I think by being a big fish in a small pond, Anders figured he could raise a family and make a more stable living than he could out west where many of the Paleo-Indian experts gravitated. He came to love Port City as much as he did archaeology, and so he made a great career and life here."

"But we still don't know what he was doing at Strawberry Flats," Kip said.

Powers thought for a moment, then snapped her fingers. "Maybe it's simpler than it seems."

"It doesn't seem so."

"Why not? Anders was doing all he could elsewhere in the city to stop the P2 dead in its tracks," Powers said, "And what better way to do that than by finding archaeological evidence to tie up the project."

"A moment ago you dismissed Strawberry Flats as archaeologically unworthy."

"I'm trying to look at it from Anders's perspective – which, I believe, is why we're having this meeting in the first place," Powers said, returning to her chair. "We know from anecdotal and word-of-mouth evidence that Strawberry Flats was inhabited as far back as the Eighteenth Century by an odd assortment of people who chose some of the absolute worst terrain to settle in – swamp and flooding riverfront. And it's still intact.

"They must have dodged floods and the like for at least a century and a half before Queens Creek dried up and made the area more hospitable," she continued. "Today, Strawberry Flats is so under-the-radar that it doesn't even appear in our archaeology resource overlay maps."

She was on a roll, but Kip only half heard what she had to say. Her hands were a blur of animation, and he could have sworn her eyes were sparkling. If he hadn't been worrying about losing track of the conversation, he could have continued to stare at the woman in front of him. Fortunately, she hadn't gotten too far ahead of him.

"So, you see, Anders had every reason not to tip off people to his efforts to derail P2 with anything from Strawberry Flats," Powers said. "And, judging by your shiner from the funeral, we've already got a good notion of how hard the pro-project people would attack him. They would have loved to see him brought down a few notches for any number of reasons, bogus or not."

"Misappropriation of public funds? Kip suggested.

"For starters."

"But the big question is, did he find anything?"

"You say he pulled up stakes overnight. How did you find it, anyway?" Powers asked.

"It wasn't easy, even with the directions the owner gave me," Kip said. "I was standing on top of it and still I didn't know it at first. Call it a lucky accident."

Kip stood and gazed out the window on to a narrow alley.

"You've got that weird look again."

Kip didn't answer, and Powers asked again. "What is it?"

He exhaled and said, "Something's wrong. I'm getting the feeling Anders did find something, and it ended badly for him."

"Are you suggesting . . ." Powers stumbled momentarily over Kip's statement. "That's ridiculous. When I said he'd get war declared on him, I didn't mean it literally."

"It's a feeling, a hunch for lack of a better word," Kip said. "I've seen it plenty of times before when nothing added up – and this doesn't."

"If you think there's foul play, you need to let the police know," she said.

"Hardly. There's nothing to go on. I know the Port City police department all too well. They will be too polite to laugh at me, but they would tell me to keep my crime fantasies to myself. Besides, can you image the firestorm that will rain down on me when word gets out that the Port City *Beacon* is claiming foul play in the death of Anders Martin – when it has been officially declared an accident? I'm already losing advertisers and readers over the *Beacon*'s stance on P2. All my detractors will become enemies when they realize I'm trying, with no evidence, to derail the project that they all want so badly."

"So, what are you going to do?"

"First thing is back you out of this mess," Kip said. "Pretend we never had this conversation. Whether or not there is anything to this, you will be better off out of the picture. Then, I'll do what I always do – work it until I get answers. It's not a pretty process and I usually get beat up on these things. That's figuratively, not for real. But you get the idea."

"Yeah, I get the idea," Powers snapped. "If that's the way you operate, you can clear out now. Anders was my friend and mentor, and if there is anything to what you say, I'll know about that soon enough, without the help of the mighty *Beacon*."

The reversal in conversation was so sudden Kip didn't know which third rail he'd grabbed – manners, gender, or politics.

Powers rose so quickly Kip was thankful for the desk that separated them. She swept to the doorway and shouted to her receptionist.

"Daphne, would you please escort Mr. Alexander out of here, now," she said.

"That's okay," Kip said with none of the confidence and humor that he had brought to this ill-fated meeting. "It's only twenty feet and I can find my way out. I apologize if I . . ."

"No. Just go."

Kip had a pretty good idea what it felt like to be a dog with his tail between his legs. In his encounters with people who had booted him from meetings and newspaper interviews for asking questions that struck too close to home, none had been as abrupt as this one. But even his interview subjects took the time for parting shots, such as how their attorneys would be calling on his publisher to set matters right. Many shouted diatribes about the media and how they were dragging down civil society. In Erin Powers, however, a switch flipped off, or on – Kip couldn't tell which—and now he was gone.

But what could he have done differently? She had no idea of how ugly matters could get if the wrong people got wind of a foray into Anders Martin's death. Law enforcement, City Hall, civic and business honchos would have both their heads on a platter. The *Beacon* could weather it, but Powers would most likely lose her job. She should have thanked him.

Next to worst of all, he needed Powers to help him break through the wall of secrecy around Martin for more information and insight into the man. Fat chance now.

Worst of all, Kip lamented, he liked the woman from the moment he set eyes on her. And to think, he almost asked her out for a drink. Now she was probably considering a restraining order on him.

As he furiously pedaled his two-wheel pride and joy along Ledbetter Street, he savored the sting of the chill March air in his face. Weaving in and around other cars brought him some satisfaction, not to mention curses from their inconvenienced drivers. He blew stop signs with abandon and might have added the traffic light at Columbus Street to his list of vehicular misdemeanors had a dump truck not turned left in front of him as the light changed.

The combination of panic braking and the turn of his handle bars sent Kip sliding fifteen feet until he came to rest in a heap next to the truck's passenger door. The driver and his partner hopped to the pavement, and might have asked about Kip's wellbeing had he not let loose with a string of oaths.

The driver and his passenger weren't quite as tall as Kip, though shoulder to shoulder they were as wide as the truck they drove. Possibly WWF retirees. Not taking kindly to Kip's reference to their mothers, they slowly turned and looked at each other and wordlessly took three easy strides toward him. Grabbing the front of Kip's jacket, they lifted him off the ground.

"Okay, buddy, traffic court is in session," said the one on the right. "Whataya say, Elmer?"

"We find you guilty of shitty bike riding and being a bigger asshole," Elmer replied. "Over to you, Kenny."

Kip's pitiful efforts to wrench loose from the grips of Elmer and Kenny confirmed his doubts about escaping. As a fist cocked inches from his face, he flinched at the coming mayhem.

Instead of a rendezvous with cartoon stars and tweeting birdies, the situation worsened. Judge and jury of the traffic court glanced at each other for confirmation of what they had seen and they released their grips and burst into raucous, raspy laughter. Kip backed up warily, and they slapped their thighs and laughed louder. Watching them lumber back into the truck's cab, Kip failed to make sense of his bizarre reprieve.

"We'd have loved to have painted you a fresh, new black eye, but we can see you already got a fine one," Elmer hollered from behind his steering wheel. "Our boss might get jealous of us finishing off his light work. Have a real nice day, Mister Publisher."

Some of the pedestrians gathering at the street corners murmured nervously while others laughed outright. With the drama concluded, they quickly dispersed as the massive truck with chimneys for exhaust pipes roared off, prolonging first gear noisily for effect.

Standing over his bike in the middle of the empty intersection, Kip managed to glimpse the logo on the receding truck: Schultz Development & Construction Co.

TEN

By the time Kip parked his bike in the print bay in the rear of the Beacon Building, he had regained some of his composure before his run-in with Kenny and Elmer. He lost it as quickly with his first steps across the shop floor.

Willie and Della looked up from their conversation and quizzically regarded their employer.

"Where have you been, Kip?" Della asked so sharply that he wondered who was working for whom.

"What do you mean, where have I been?" Kip replied with the defensive irritation of a spouse arriving late to dinner. But he knew the answer would not be something he wanted to hear.

"Miles Tennyson and his assistant are waiting for you in your office," Della said.

"Crap!" Kip hadn't been entirely unaware of his appointment with his board's choice of auditor. "How long have they been here?"

"Five, maybe ten minutes," Willie said. "And, by the way, you look like you got run over by a truck."

"That's all?" he sighed. Ignoring Willie's assessment of his appearance, Kip looked at his watch for the first time that afternoon. He had known he'd be cutting close the meeting with Tennyson, though the time gained from his premature exit from the city archaeology office was rudely offset by his traffic altercation. "And Miles Tennyson is early, which shouldn't surprise anybody."

Della's next question cleared up the real reason for her agitation.

"Why are they here, Kip?" she asked. "Mr. Tennyson asked for the last three years of our books. I told him no way would he see our ledger without your permission. Why didn't you tell me he was coming?"

"I've only known since late this morning, when he asked for a short meeting," Kip said. "So I agreed to squeeze him in before my interview with Helen Martin."

Kip's answer merely begged the question Della and Willie couldn't hold off asking any longer. As the three of them stood among the sleeping machinery, the poignancy of the moment sent a chill of introspection through Kip. They were the most senior of his staff and, for all purposes, family. In sizing up the two people in front of him, Kip saw them in the moment and not the numbing day-to-day continuum of familiarity.

His pressman wore industrial-issue dark blue trousers and accompanying long-sleeved collared shirt. A fraying cable-knit sweater may have stifled the winter chill of the print bay, but Kip suspected it of also being a treasured gift knitted by his wife. On the cusp of turning 60, Willie seemed smaller and frailer than the wiry fireball Kip knew as a youth. His shock of black hair was skipping gray and going straight to white.

Della had eased into her 70s without the loss of the earnest energy that endeared her to the staff. Kip thought he knew the answer but nonetheless wondered why so many older people dressed in styles cemented in time, decades ago. In her case, Della's fashion sense was firmly rooted in the narrow attire of the 1950s and '60s, a style made more pronounced by the *Beacon*'s (barely) business casual dress policy. Prim Della and semi-goth Carrie Brant at lunch in a Port City diner was always an interesting sight.

Together, Della and Willie set the spiritual goalposts for the *Beacon*, and Kip couldn't image the place without them. In their own caring ways they kept Kip in line, a favor that never went long without his appreciation. So when Willie challenged Kip about Miles Tennyson, he listened.

"What's really going on, Kip?" Willie asked. "Is this your work or the board's?"

Kip was only too glad to lay this one at the feet of the board of directors. His answer was mostly truthful, too.

"The board's," he said. Without delving into the details of the Alice in Wonderland proceedings of the recent board meeting, he conveyed the gist of their ostensible request to size up the paper's long-term prospects. "However, I suggest not reading too much into Miles's work here. Nothing ever comes of my family's periodic panic attacks."

Della laid a clutch of manila file folders on a table and delivered Kip one of her parental looks used to restore normalcy in the front office when silliness got out of hand. "How can we not worry about this?" she asked. "Miles Tennyson may seem like a nice person and all, but you know and I know he makes his living off of other people's misfortunes."

"Oh, how so?" Kip said. "The last I heard, that's the way much of business works."

Still, Tennyson's reputation for acquiring distressed enterprises around town came well earned. Some would say the man had ways of hastening the process, but that was local urban legend. In playing the devil's advocate, Kip mainly wanted to gauge the depth of feelings of his business manager and pressman for any overlooked signs of trouble.

Della nearly spat her response. "Really? Maybe you should tell Marty Hawkins that's how business works. I'm sure he would feel a whole lot more comfortable knowing that, now that Mr. Tennyson has his three restaurants. Or maybe you should ask Selma Landau if losing her ad agency to him is the way business works. Should I go on?" When no answer was forthcoming, she said, "Judging from the late payments for advertising from your friend Teddy Abrahamson, I'd say his lumberyard might be next. So: Are we in line, too?"

Kip's rhetorical if not obnoxious baiting of Della had its effect. He could only hope this perception of matters ended right there with her and Willie. The staff couldn't work any harder without melting the magic glue that held them together.

"Listen, Della, Willie," he began. "Think what you will of me, but the *Beacon* is far bigger than all of us put together. Sure, we struggle at times, but that's nothing new. The *Beacon* has always cut it close. That's the nature of our beast. We're a community newspaper, not some flush tech venture. The *Beacon* board can wail all it wants, but believe me, they will be the last people to push for our demise."

Willie cleared his throat, for effect. "This time looks to be different, Kip," he said. "Why else would that piranha be swimming in our waters?"

"Well, we'll have to see, won't we?" Kip answered, unfazed by Willie's memories of the *Beacon*'s periodic scrapes with fiscal reality. "Trust me, I don't plan on making this easy for him or the board."

Sometimes, what you get is not what you see. Of this Kip was certain, even before entering his office.

The man who rose gracefully from the concave slope of Kip's couch was in his early 50s. Kip could never tell with rowers after a certain age. Decades of daily workouts on the water and in the gym tended to make them appear younger than what their driver's licenses reported.

At a wink over six feet, Miles Tennyson possessed military erectness and a salt and pepper buzz cut to go with it. Despite his rower's physical prowess, Tennyson maintained a relaxed, almost languid manner that pointed more to an Oxford don than a small town corporate raider. His sturdy brown tweed sport coat with patches on each elbow, thin tortoise-shell glasses, and black turtle neck sweater easily put people at ease. Where's the pipe? Kip thought.

Mindful of Willie's assessment, he ran his hands through his wind-blown hair in a vain attempt to offset the look of a man run over by a truck.

"Still commuting by bike these days?" Tennyson asked. Extending his hand, he added, "No wonder you are the fittest person in the boathouse."

His fluid Piedmont drawl wasn't lost on Kip, who scoffed at how quickly people dismissed even diluted Southern accents for lack of gravitas and quick wittedness. As a mannerism, they had disarming qualities, though Tennyson's polish put him in an advanced league.

"I do sleep well at night," Kip said, "even if my staff thinks me a quaint curiosity."

Tennyson turned and gestured to his assistant sitting in a chair. "Kip, this is Rex Thomas, who will be helping me on this project."

Thomas struck Kip as intern young, with his unstarched white button-down shirt, rep tie, blazer, and khakis that said, 'first job, first set of work duds.' Oh, boy, Kip thought, this kid graduated from college, probably with flying colors and letters in lacrosse and chess, and now he thinks he's getting an introduction to the real world. Actually, he might be, Kip reconsidered, allowing that Thomas could have gone the corporate route with its labyrinthine training programs and its officious need-to-know exposure to business. At least in Port City, Thomas would learn how business gets done on the retail level, warts and all.

"I'll see that Della gets you and Rex a spare office so you can get going first thing in the morning," Kip said. "You will find that she runs a tight accounting ship."

Tennyson smiled and said, "That was never in doubt. We only want to get the lay of your office this afternoon."

Even someone without Kip's notorious frugality would flinch at the cost of two people poring through their books for days. Worse, his board members would not be picking up the tab on this lark; the *Beacon* would.

"Anything we can do to hasten your work, let us know," he said. "And if that's all, I've got to dash to an appointment. Della will take it from here."

Tennyson brushed aside the slight. "Before you go, you should know that this isn't something I sought out," he said. "I know that I have what you might say is a reputation in this town . . ."

"Thoroughly deserved," Kip cut in.

Tennyson looked more miffed than offended by the interruption. "Your relatives asked me to pursue this – not the other way around," he said crisply.

"That much we can all agree on," Kip said. "But when you're finished, you will find we may not be awash in cash, but we are solvent, and the board will again have wasted *Beacon* money on a bullshit fishing trip for who knows what reason."

Rex Thomas was getting quite an introduction to the behind-the-scene nuances of business as practiced in Port City. Kip could tell by the kid's efforts to shrink himself into inconspicuousness that he was probably reconsidering his decision to forego a management trainee stint with a D.C. investment house. His mentor, however, wasn't quite done for the evening.

"Uncomfortable as it is to say," Tennyson began, "I'm required to let you know that I am working for all of the *Beacon*'s board of directors. If it leads somewhere you don't like, so be it."

"Noted," Kip said, thoroughly worried where Tennyson could lead it. "Let's go find Della, so she can show you around. And my advice for you and Rex is if she should offer you coffee, take a pass."

ELEVEN

Helen Martin met Kip at the front door of her slate-blue shingled bungalow on Orion Street in the West Ridge neighborhood. Even though it was the tail end of winter, the yard and its well mulched flowerbeds reflected the diligent care of someone impatient for spring's arrival.

"You can park your bike here on the porch," Helen said. "Did you ever think of driving? It's going to be dark when you go back."

"I will next time," he said. "That hill on Randolph Road nearly did me in. But at least it will be downhill when I leave."

Kip attributed the quality of the yard work to Helen, as well as the seamless appearance of the Arts & Craft styled interior. Had to be, since Martin had never seemed the domestic type.

She led him into a kitchen that must have been carved from several rooms when they bought the house and gave it a serious remodeling. It was clearly the heart of the Martin household.

Photographs framed and unframed and a progression of memorabilia of school, sports, vacations, and family milestones covered the walls like an open scrapbook. Yet the homey aroma of dinner in the oven and a cello sonata drifting throughout the house couldn't quite mask the empty feeling that Kip was certain did not originate in his imagination.

The woman standing before Kip was on the tall side, though neither athletic nor matronly; sturdy, Kip thought, at a loss for a more flattering word that she deserved. She wore faded black jeans and an off-white cable-knit sweater that gave her the look of the plein air painter that she was. Her raven black hair was cut short, as much for efficiency as for aesthetics. Thick, Tina Fey style glasses furthered her creative appearance. He apprised the handsome face that weeks before blushed pink in the cheeks with good health. Grief had made itself known through the gray gauntness that a touch of lipstick only magnified. Please, let this be only temporary, Kip thought.

"How about a drink?" she asked. "You look like you've been hit by a truck."

"It has been that kind of day," he said, tiring of that particular allusion to his appearance, particularly when it was he who had sized her up as worse for the wear. "Yes, a beer, please."

He accepted the bottle and politely waited all of one second before taking a long, delicious pull, feeling the pieces of his day slide back into order.

In the easy confines of his office earlier in the day, a visit with Helen had seemed perfectly reasonable – another interview, detached and perfunctory. As he plopped down into the stern comfort of a Morris chair that he belatedly realized must have been Martin's favorite, the weight of the moment smacked him in the head. What had he gotten himself into on this day that would not end?

"Before you begin," Helen said, "I'd like to say thank you and the boat club for all your thoughts and kindness. I'm sure my card to the club fell short and I know Anders would never have stood for the attention. But I appreciate it."

"Those rowers can be big hearted," Kip said. "You know we miss Anders. But how are you holding up?"

"Better now."

She told Kip of the shock, incredulity, and numbness that hit her in waves. Full acceptance was still a way off. The high school where she taught art, however, had also been supportive, allowing her time off to deal with the tragedy.

"When the semester is over, we will probably move back to Colorado," she said. "The girls are in college now and can handle the transition more easily than they could have a couple of years ago."

"You would be missed. I hope you think that one over."

"Not likely. If it hadn't been for Anders's job with the city, we might still be there, and none of this would have happened."

Kip's face darkened, and he ran a hand through his hair, recognizing that Helen also meant that had they never come to Port City, Helen and Kip would never have met, and their torrid six-month affair would never have happened.

She read his next thought right off.

"No, Kip, Anders never knew, and if he did, then he kept it to himself," she said. "After all, that was a long time ago and we'd only been married long enough for me to second guess living with such a difficult and complex man."

"I still feel apologetic," Kip said, "and I still don't know what I was thinking at the time."

Helen set her cup of tea on the arm of her chair and said, "Look, I was young, and you were younger. Your marriage to Meryl was over before it began. We were easy, unconscious targets for each other. I don't regret it, and I hope you don't either."

There was no hesitation in Kip's assent. But he regretted, and he was sure Helen did too, having sneaked around like high school kids avoiding curfew, living a tawdry secret that was going nowhere and, if discovered, would have been beyond messy.

"Sarah turned out to be the best thing for me and for our marriage," Helen said.

The doubled-edge shock that had hit him when Helen became pregnant, followed by her announcement that it was not Kip's child but Anders's, revisited Kip. All along, she wanted to get pregnant, but not by him.

Kip studied the label on his bottle and concluded uneasily that Helen only meant that good had come out of their relationship. "I suppose so," was the best he could muster in reply.

She tried to re-route the conversation. "I can see your mouth still gets you in trouble," she said. "What did you say to Paul Schultz, anyway?"

"I called him a greedy bastard, that's all."

Helen laughed knowingly. "That's a lot of all, considering that man. Anders would have been impressed."

Kip accepted the offer of a second beer and nudged the conversation to Strawberry Flats. "Helen, did you ever notice anything unusual about Anders's opposition to the P2 project? Did he ever mention anything other people might not know?"

He studied Helen's face for tell-tale signs of contradiction or ambivalence, of which there were none. Only an air of weariness.

"Anders's view or my view?"

"Both, if you want."

Helen removed her glasses, rubbed her eyes, and for probably the umpteenth time, revisited Anders's feisty relationship with modern urban life.

"Naturally, I'm against it. P2 doesn't belong here, plain and simple. Let some other chump place have it – one that needs it."

"Well said. And Anders?"

"My objections paled in comparison with his."

"How so?

"It's the nature of someone who makes his living from history – creating the present out of the past. Certainly not from obliterating it like so many people have done in this country."

"I'm coming to appreciate that view. It took someone like Anders to bring it home."

Helen nodded. "He had the effect on people."

She rose from her chair and crossed the floor to stand by the glowing fireplace. His mind might have wandered had not Helen changed the conversation so sharply.

"I hear you had a run-in with Erin Powers this week," she said. "How did you manage that?"

"There was more out than in to it," Kip said, wondering how Helen even knew about that bit of fresh news. "I made an appointment to interview her about the archaeology program, and I evidently derailed it. I chalked it up to frayed nerves from the past week."

"That's right," Helen said. "She's taking Anders's death hard. Still is. Anders and I were extremely fond of Erin and we have always been a safe haven for her. She's welcome here any time for any reason. She and I talk regularly."

"I can certainly understand that," Kip said. "If our brief

encounter hadn't gone south so quickly, I was going to ask her out for a drink."

Helen paused on that piece of information.

"There are a few things you should know should that event ever occur," she said. "Most men have a difficult time with Erin. They fail to appreciate the extent of her passion for her work. When they realize she has no interest in yielding or compromising on her career, things unravel quickly."

Nodding in agreement, Kip said, "This is the Washington area, after all – we're living in one of the most driven and ambitious cultures on the planet. Archaeology has no lock on ambition in this town."

"Perhaps, but an archaeologist works in time spans of tens and hundreds of thousands of years, with only a professional life span to crack open even the most mundane of mysteries," Helen said. "And that's under the best of conditions – funding, political, personnel, and technology, you name it."

Helen returned to her chair, and Kip knew more was coming

"I should also tell you, Erin has been seeing someone for the past year," she said. "It started well and now it's not, and she's taking it hard. Randy teaches in the archaeology program at George Washington University. He understands the complexity of her career aspirations, but he has his own ambitions. Neither seems to be cooperating.

"So, they are on and off a lot," she continued. "They have their moments of ultimatums, break off, and then get back together."

Kip made a highly intuitive leap and determined that Erin Powers would never have to worry about lack of flexibility from him.

"Not that it matters, are they on or off?" Kip asked.

Helen looked at Kip intently, then softened. "They're off. But I wouldn't make any rash wagers on how long it will stay that way. But to be fair, I wouldn't worry too much about Erin's dismissing you so quickly. It's not like her – she's a good person and not one to hold grudges."

"Too bad I'll never know," Kip said.

"Around here we never say never," she said, adding, "and that's my advice for you."

"And I will take it, thank you," he said, thinking it best to steer the conversation elsewhere.

"And what keeps you busy in the short run?" he asked. "There are still four months of school left."

"Well, besides actually working, I'm sorting through Anders's professional papers and collections. I wouldn't call him a hoarder, but he saved an awful lot of stuff. He was extremely organized about all his projects and files."

"I remember when my parents died," Kip said. "Sifting through their things was far more emotional than Cass, Alf, and I ever expected. Not to mention hugely time consuming."

"His stuff doesn't mean much to me, and I knew I'd be at it forever without help from someone who understands Anders's field," she said. "Owen Draper has been a big help there."

"Owen Draper?"

"He knew I didn't know where to start and offered to help."

"I didn't even know they were so close," Kip said. "They may have been in the same field, but I'd have thought still worlds apart. Isn't Owen a museum curator?"

Draper was a director at the National Museum of Archaeology, Helen explained. And, yes, Draper's specialty in Pre-Columbian archaeology was far removed from Anders's work. Most of their contact came through rowing and living in the Port City fish bowl.

Kip, too, knew Draper through rowing. Like Martin, Draper was a sculler, preferring two-oared solo rowing over one-oared group sweep.

"Yes, they did know each other," Helen said. "They'd have coffee every now and then. Shop talk. I'm glad they connected – at least for my own selfish reasons. I won't have to be the one to sift through Anders's life work."

That bit of unexpected news would be worth revisiting later on. Perhaps Martin had confided in Draper about his side dig. This might be easier than he thought.

"Interesting," Kip said. "You know, I'm beginning to think

that Anders was even more heavily invested in fighting P2 than anybody thought."

It was Helen's turn as ask how so.

Kip told Helen what he knew of his secret dig at J.D. Bushrod & Son.

"Did you know anything about what he had been doing?" he asked. "Anders had been working on it almost up to his death. Then it looks like he abruptly quit."

"God, no," Helen said. "I certainly did not, and if Erin didn't know, then nobody else does, either."

It didn't take a mind reader to see how much this news shook Helen. She closed her eyes and drew in a breath lasting so long that Kip thought she might be holding it. But as the tumblers of logic in her churning mind finally slipped into place, Helen exhaled.

"Anders always told me what he was working on. He gave me the bad news with the good. It didn't matter if it was an argument at work that he unjustly lost or something as silly as a broken wine glass. What I'm saying is, I never had to ask. Anders always told me before I could ask. It was the bedrock of our marriage."

"I'm sure he would have told you, and told you sooner rather than later, if he could have," Kip said.

She lifted her cup and took a sip of tea gone cold and said nothing.

Kip, continued, "Where do you think Anders found the time to do all the things that he did and still manage a side project?"

"He ran his own department, and he ran it well enough that nobody ever questioned him," Helen said. "There's always time to be grabbed by ducking out of a public hearing, tours, and so on. I'm sure he could find the time.

"But, the bigger question is why nobody noticed him at Strawberry Flats," she said. "Didn't Liza Bushrod have suspicions?"

"I would not call them suspicions," Kip said. "After all, she's the one who gave him permission to work on her property. To her it was a project that didn't interfere with anything. And then it was gone. And but for some luck on my part, it would have been forgotten."

"Didn't Anders ever run out of steam?" Kip asked. "Didn't he get tired? Getting up every day before dawn for rowing is tiring enough for the rest of us"

"Of course, he got tired," Helen said. "But no more than usual. He was 52, after all. I will say, though, that in the last couple weeks, Anders was all over the board – grouchy one moment, apologetic and kind the next. But the odd part was, in the days before he drowned, he was very much at peace. He actually seemed happy. I never asked. I was just glad to have him like that."

"Let me ask you about Paul Schultz . . ."

"They couldn't stand each other, plain and simple," Helen interrupted. "They stood for ideas at opposite ends of the spectrum."

"Did Anders ever feel physically threatened by Schultz?" Kip asked.

"I would have said no way in hell – at least until your run-in with Paul. Now, I'm not so sure. That said, Anders could not be intimidated by anyone or any group."

"Did he ever discuss Schultz with you?"

"Their bitter arguments, yes. Looking back, I suppose those two could have come to blows someday." Helen rose, and Kip thought it the end of their meeting, but instead, she said, "Would you like to see Anders's den?"

Kip did.

With one glance of the den, Kip silently declared it the man-cave of a diehard professional. Shelves bowed with the weight of books, binders, pots, shards, maps, and charts. Hanging from the wall, a glass-covered box held neatly arrayed rows of arrowheads. There were a few empty spots, but overall each looked like the other, as far as Kip could tell. Draper would know what he was seeing.

"Anders would have been flattered by the attention of such a high-powered museum curator," Kip said, futilely tilting his bottle for traces of any remaining suds.

"Or embarrassed that someone had to clean up after him," she said.

"I cast my vote with grateful," Kip said. "I should go while there's still a little daylight."

She ushered him to the door and said, "I could drive you home."

He considered the offer and even though he found nothing risky in it, he declined. "Nah. I'm looking forward to a downhill ride."

Helen ran her eyes up and down him as if it might be the last time they saw each other.

"Take care of yourself, young man," she said. "You look better intact."

Kip brushed hair from his eyes, slipped on his helmet, and said, "Thanks, that's advice to treasure."

They did not hug, and Kip left without saying another word.

TWELVE

The cobblestone alley leading to Kip's house passed between two townhouses and their dollhouse-sized patios was a cool sight for tourists. But it was hell on the skinny tires of bicycles, and he walked his bike the final seventy-five feet of his ride back from Helen Martin's home.

The twin carriage lights on each side of his front door were on, the best news of his interminable day. They signaled that Mrs. Campbell, his gruff angel of a neighbor, had fed Ike and Samantha.

Once settled at his cluttered kitchen table with a sandwich, Kip half-heartedly sifted through the day's mail. Nothing but third-class trash, including, in his humble opinion, that week's edition of the *Mirror*, which would have to serve as Kip's mealtime reading.

As much as he loathed Ambrose Ralston's column, "Mirror, Mirror," Kip read it, like many others in Port City. It was always an opportunity to see what new ways his rival could embarrass himself – with phony urgency, salaciousness or, most often, garden-variety banality. The man's formula was almost too elementary: Spin opinion from canned community news and pass it off as insider wisdom. Since Kip also knew the pool of news from which Ralston would be choosing, topics for "Mirror, Mirror" were a weekly guessing game he seldom lost.

This week's 1-2-3 lineup had to be the widening of King Street to accommodate tour buses, the announcement of a mayoral candidate and, finally, the prospects for Port City High School's spring baseball season.

Wrong.

There, in the number-three spot in full wattage, was "Beacon on the Auction Block?"

The sandwich in Kip's mouth turned to sawdust.

In one short paragraph, Ralston had managed to accurately summarize the main points of the *Beacon* board decision to bring in a third party – Miles Tennyson, as noted by Ralston – to evaluate the health of the paper. Conveniently left unwritten was the reason for the audit, an omission that would shrewdly lead readers to one conclusion: The paper was being readied for sale.

So precisely damning was the wording that Kip had to pronounce it the work of a weasel, and only one came to mind: Melvin Alexander. He must have gotten his meds mixed up if he thought such a tip would generate buzz for selling the *Beacon*. Tennyson had too much sense to needlessly invite competitors into the arena. Besides, such a move wasn't all that swift professionally, since revelation of the source of its exposure would deal Tennyson a nasty ethical blow. Melvin, on the other hand, didn't have the sense to remember to buy low and sell high. Long-term, the *Beacon* might suffer from his stunt should its sale ever come to pass.

Kip's immediate worry centered on how his advertisers would react to Ralston's one-paragraph doozie. If too many defected to, say, the *Mirror*, the *Beacon* would be in big trouble. Paul Schultz had already caused enough grief in that area. More bleeding would force Tennyson to revise the healthy assessment that Kip had promised. What was Melvin thinking?

There was still time enough left in the evening for Kip to go pound on Melvin's front door and confront him. It was fun to imagine his cousin dropping his crystal tumbler of bourbon onto his marble doorway as Kip shook him into tiny pieces. But sleep, or an approximation of it, was calling. Hell or high water, rowing practice began at 5:15 the next morning. That fantasy would have to wait until another day.

"Lights out, guys," Kip sighed, as his housemates roused themselves to join Kip in his bedroom.

THIRTEEN

For most of the 200 miles before it reaches Washington, D.C., the Potomac River flows peacefully through flat farmland, punctuated by small towns, bridges, woodlands, and tributaries. The pastoral stretch of its journey ends sharply at the Potomac Fall Line, a few traffic jams upstream from the crawling beehive of the Washington Beltway, where the rolling Piedmont yields to the expansive Tidewater region. Beginning with Great Falls, the river races through chutes and over a boulder-strewn riverbed down steep and narrow gorges before settling into its dignified entry into Georgetown.

This is the Potomac of panoramic vistas, monuments, Japanese Cherry Trees, and lovely arched bridges. Hollywood gravitates to this two-mile stretch of river for scenes of rowers gliding along in the orange glow of impossibly beautiful summer mornings. Along its shores, cyclists and joggers ply parkland trails. On the Georgetown waterfront on weekend afternoons and well into night, crowds pack the outdoor restaurants and bars to socialize and ogle million dollar yachts at dock.

This was not the river the rowers of Port City and Algonquian boat clubs found on a cold and blustery Saturday afternoon on the front end of March. With the tide coming in, the current flowing south, and the wind gusting from the northwest at cross-quarters, both teams knew they had more than each other to contend with.

Only the eight-person boats could handle conditions like this. Both teams agreed to abandon racing the fours and eliminate one

8 from each team to make the scrimmage more manageable for the coaches who would be driving launches alongside the two 8s competing in the best two-of-three format. Kip won the coin toss with Schultz and got to compete. What Schultz felt about sitting out was another matter.

Kip could trace the course with his eyes closed: Beginning at Key Bridge, it ran downriver along the Georgetown waterfront for 1,000 meters and then angled east for another 500 meters before ending opposite the Kennedy Center where he would be wondering where all the oxygen in the world had gone.

He had always been wary of races so short and intense. None of the *Madison*'s rowers could afford a mistake. A rower even slightly out of sync with his or her teammates could slow a boat by seconds over a course where margins of one-hundredths of a second sometimes separate first from second place. Worse, if the rower got far enough out of sync, the sheer force of the seven other oars could slam back the oar, sometimes even knocking him or her out of the boat. Such "crabs" had cost Port City races in the past.

Still, precision timing and blade work would be luxuries on this near stormy day. The weather report hadn't lied – rain was in the air, spitting and sputtering. The wind, while never topping 12 mph, nonetheless pushed rollers across the river while the incoming tide fought the current. With a high of 50 degrees forecasted for midafternoon, the racers had about as miserable conditions as could be expected.

After launching the *Madison* from Algonquian's dock at the end of Key Bridge, the Port City crew took a warm-up paddle upstream and practiced starts and power spurts before crossing back under the middle span of the bridge for the start. It was the last chance to work out kinks and jitters and to eyeball the men in the *C&O*, Algonquian's boat. True to reputation, the Algonquian team was big and fit. Like the rowers in the *Madison*, they wore layers of high-tech fiber and fleece pullovers, topped off with stocking caps or baseball caps. In a formal race, they'd all be in spandex team uniforms, hardly handsome at a regatta and eye-stopping in a 7-Eleven.

Bo Hansen and Peter Baker, Algonquian's coach, communicated on the water with two-way radios. Both brought along volunteers with camcorders to chronicle the race for analyzing the next week. Baker agreed to be the starter, calling out the start sequence over an electric bullhorn and into his radio so that an assistant in a launch at the finish line could record the results. He and Hansen would then accompany their crews to the finish line.

Even on a calm day, Kip found the aligning of the sixty-foot boats in parallel positioning a daunting proposition. In a slight breeze, boats will drift. One could get into position, only to have others float apart while still others patiently waited for their turns. He felt for Dana Parsons, the *Madison*'s coxswain, on the days when exasperated race officials gruffly shouted instructions through electric bull horns.

Only two boats were in this race, however, so Parsons and her counterpart in the *C&O* were able to quickly get into position.

Baker opted for an abbreviated start call to avoid any cat herding:

"Ready!"

"Row!"

And the boats were off.

All week long and in the warm-up before the scrimmage, Port City had worked on its start sequence: half slide, half slide, three-quarter slide, full slide, and then thirty strokes at a rate of 36 a minute before settling at 32. In the final 250 meters, the rowers would take it back up to 36 for the final sprint home.

But, today, Hansen told his coxswain to come out at 32 and settle at 28 to better cope with the North Atlantic-like conditions on the Potomac.

The *C&O* tore off at a high stroke rate – probably 36, Kip figured – and quickly pulled ahead of the *Madison*. A collective geezus rang out in the *Madison*, prompting an angry retort from Parsons.

"All eyes in the boat!" Parsons barked, loud enough to make redundant the little loudspeakers spaced throughout the boat.

"Do not worry about them. They will pay for that fast start."

All of five feet and 105 pounds, Parsons constituted the ideal commander of the *Madison*. Her weight detracted little from the vaunted power-to-weight ratio valued by coaches. But her best trait was her analytical eye. From many years of experience, she knew exactly what was going on with each rower and how to correct any flaws among them. At the same time, Parsons had an uncanny knack for sizing up competitor boats.

With her admonition, the *Madison* settled into a rough rhythm. Depending on the location of a wave, some oars dug deep, partway up their shafts, while other rowers completely whiffed strokes. When done unawares, air strokes could be devastating, but the crews had expected them and easily recovered.

Kip's role in the stroke position meant he was the executor of Parsons's commands. When she called out to "settle" at 28 strokes, all knew to do so, though the port rowers followed Kip's lead while the starboard rowers followed the lead of the 7 seat behind Kip. In three easy strokes, the *Madison* entered the main body of the race. Instead of long, sweeping strokes, he abbreviated the length of his strokes to reduce chances of catching crabs. He wasn't so sure that the *C&O* would be doing otherwise. Either way, no records would be set this afternoon.

In spite of their shortened strokes, Kip felt the *Madison* pulsing healthily with each drive. The whistling wind, the clicking of sixteen oarlocks, the splashing of oars, and the exhortations of two very vocal coxswains made for a good adrenaline rush.

He couldn't vouch for his teammates, but for him what happened on land, stayed on land. As soon as any boat Kip rowed in pushed away from a dock, all joys and sorrows of daily living vanished. In their place, satisfaction born of synchronizing with seven straining oarsmen and the exhilaration of speeding through the water took over entirely. The more intense the workout, the more he left the world ashore.

Today was no different. The rude and unwieldy queue of characters in his mind never made it past the velvet rope on Algonquian's dock. Erin Powers, Paul Schultz, his cousins,

Ambrose Ralston, and Miles Tennyson would have to wait. For the next five minutes, all that mattered to Kip was maintaining focus and stamina.

By the end of 1,000 meters, endurance was becoming an issue. That was to be expected, given the added tension of all-out exertion in rough and unpredictable water. So far, no one had missed a stroke, which said much for Hansen's conservative strategy. Still, Kip knew that with near-equal crews, a 28-stroke rate would never overtake a 32.

With Key Bridge receding in the background, Parsons delivered the good news.

An Algonquian rower caught a crab with 400 meters to go, forcing his teammates to momentarily cease rowing while he got his oar back in sync with the others. It was enough for the *Madison* to overtake the *C&O*.

"Power 10, in three!" Parsons screamed. "3-2-1, let it rip! They'll be back, so give it your all!"

Sure enough, the bow ball of the *C&O* bobbed and pulsed into the periphery on Kip's left. Only thirty feet separated the two hulls, a deceptively narrow span, given the twelve-foot length of the oars reaching toward each other. Less than 250 meters remained, and Parsons announced the final sprint.

The 250-meter sprint demands everything a rower has: strength, oxygen, and concentration. The greatest sin in rowing is to finish a race with gas left in the tank. In the blustery conditions, the *C&O* crew was nearly spent when Parsons called out, "32 in three. 3-2-1!"

The *Madison* did not surge, and Kip knew it wouldn't.

In a voice loud enough for only Parsons to hear, he told her so. "Dana, we've got to take it up more!"

Strokes do not tell coxswains what to do, especially in a race. Parsons stared through Kip, ignoring the incursion on her authority.

Kip didn't have the oxygen to spare for an extended conversation. "Do it!" he rasped.

Parsons's instructions from Hansen called for 32 strokes a minute and Kip could see her weighing the implications of obeying their coach against the indignity of giving into him. No contest. So, he said it again, slightly more politely, "Dana, it's only twenty-five strokes! Twenty, now."

There was only one way to know if her bone-dead rowers could keep it together at a rate that would be challenging even on a calm summer day. Parsons barked the abbreviated order: "Dammit, 36 in 3-2-1. 36!"

The crew of the *Madison* wheezed with the unexpected effort, but the boat did surge.

With 120 meters to go – twelve hard strokes – it was clear the *Madison* would hold off the *C&O*. Taking the rate up to 36 was paying off. A few scattered come-ons! interspersed with the rapid-fire the clunking of oarlocks and the splashing of paddles were all that could be heard.

"Ten to go," Parsons willed her rowers.

"9-8-7 . . ."

And then from the middle of the boat, an "Oh, shit!" followed by the sight of a rower flung forward onto the rower in front of him and then into the river.

"Let it run!" Parsons screamed the traditional command to stop rowing. "What the hell is going on?"

"Crab . . . Gardner," came a reply from the middle of the boat.

Phil Gardner, the 4 seat, was barely treading water in the river. Sheer exhaustion and the shock of 50-degree water took the fire right out of him. Hansen quickly eased his launch alongside Gardner, and with help from his volunteer videographer, pulled the shaken rower aboard. They wrapped him in a reflective space blanket. While they were turning around, Baker approached Hansen's launch. They agreed that Hansen would speed Gardner back to the warmth of the Algonquian boathouse while Baker accompanied the two shells back ashore.

"Bo, there's only half an oar here," Manny Vargas shouted. "It's missing the entire bottom half."

"That's impossible," Hansen said. But he easily could see what Vargas meant. "So where is it?"

From the bow of the *Madison*, Steve Chang spotted the white, black, and red trimmed blade with its partial handle bobbing in the water. Hansen had a near-frozen rower to ferry ashore, so he left the matter with Baker and sped away.

Baker maneuvered his boat into position for retrieving the oar while his assistant leaned over snagged it before it could sink. Saying nothing, the coach turned the tiller and joined the other two boats for the somber journey back to his boathouse.

FOURTEEN

Outside the Lee Street Pub, mist, rain, and fog took turns creating a storybook scene in the early evening. A quiet side street off King Street, Lee glistened beneath old-style lampposts. The saturated atmosphere had the odd effect of muffling nearby sounds while amplifying those from far away. Jetliners racing down the runways of National Airport and the click-clacking of Metro subway cars on their above-ground routes sounded as though they were only a few blocks away.

Only hours earlier, the Port City rowers had managed the arrival of a classic low-pressure front that had now settled into a moody nor'easter. Passersby, hunched and arm-in-arm under umbrellas, could see through the establishment's steamy mullioned windows to where they had crowded into a narrow alcove for the club's monthly happy hour.

It had been Kip's idea to invite the Algonquian rowers. Had it been a full regatta with hundreds of rowers, no pub could have held so many thirsty bodies. For this minor monthly ritual, however, the restaurant's staff had combined several tables to form one long banquet table that didn't quite accommodate the twenty rowers and their spouses and significant others. So some appropriated bar stools and others half sat in the recess of the bay window.

At the bar, Kip did not have to signal for service. It came to him in spades.

"Well, hello, row boy. What can I get to stroke your oar?"

"Actually, Glynda, you've got to stroke a whole lot of oars tonight. How about eight pitchers of Port City IPA?"

"Ha! Happy hour for the beasts. I should have known. You

guys never miss your period."

Glynda Barnes never failed to make Kip laugh. She was the reason the rowers didn't defect to other pubs and bars in Port City. Initially, the group had frequented a variety of venues for their get-togethers – until the lithesome blonde with the salty mouth began working at the Lee Street Pub. How she could make Lee Street's standard uniform of white oxford shirt and khaki pants so sexy was a source of wonderment. As endearing was the unpredictable banter that came with the package.

"Tell your lovable beasts the first round is on me tonight. I am so sorry to hear about Anders. He didn't come in here much, but we all liked him. And he gave this place class."

She had more to say.

"I don't know doo-doo about your sport, except you are all crazy. But rowers don't drown out there, do they?"

Kip measured his reply as she topped off the pitchers. "Actually, they do," he said. "Not very often, of course. You hear about it every now and then at some club around the country. And when it does happen, everyone is shocked and surprised as though it couldn't happen. And certainly not in Port City."

"Maybe you are right," Glynda said, gathering up two pitchers in each hand and nodding for Kip to grab the other four before heading over to their table. "But it's horrible."

As they weaved their ways among the tables, a shimmer of red caught Kip's attention, and he pulled up so abruptly that beer sloshed on to his hands. A man and a woman deep in conversation, each leaning in to hear the other better, looked up at Kip and Glynda. Instead of the pony tail he remembered from their meeting, Erin Powers wore her hair long and flowing. Kip's heart soared, plummeted, and then leveled out, awaiting his next move.

Mindful of Helen Martin's comment about his trouble-making mouth, Kip mentally tried out a series of bon mot approaches that might reestablish conversational footing with Powers. "How do you like these digs?" Nope – corny … already tried. "Of all the gin joints in all the towns in all the world, I walk into yours." Ugh, ugh – she might take it as bitterness, rather than a superbly cultured sense of irony. As he considered the merits of a straight-on "Hello, there," her companion preempted Kip.

"I'm sorry, but we did not order . . . eight pitchers of beer." The man disavowing the order looked to be in his late thirties. He was wire thin with receding hair and goatee which were already on the losing end of turning gray. Gesturing with the flick of his hand, he said, "Perhaps that . . . that group over there might be more suitable."

He's as pompous as he looks, Kip thought. Trading a glance with a bewildered-looking Glynda, he deadpanned, "But you two look so thirsty, it's the least we can do."

"Now, look here, fella . . ." He was actually rising to his feet when Powers cut in.

"It's all right, Randy," she said. "This is the newspaperman I told you about last week."

Given his brief and ill-fated initial encounter with Powers, Kip fully expected a tart exchange and even quicker dismissal. What a shame that would be, he thought. She looked even more gorgeous than when he first met her. Should he attempt another apology, even if it's in front of what looked to be her reputedly off boyfriend? He never got to exercise his contriteness.

"I would invite you to join us, but I can see you're on a mission," Powers said. "Kip, this is my friend, Randy, a fellow archaeologist. Randy, meet Kip, the editor of the Port City *Beacon*. Or is it publisher?"

"Both, actually," Kip said.

Powers looked over to the happy hour noisily underway at the far end of the room, and asked, "Who are all those people you're with?"

Not bad, thought Kip, happy to have been spotted first by Powers. He explained as briefly as he could, considering that the weight of four pitchers of beer was catching up with him and, surely, the patiently waiting Glynda.

Ready to exit the awkward scene, Kip said, "Randy, it was good to meet you. Sorry for the lame humor."

"Not at all, Chip," Randy said.

Kip took a step forward and would have emptied four pitchers over Randy's head had Glynda not quickly stepped in front of him. She joined the other two in a shocked stare at Kip.

"Thanks, Glynda," he said. "That would have been a waste of good beer."

As they headed back to happy hour, Glynda said, "Jesus, Kip, what was all that about? If I didn't know better, I'd say that Young Red there has your number."

Before Kip could answer, Glynda issued an astonished squeak, "Oh, no, not again. Guys . . .!"

Standing like a goofy glee club, Kip's brothers-in-oars broke out in a heavily altered Beatles song:

Lovely Glynda Lee Street maid
Lovely Glynda Lee Street maid

Lovely Glynda Lee Street maid,
Nothing can come between us.
When it gets dark I row your heart away.

Standing by a bar,
When I caught a glimpse of Glynda,
Filling in my bill in her little white book.
In a cap she looked much hotter,
And the towel across her shoulder
Made her look a little like a rich man's dream.

Lovely Glynda, Lee Street maid,
May I inquire discreetly,
When are you free to have some beer with me?
(Glynda!)

Horrible job with the lyrics. Terrible harmony. Nearby patrons winced. But Glynda rocked so hard with laughter they were lucky not to be getting their beer off the floor.

Rabid toasters, the boys raised glasses to Glynda, who wisely retreated.

And on and on they toasted: to each other's teams, the stinking weather, and even the broken oar, where they stopped to chew on possible explanations.

Earlier in the afternoon, at Algonquian's boathouse, when Bo Hansen and his charges had studied the two broken pieces, the first thing they noticed was the number on the oar. Gardner in the 4 seat had picked up the number 1 oar – Kip's. Kip never knew he was rowing with the 4 oar.

Usually in rowing, the choice of a boat's eight oars make no difference. But some rowers prefer to make adjustments to an oar's collar and its positioning in the rigger to compensate for longer or shorter arms and desired distance in the water. Several in the *Madison*, Kip included, adjusted their oars, so it did matter which they used. In the rough rowing conditions, neither had noticed the switch. But it certainly gave them all something to talk about afterwards.

"I still can't believe that oar snapped," Hansen said. "Even a moose like Gardner shouldn't be able to do that."

Ignoring the beastly comparison, Gardner posited, "Maybe it got damaged when we loaded the trailer this morning."

"We'd have known at the time," Steve Chang countered. "Besides, aren't they made from some indestructible material? And why weren't other oars damaged?"

"Who knows others weren't?" another suggested. "We can check on Monday morning."

"Those oars cost a hundred bucks a pop," Hansen said. "Our heads will roll if we break another. Besides, not to overlook that Phil could have had a worse outcome than a swim in the Potomac."

Hansen wasn't finished.

"And another thing, whose bright idea was it to take the stroke rate up to 36 today?" he asked. "And don't tell me you all held a group vote." His tone was somewhere between sarcasm and bemusement. "Dana, you have any insight into that maneuver?"

Parsons was half-sitting on the window sill, and from the

glare she delivered Kip, he figured she wasn't over their exchange of six hours ago. A dozen heads turned toward Kip's end of the table.

"I confess to mind control," Kip said. "Since we were never going to hold off you guys," he said, gesturing to several Algonquian rowers, "without some additional mph, I willed Dana into action. She tried to resist, but she was totally powerless in the grip of my mental persuasion. How was I to know our guys were stronger than our equipment?"

Parsons raised her glass in mock salute.

Hansen, Kip noticed, wasn't laughing, and he knew repercussions still might follow on Monday. But before he could consider the form it might take, Glynda approached.

"Fellas, do I dare interrupt? Who needs refills?"

Half a dozen hands shot up, and she took orders for another round as well as appetizers and sandwiches. Glynda never questioned why they all weren't on the south side of the obesity epidemic. Maybe, after all, they worked as hard as they partied.

FIFTEEN

The nor'easter that scoured Port City over the weekend was busily wearing out its welcome Monday morning as Kip arrived at the *Beacon*. The front door, swollen with accumulated moisture, put up a tougher fight than usual. As it yielded, he lurched forward, and cold rainwater cascaded from his slicker and out-gunned umbrella onto the tiled foyer. His corduroy pants were soaked from the knees down and his sneakers squeaked like fleeing mice.

Today was the rare one when he envied office workers, emerging pristine dry from their cars in underground garages. Their commutes may have been soulless, but they would not have to wait two hours for their clothes to dry.

Still, the two paper sacks of caloric sin from Mister Perks coffee shop had survived his sprint up King Street. A round of pastries and doughnuts were sure to be welcomed by the staff who would soon be arriving equally soaked. Kip seldom touched the coffee machine in the second floor conference room, but this time he preempted Della's wreckage by brewing a pot.

As the machine chirped and gurgled, he leaned on the conference table and studied the rain-lashed scene on St. Edmunds Street. The week ahead couldn't be any more distressing than its predecessor. Some issues he couldn't control – Melvin's questionable I.Q. and Tennyson's audit. Others he might be able to influence.

Working on an éclair back in his office, Kip focused on Anders Martin and even more closely on his successor. Erin Powers had insight into Martin's final days and valuable knowledge of the field of archaeology – if he could tap it. If only there was any truth to Helen Martin's assessment of Powers.

It was shy of 8 o' clock, too early for even telemarketers to be out and about, so instead of calling Powers, Kip began planning the framework for the *Beacon*'s spring publishing season. Pulling together the many pieces of the paper's functions was a critical and productive task. Even satisfying most of the time. But this morning, it felt like busy work. Try as he might, Kip's focus kept shifting from the job at hand to his three-minute encounter with Powers on Saturday evening. He could have sworn that despite his near beery brawl with on-again/off-again Randy, there was a twinkle in her smile that said she really would have liked him to join them. Then, again, that was before he nearly blew the lid off the evening. Thank you, Glynda, for sparing Randy the waterfall.

He had worked himself in a nervous knot of ifs and buts when the phone on his desk rang. He almost let it go to voice mail, but the prospect of the *Beacon*'s dwindling advertisers made him think twice.

The voice on the other end of the line was soft and vaguely familiar.

"You're an early bird, Mr. Alexander."

It was female, that much he could tell.

"I assume your digs are peaceful at this hour," she added, sparing him further guesswork.

Erin Powers had beaten him to the call, depriving him of the clever suaveness he had planned. Left was the lamest of lines. "I was just going to call you," he said, "but it seemed too early."

"And why were you going to call me, may I ask?" she continued. Again, the playful tone, as though she'd never thrown him out of her office and later on witnessed the near spectacle at the Lee Street Pub.

"I wanted to see you again." So much for his elaborate spiel on contriteness and what the real Kip Alexander was like.

"Really? Now?"

"Well, it doesn't have to be now, I mean . . ."

"No?"

"Is everything a question for you?" Kip asked, more

frustrated than irked.

"Here, let me be more direct."

"Please do. We might get further."

"Your front door is stuck shut. You could see me again if you could manage to open your castle door."

Kip made it to the front door in three strides and flung it open to a wet and bedraggled figure on his door step.

"Sorry, most people throw a shoulder into the door on days like this," he said. "Come on in. People don't start arriving for another half an hour, or else someone would have heard you."

Powers stepped into the foyer, pulled her hood back, and hesitated. "Do you have any newspaper you can put down so I don't ruin your floor?"

He regarded Powers for signs of irony and, seeing none, said, "Possibly, though we prefer the *Mirror* for such things. Come on upstairs. The coffee is fresh and a whole lot better than it will be in about an hour from now."

He held her briefcase as she emerged from her Gortex chrysalis and gave her a hair an organizing shake. "Ye gods, what a storm out there, and we've still got a couple more hours before it clears out," she said. "Show me to the coffee."

Powers chose the couch in Kip's office and began working on a bagel and mug of coffee. Taking a long look around the room, she said, "I will venture the guess that you are a benevolent boss and not at all like the gruff jerks that people associate with TV newspaper editors."

"You're half right," Kip said. "My staff thinks I'm a push-over, while the outside world thinks I'm obnoxiously aggressive."

"That sounds almost plausible," she said.

"I try not to overplay the so-called career stepping-stone card that small town publishers push off on their staffs," he said. "That's not the legacy I'm passing on from my parents. But we do try to put up a tough-guy persona with the outside world – you know, the things we will and will not do. Better to be respected than liked in this field."

"Then, do I dare ask a favor?"

"Perhaps. But, I'm not very good at knee-capping and changing fuses."

"Nothing so dramatic, and actually it's right up your alley," she said. "I was hoping that the *Beacon* might like to produce a feature on Port City's archaeology program."

So, that's why the Mountain had come to Muhammad on this rainy Monday morning, Kip thought. He had been sitting on the edge of the front of his desk with his feet dangling, and now he rose, intrigued at this turn of events.

"Of course, if this is an affront to your tough-guy image, let me know and I can be on my way," she said.

Damn, Kip thought. She wouldn't take this to that oaf at the *Mirror*. Or would she?

Before he could reply, Powers said briskly, "And no, I wouldn't ask the *Mirror* to do this story if you don't want it."

Kip looked puzzled at this juncture in the already whip-sawed conversation.

"Call it an olive branch for my rude behavior the other day," she said. "My temper gets me in trouble too often. But, you've got to admit, it's a great idea for a story."

"Tell me more."

"Well, with P2 looming in everybody's future, an article showcasing the archaeology office's efforts to discover and share knowledge of the city's rich past would be most appropriate," she said. "And I know the person to write it."

Powers could have asked him to write *War & Peace* backwards and he would have jumped at it. "I'd like that very much," he said. Returning to his comfortable perch on the edge of his desk, he added, "I'd like something in return, though."

She looked at him quizzically. "What would that be?"

"Would it make sense for you to call Owen Draper?" he asked. "He's an archaeologist and he knew Anders, according to Helen Martin. Maybe if you were to call him – archaeologist to archaeologist, it might turn up something about Strawberry Flats."

"So, you really do want my help on this," Powers said. "Are you sure about this?"

"I'm very sure about it," Kip said. "The more I've thought about it since last week, the more sure I am."

"Well, then," Erin said, "I'll call him first thing when I get to my office. We can go over it tomorrow."

Tomorrow would be a no-go, he told her: Among other conflicts, he had an appointment with Joseph Patel, Port City's medical examiner.

"I suppose this has to do with Anders," Powers said. "Is it necessary?"

"Necessary might not be the best phrasing," he said. "A visit with the M.E. is something I do with most news events involving a death. So, what better way to ask a few more questions of Doc Patel? Besides, I like the guy, even though our get-togethers are seldom fun."

"I see," Powers said. "Do you ever learn much from your sessions?"

"Sometimes. But with Anders, probably not. The M.E. report has been concluded and I would already have heard about anything special. I'll be going through the motions. It's something I do whenever he releases a report on the death of an important community figure or if the situation is particularly interesting, and this time it's both."

"Makes good sense," she said, though Kip could detect neither approval or disapproval.

They agreed to reconvene at Powers's office Wednesday afternoon after the printing of that week's *Beacon*.

SIXTEEN

An annex to Port City Hospital, the city's medical examiner's facility consisted of offices, a cramped lab, visitors area and, of course, the refrigerated vault-like examination area so indispensable to TV and Hollywood. With its street-side retail-office appearance, the facility reminded Kip of an urgent-care center – neither too small nor too large, professional in appearance, but not a place to linger.

After chaining his bike to a nearby lamppost, Kip entered the empty waiting area, where the décor was minimal: gray carpeting, wood and Formica furniture, and overhead fluorescent lighting. Somewhere in the interior, music could be faintly heard.

Within seconds, Joseph Patel emerged to greet Kip. The M.E. was thin and in height he barely reached Kip's shoulders. Rimless glasses and a white lab jacket worn over a blue oxford shirt and paisley tie gave Patel professional stature to spare.

For the last fifteen years Patel led a small staff tasked with determining causes of death that occur suddenly or without explanation. Very few cases stumped them. Most involved traffic fatalities, suicides, homicides, home accidents, and the identification of missing persons. Nothing shook Patel's office as much as the sudden death of young people, whether through cars, drugs, violence, and even athletics. While the writing of these news stories often included a visit with Patel, Kip never overcame the feeling of intruding in personal matters. Because of privacy restrictions and sensitivity to grieving family members, he seldom walked away with sensational or unique information.

Yet, by making the city's M.E.'s office a regular part of his beat, Kip had easier access than his competitors. Patel trusted

Kip and Kip trusted him, and this required an on-going relationship that frequently involved perfunctory visits. Today's meeting fell somewhere between routine and unusual – which would further depend on what Patel had to tell Kip. He expected today's meeting to last less than fifteen minutes. Patel would agree with him.

"Cause of death is accidental drowning," Patel said, wasting little time once they'd settled in his office. "In water that cold, Mr. Martin succumbed quickly. I doubt he suffered much. Further, the time between death and recovery was so brief that his body experienced no degradation."

"I understand," Kip said agreeably. Patel's assessment was going so quickly that Kip wondered how he could diplomatically steer the discussion toward his suspicions of foul play without appearing conspiratorial or sensational. Not much to be done about that, so he plunged in. "But were there any quirks or other indications that might explain how he capsized?" he asked. "Can you tell if maybe his boat hit something?"

"No, not really," Patel said. "Besides, that would be crossing over into the jurisdiction of law enforcement, and I'm sure you've already been in touch with them. We consider Mr. Martin's death a freak accident."

Patel's next comment brought Kip to attention. "Off the record, though, there is one unexplained aspect."

Normally, he resented the casual and frequent way some interview sources employed the phrase "off the record." Even though the practice formed the bedrock of first-class reporting, too many sources invoked it for reasons of mere convenience to avoid having to think harder and to avoid having to construct more thoughtful responses. For others, "off the record" was a shallow attempt to ingratiate the reporter with useless information. Then, some used the interview provision as a means of sidetracking trains of thought and inquiry. Sure, some reporters – a minority, Kip maintained – reciprocated with their own gray interpretations of the meaning of "off the record" in order to get what they needed.

Patel, however, fell into none of these categories. Besides, his interest in Martin had deeper dimensions than everyday reporting. "You're on," Kip said.

Patel swiveled to face his computer, tapped several keys, and an image appeared. Kip blanched momentarily at the clarity of the detail of Anders Martin's left arm. In the middle of the forearm section, a wound had been wiped clean of blood. What remained crudely resembled an oblong triangle.

"What is it?" Kip asked.

"As I mentioned, we don't know – that is, we don't know what caused it," Patel said. "We assume he got tangled in the boat rigging and cut himself repeatedly trying to right his boat. In his physical state, he couldn't do much."

"As a rower, you might know whether that would be plausible," he continued. "It's unlikely his body encountered another boat, and it clearly did not look to be caused by shoreline rocks, since the Heron Bay shoreline is mostly mud and muck."

Kip couldn't argue with that logic, and he told Patel so. "I guess we'll never know, though in my line of work, like yours, I don't like unexplained questions."

"Correct," Patel said. "But, ultimately, it had nothing to do with the cause of Mr. Martin's death."

Patel was no Jake Johnson, and Kip had no qualms about his next question.

"Did anyone notice Anders's watch was missing when they brought him in?" he asked.

"We could see from the tan line he wore a watch, but we didn't think anything more of it," Patel said. "What more should we be making of it?"

"I don't know," Kip said. "It's out of character for him. A watch is good to have when you're out on the water alone. That's all. Jake Johnson certainly didn't think much of my asking."

"He's not likely to tell you what he thought one way or the other," the M.E. added.

"You're right about that."

Their conversation was almost at an end when Patel asked to excuse himself for a moment.

With Patel in the hallway, Kip looked absently around his

office before settling his gaze back on Patel's computer screen. He located the small personal printer on Patel's credenza, and leaning over his chair, he hit Control-P on the keyboard and backed off to wait for the printout.

He thought his desktop printer at the *Beacon* was the slowest in town, but Patel's won that competition hands down. Clearly, it wasn't intended for spitting out memory-intensive photographs. Kip could hear Patel excusing himself from a discussion in the hallway. The sound of his approaching footsteps echoed louder and louder until Kip was sure his maneuver was about to be discovered. Patel could react in many ways, though Kip never found out. Patel turned back for further discussion.

Mercifully, the photograph inched into Kip's waiting fingers. Tucking it into his backpack, he retreated to his side of the desk.

"Sorry about that," Patel said, reentering his office. "But I think we're done, unless you've got any other questions."

Kip assured him he didn't, and he thanked Patel for his time. They shook hands, and Kip departed more confused than when he arrived.

SEVENTEEN

Inside, the Beacon Building was dark and quiet by the time Kip returned from his visit with Joe Patel. It was late Tuesday afternoon, and the staff had long departed. Weekly practice had long ago evolved into custom, and offices and desks had been decluttered in anticipation of the next news cycle. The staff's challenge to entropy, while laudable, never lasted. Within twenty-four hours the office would revert to a war zone of messy desks, overflowing waste baskets, and abandoned mugs multiplying like fruit flies. The *Beacon*, Kip knew, was in no danger of becoming the sterile corporate-style newsrooms he'd increasingly seen at big city dailies.

He tossed his pullover on to the nearest chair and was about to settle down to check emails when the faint clacking and clicking of a computer keyboard down the hall broke the silence. Inspecting, Kip found soft light spilling into the hallway. Ben Bailey, Kip bet himself.

Yep, there sat the *Beacon*'s 30-year-old wonk, oblivious to Kip's presence in the doorway, thanks to the pair of earbuds piping in music. Kip did his best not to scare the humming, typing figure hunched over his desk. Knocking didn't work, nor did loudly clearing his throat. Flicking the overhead light on and off did the job.

Swiveling in his chair, Ben looked sternly over his reading glasses and gave Kip a "What is it now – can't a man work in peace?" look.

Not waiting for an actual greeting from his managing editor, Kip said, "You know, we don't pay overtime around here."

Ben removed his glasses and rubbed his eyes – for effect, Kip assumed.

"It's interesting. You say don't rather than can't when it comes to overtime pay," Ben said.

Instead of countering his comment, Kip eyed the files and newspaper sections and press kits stacked precariously on his guest chair. So much for ritual cleaning at Chez Bailey. Kip shifted the pile to the floor and settled onto the chair and stretched his legs out. Ben relaxed and put his feet on the edge of his desk.

Kip and Ben deeply enjoyed the other's company. The eight-year difference in age should have been enough to put seniority into their relationship. But Kip always suspected Ben had been born fully mature. The guy skipped right over the usual pitfalls of ambitious reporters in their twenties – the impulsive whipsawing between neediness and knowing everything while rejecting guiding hands. He came readymade, and most of the time Kip had only to point him in the right direction.

Ben had no problems with bouncing ideas off colleagues and would always accept the same from them. While Kip and Ben could discuss anything, they always reverted to work-related topics. They could start out on the Washington Nationals and end up dissecting the chances for Port City's high school baseball team. Discussing politics on any level invariably worked its way back to Port City.

Maybe a sense of humor lurked somewhere inside Ben, but it didn't extend to his workspace. A Howard University Bison pennant hung on the wall next to his bulletin board. Above the neatly arranged clippings and photos tacked to the bulletin board, hung a framed photograph of the Kipling quote inscribed over the players' entrance to Centre Court at Wimbledon advising, "If you can meet with Triumph and Disaster / and treat those two impostors just the same." Kip didn't know much about Ben's tennis game, but the quote said everything about Ben's personal style of effectiveness.

Ben gestured to the mini-fridge next to his desk. "Help yourself," he said. "I'll take a diet soda – I've still got another forty-five minutes of work in the land of no overtime pay."

Kip handed him a can and helped himself to twelve ounces of radiator water currently in favor with Millennials.

"Have you read the *Mirror* today?" Ben asked. "Ambrose Ralston came out with all guns blazing in favor of P2."

Kip shifted to a more erect posture and stared into the darkness of the hallway before replying. Running his fingers through his hair, he said flatly, "Why am I not surprised? Ralston would hump road kill if he thought it would bring in money. Hand me a copy, please."

The headline said it all, as far as Kip was concerned: "Port City Needs the Pentagon. The Pentagon Needs Port City." The following paragraphs described the myriad benefits that would flow from the installation to all quarters of the city. The only part missing was the downside, something Ralston had taken into account. "As the publication of progress in Port City, we'll leave it to others to attempt an explanation for why our fair city should not avail itself of this windfall."

Kip handed the paper back to Ben. Taking the high road in this town was getting more difficult by the day, and Ralston knew that about Kip. Reading Ralston's invitation to a pissing match had the effect of making Ben's beer start to taste a whole lot better. Popping another can, Kip asked Ben what he thought of the *Mirror*'s editorial.

Taking his feet off his desk, Ben faced Kip. "I think things are getting more interesting around here, Boss," he said. "Until today, people were only noodling around the edges of the federal edifice complex in this city. But soon they'll be making up their minds. And . . ."

"The *Beacon* will be caught in the crossfire if we don't respond and help control the conversation," Kip interrupted.

"Right. And . . ."

"And we'll deal with this all in due time."

"As though our editorial last month had much impact around town," Ben said.

"Not if you don't count my angry board of directors or one still very pissed off Paul Schultz, not to mention the loss of his advertising network."

"Oh, that."

"Yeah, that."

"What's your next move, then?" Ben asked. "Staff members are beginning to ask, too."

"I'm not surprised. But for now, there isn't much we can do – it's still early in the game to be hitting the panic button," Kip said. "As much as it goes against my grain, we need to take a softer approach and kill it with a thousand cuts.

"And for what it's worth," he continued. "I'm looking into a feature on the city's archaeology program and how it's faring without Anders Martin. The guy was a pioneer critic of P2, and I believe his legacy could use a little exposure."

That was mostly true, though Kip had no intention of sharing his suspicions about Martin's demise. If Ben didn't slough off the idea, he'd probably demand to join in on the story, something that would surely backfire, given his too by-the-book approach to reporting.

"You sure you aren't just checking out the fox who's running the program in Martin's place?" Ben asked.

Kip's failure to hide his grin said all that Ben needed to know. When he burst out laughing, Kip said, "Pure coincidence. Besides, word has it that she's taken."

"When did that ever stop you?" Ben said.

"I can see we've been working together too long," Kip said. "Hasn't the *New York Times* knocked on your door yet."

"You know I love it here too much to leave," Ben said. "What would I do with all that extra money and time and fame?"

"Good to hear," Kip said, rising from his chair.

"Noted," said Ben, who wasn't quite through with dimming Kip's day.

"By the way, did you also hear that Miles Tennyson has bought one of Schultz Development's units?"

Kip was nearly through the doorway when Ben dropped that nugget. Life indeed was getting more interesting around the *Beacon*. Returning to Ben's work area, he shifted the pile of paper back on to the floor and took a seat. Tennyson didn't typically take suffering enterprises off the hands of their suffering owners for fun.

"Which company?" he asked.

"His surveying company," Ben said. "My source says Schultz figures he'd be better off contracting out small stuff like that."

"Probably so," Kip said. "But it begs the bigger question of why Miles Tennyson would want such a small operation. Unless . . ."

". . . unless," Ben added, "he's also got specific designs on the coming windfall from P2."

"Most likely. It does look very much like he's jockeying for the arrival of P2."

Kip felt a knot forming in his stomach. Had Melvin, Stephen, and Dorothy outmaneuvered him, intentionally or not, in having Tennyson dig into the *Beacon*'s finances? Stunning as it was from Kip's perspective, he could appreciate how the *Beacon* could become a pawn in the installation's public relations game.

"I wish you had told me this first, and then about Ralston's grand opinions on progress in Port City."

"Next time," Ben said, but with a twinkle in his eye meant to diffuse Kip's building ire. "On second thought, I think I've had enough for one day. How about you?"

"Agreed."

Ben shut off his computer and both men put their jackets on.

"One last thing," Kip said.

Ben grimaced. "Yeah . . ."

"Remember, 'Yours is the Earth and everything that's in it, And – which is more – you'll be a Man, my son.'"

"What are you talking about?"

Pointing to Ben's bulletin board, Kip said, "It's the second half of your Wimbledon quote."

"Yeah, right. Everything on Earth," Ben said, "but overtime.

EIGHTEEN

With only a few days until the spring equinox, winter blew Port City a few last raspberries. Cold and blustery with scudding clouds, the day called for heavy coats and hats. Kip felt for the tourists, who were counting on balmy weather for long-awaited excursions to nearby attractions. Perhaps in another few days Port City's visitors would get the spring weather that made the area so special.

Inside the warmth of Port City's archaeology office, winter's last gasp was far removed. Kip had absorbed a questioning look from Daphne, the volunteer working the front desk as he entered. She was probably wondering what fireworks he might ignite.

"Erin is expecting you, Mr. Alexander," she said, holding her gaze on him. "Go on back."

Powers met him before he'd covered half the distance across the common area. She was wearing black denim jeans and a leather vest over a black turtle neck shirt. Running shoes completed her attire for the day. Her deep coppery hair had returned to its ponytail configuration.

"Pardon our informal look today," Powers said. "We're re-labeling and packing artifacts. It's a never-ending fact of life in our line of work. Future generations will thank us, if they're not too busy cataloguing Twenty-first Century stuff. Come on back."

For simple interviews, Kip usually took notes. For more complex stories, he used a small digital voice recorder while taking backup notes. Even though recorded interviews took forever and a half to transcribe, he looked forward to every syllable of this one.

Over the next forty-five minutes they covered the basics of Port City's archaeology program. Powers next lent him books and pamphlets on city history and culture that would provide ample material for a solid article. In half an hour, Rick Adams would arrive to take photos for the *Beacon*. That left enough time to move on to other subjects.

There was plenty to tell her – the broken oar, his visit with Helen, and Patel's report. He made it a point not to include Helen's thoughts on romance. Later, maybe. He did, however, explain the increasing complexities in his life, thanks to Miles Tennyson's foray into the *Beacon* books and his acquisition of a Schultz Development unit and Ambrose Ralston's editorial. But it was Helen Martin's comments on which he concentrated.

"What struck me most was Helen's hurt and anger when I told her about Anders's handiwork at Strawberry Flats," Kip said. "She felt betrayed that he hadn't confided in her."

"Why wouldn't she feel strongly? After all, Anders was more or less sneaking around, even it was professionally. That's how I feel about it, and I only worked for him."

"It's that Anders had never in all their years of marriage held back any information," Kip said. "It makes his venture at J.D. Bushrod & Son all the more extraordinary. That normally would be the kind of thing Anders would share with Helen. Why would he take such a secret to his grave? And what would have been worse, or more important – finding something or not finding something?"

"There could have been the element of embarrassment for Port City's chief archaeologist fishing around a junkyard at odd hours in search of an elusive wrench to throw into the gears of P2's apparatus," she suggested. "It's possible he could have gotten in trouble over it, one way or the other." She thought for another moment and asked, "Was there anything in his house that would indicate what Anders was doing?"

"You're asking the wrong person. Helen showed me his home office. Pretty cool. Part library, part gallery, part man cave with lots of pots, shards, posters, and nary a wide screen in sight. Nothing that screamed, I found it! You could call it a dead end."

After pausing, he asked, "How was your visit with Owen Draper?"

"Phone call. That's all I could get, which was no small accomplishment."

"He's that big a fish?"

Yes, sirree. The man is a major deity in the archaeology world. He heads up an entire department at the NMA."

"So, what did your Zeus have to say?"

"My Zeus couldn't have been less interested, though he was polite and understanding. Still, he said that no reputable archaeologist would squander valuable time tilting at a windmill like Strawberry Flats."

"That's not exactly the enthusiastic and illuminating reaction I was hoping for," Kip said. "Didn't the fact of what Anders had undertaken stir his curiosity, even an iota?"

"I tell you, no," Powers said. "Owen even hinted that he thought Anders had possibly gone around the bend in his quest to stop P2. Also, he suggested that being associated with Anders's extracurricular project might not be good for me professionally."

"Well, we both have our worries about that," Kip said. "That booby trap won't be going away as long as we're poking around."

"Speaking of poking around, how was your visit with the coroner?" she asked. "You haven't mentioned it yet, so I assume not much came of it."

"Correct, for the most part," Kip said. "Patel wouldn't elaborate beyond their finding of accidental drowning."

"You say 'for the most part.'"

"Oh, yeah. Take a look at this," Reaching into his backpack at his feet, Kip extracted the folded printout from Patel's office printer. "See what you make of it."

Powers took the sheet from Kip, looked at it, and flinched.

"A spoiler alert would have been appreciated," she said. "This is gruesome. And what is it?"

"Nobody seems to know. It's a wound of some kind. We don't know what caused it."

Considering the brief time he'd known Powers, Kip decided

to forego telling her how it came to be in his backpack. Instead, he said, "It's my homework assignment, and so far I'm looking at an F for completion."

"Well, I certainly don't know what to make of it," Powers said, handing the sheet back to Kip. "Just another piece in the miserable puzzle."

Kip had to agree. Much about his conversation with Helen Martin wasn't meshing with what they knew overall. Besides, roles seemed reversed.

"Don't you think it odd that Helen's harsh reaction had nothing to do with Anders's nutty behavior?" Kip asked. "Her concern wasn't with the dig at all. It was that Anders hadn't told her. Owen, on the other hand, gives the dig no credence and sees something la-la in Anders. And, let me guess, Owen's lack of interest extended to a site visit."

"That's so far removed from his world," Powers said. "At his level, he deals with international sites, not urban junkyards. That would be like me inviting Roger Federer for a set of tennis."

Kip felt even more stymied. "We don't know any more than we did two weeks ago," he said. "Right now, I can think of only one person with a grudge serious enough to want to harm Anders."

"Paul Schultz?"

Kip nodded and said, "But for yours truly's black eye and Schultz's very public opinion of Anders, there's doodly to go on."

"But, you've got to start somewhere," she said.

"And it gives me great pleasure to begin with Schultz," Kip said. "The thing is, how could that man know more about Anders that his wife, you, and I don't know?"

She shrugged.

"It would seem Schultz has been guessing, based on information from rummaging around the Liza's junkyard and doing his own work throughout Strawberry Flats."

"But would you do in someone on a guess?" Powers countered. "I certainly don't think so. But, then again, the stakes are starting to look mighty high to a lot of people. Yet Anders is looking more and more cuckoo." She sighed and continued. "Maybe we should tell the police about this and be done with it. Slip them an anonymous note under their door, saying Anders's death looks suspicious, but there's not a shred of evidence to support it."

Kip felt the same way. In all of his investigative reporting, something always came along to encourage him. What he had here was bare dirt and mussed-up bushes. But he wasn't ready to give up, even with the mess rising around the *Beacon.*

"Let's wait until I check out Schultz," he said. "Maybe something in his past will turn up. I can start on that tomorrow."

"And what can I be doing in the meantime?" Powers asked. "No way I want to be dead weight in this."

"Far from it. How about a visit to J.D. Bushrod & Son to see the site in person? How about Saturday? That's the earliest I can get away."

"Works for me," she said.

"In the meantime, would you like to have dinner? Tomorrow night? I might have something to report about the lovely Paul Schultz."

There. He had done it.

By the way Powers bit her lip and let her answer hang in the air, Kip knew the answer.

"I'm sorry, but no," she said. The delivery was soft and not dismissive. If it hadn't been for that inexplicable rush of adrenaline that comes even with rejection, Kip might have quit there. Some things aren't worth the trauma. But some things are. He pressed on. Well, half pressed.

"I understand – but there will be other invitations, I promise."

Powers's neutral reply was fraught with possibilities. "We'll see," she said.

"Fair enough," he said. "But – I've got one last question I forgot to ask the first time we met."

"Fire away."

"Where had I seen you before?"

"That's an easy one," she said. "In the basement of the

Hampton Funeral Home. I wanted to see who took the punch for Anders."

NINETEEN

With a hard row behind him and a second cup of Mister Perks's strongest brew whipping his neurons into shape, Thursday morning looked not only doable, but enjoyable. Memory of his unsatisfying and awkward conversations with Helen Martin and Erin Powers of the past week had receded enough to allow him a clearer mind. Barring the disruptions of unhappy advertisers or crazed Old Town matrons, the day ahead looked good.

For starters, meshing the archaeology story into the editorial lineup had gone well.

Like many small town newspaper owners, Kip wore two hats – editor and publisher. It wasn't always a comfortable fit, since news and advertising in respectable newspapers are supposed to function independently of the other. For the most part, Kip managed to keep church and state separated, due in large part to the reliability of the *Beacon*'s business manager and managing editor. Della's faithful shepherding of advertising, circulation, and general administration never faltered, and bills got paid mostly on time and paychecks never bounced. Maybe because he had less intrinsic interest in rote administration, Kip felt comfortable in his delegation of responsibilities to Della.

Ben Bailey had proved to be a different matter from Della. For precisely the same reasons he could entrust the business side so easily to Della, Kip had the opposite situation with editorial. While his brain resided ably on the business side, his heart was in editorial and reporting. It was what he grew up with, studied in college, and practiced at a big city paper before returning to the *Beacon*. And that would never change. Still, he never had to worry that the *Beacon* would be too small a stage for two strong wills.

The archaeology article came under Ben's usual scrutiny. This time, however, he convinced Kip that a single article, two for that matter, wouldn't do the topic ample justice. Three, on the other hand, would be just the ticket. "Boss, you can do it in chronological stages. Work your way up to the present, and then blast away at P2."

That last prescription told him where Ben stood on the issue of Strawberry Flats, and that when the time came to resume battle with his development hungry board of directors, Kip could enjoy the comradely support of his incorruptible managing editor.

After two hours of fleshing out the first article, Kip realized a heap of further research lay ahead. The books and maps Erin lent him helped, which was a good thing. He hadn't anticipated the multitude of components involved in such a story – condensing a rudimentary knowledge of not only the history of Port City but also Europe and Africa and the customs of their inhabitants who settled Virginia in the Seventeenth Century. Then there was researching the climate of the times – hard winters and droughts and the hunger they wrought – and the city's Tidewater soil conditions that presented archaeologists with their own unique challenges. For all that work, Kip had made it only as far as the colonial era.

Kip had hit a quitting point when Della Simpson tapped on his open door to alert him to the next phase of his day, reviewing the accounts receivable and payable. This weekly reality check had been done so many times that the exercise had a smooth routine about it. Today was no different, and they wrapped up the accounting of money in and out in time for a quick lunch and another shifting of gears. Exploring Paul Schultz's background was going to take an afternoon of work.

Kip knew the basics of Schultz from the boathouse: Age 48, a native of Chicago's south side, attended college in the Midwest, married and divorced, and worked in real estate in Chicago. Over the last ten years, Schultz earned a reputation in Northern Virginia as a hard-charging commercial real estate developer who undertook a series of progressively larger development projects. Buying and flipping townhouses and retail space gave way to multi-housing projects and small shopping centers.

In the process, Schultz gained the reputation for knowing how to get things done in Port City. If he didn't personally know how to help a client overcome a sticky building permit, he knew those who could. Kip was sure his reputation as a fixer and acquirer of land explained why the military hired him. In Schultz they had a bulldog on their side.

Kip also knew that the bigger the dog, the more fleas it had. For all his public-facing image of a smooth and successful business leader and patron of the community arts and backer of 10K races and high school booster clubs, a messier situation was bound to exist. Perfectly normal. He knew this all too well from publishing the *Beacon*. But in the case of Schultz's enterprises, how could he find those elusive fleas? More importantly, how to do it without alerting anyone – specifically, Schultz. Carefully, he thought.

He began with the most natural of places: his own newspaper. As the "newspaper of record," the *Beacon* was the community repository of legal notices and official announcements. Building permit applications, notices of public hearings, and all other manner of required public postings could be found in the back pages of the *Beacon*.

Thanks to her remarkable aptitude for record keeping, Google had nothing on Kip's mother, who had digitized back copies of the *Beacon* for the past twenty years. Key-word searches could turn up any newsmaker or advertiser in seconds. I love you, Ma, Kip whispered to himself.

In less than thirty minutes, every reference to a news item involving Schultz populated his search findings page. Yet for all the dozens of search hits on Schultz and his companies, little of it was useful. Perhaps that was to be expected; otherwise, the whole world would have already known of any untoward circumstances in the world of Paul Schultz.

Kip next tried the real Google, to no avail, either. He likened much of the information gotten from the search service to holiday fruitcakes that get re-gifted and re-gifted until brick hard. And, still, they kept circulating. So it was in researching Schultz. Three hours at it and well into the afternoon, Kip was no closer to a better understanding of Schultz. It was time to go outside for help.

While not exactly Woodward and Bernstein in their impact on U.S. history, Kip and Katherine Tisdale nonetheless had conducted difficult and complicated investigations into all manner of public and corporate intrigue for the *Post*. Many embarrassed and occasionally chastened members of Congress could attest to the results of the duo's dogged work into their murky campaign finance practices. On the larger projects, Kip and Tisdale often worked with teams of other reporters, researchers, and the members of the most indispensable workforce in Washington, interns.

It wasn't always glamorous work, and recognition often felt diluted if not anonymous at times. When the Pulitzer Prize was bestowed on the paper for a year-long investigation into a tangled Defense Department procurement program, six reporters shared the spotlight, a fancy certificate, modest amount of cash, and bragging rights. Kip found that plenty enough.

So, how difficult could it be to bring this low-level real estate developer to bay? Kip wondered. If the jerk was so fanatical in matters like putting out the welcome mat for the Department of Defense, why hadn't he left more of a trail? Surely he's screwed over a business partner, snatched property from a widow, or muffed his taxes.

Tisdale called Kip as soon as she got his email. Paul Schultz couldn't be that hot a topic at her paper. Nor could it have been Kip's killer charm and good looks that prompted such a quick call back. They did work closely the years, but both had kept relations strictly professional. Nope, she was glad to hear form an old colleague.

"Well, Big Guy, how's life in the real world?" she greeted Kip. "Garden Club behaving?"

"They're on our list to investigate, if you'd care to humble yourself and help out," he countered. He knew that for all their gold-plated resources, many of the best reporters got their feet wet in the waters of community papers before catapulting to big city dailies. Tisdale may well have covered garden clubs and high school sports in her early years.

Kip wasted no time, and got on to the reason for his call.

"All I know about Schultz is from our business section," she replied, "mostly his various projects. He's got a good reputation for philanthropic work, but then again, most developers do. Other than P2, he's small potatoes compared with the regional and national development companies. Though I must say, P2 could put him on the map."

"That's it?" Kip asked, trying to mask his disappointment.

"Yep, if it wasn't, do you think we'd be sitting on a story?"

"Duh."

"You know, Kip, somehow I don't believe you would be wasting my incredibly precious time on any old story," she said. "Am I right?"

This was where it got tricky. He knew Tisdale would be in for a nasty dustup with her bosses if she were discovered to have had advance knowledge of such an important story that ran in a vastly smaller paper. She had witnessed every stunt and short-cut in Kip's fractured bag of tricks and would instantly smell any half-assed prevarication in his answer. Far better to try a straight-forward approach.

"Right," Kip answered. "This Pentagon project has the potential to change the face of Port City, and Paul Schultz who, small player that he may be, is nonetheless a key player. We can't stand each other, and to tell you a not very well kept secret in Port City, we came to blows over P2 last month. And I want to know more about him."

Kip could sense from her long pause that Tisdale was weighing whether to get involved in this chase.

"Let me see what I can do," she said. "People here and there owe me favors. Give me a day or two and I'll get back to you."

"I couldn't ask for anything more," Kip said.

"At least for the moment, right?" Tisdale laughed. "And I'm sure you'd return the favor first chance you got."

"Gladly," he said.

Kip thanked Tisdale and rang off, confident that if Tisdale couldn't turn up something on Paul Schultz, then nobody could. And perhaps that would mercifully be the end of the matter.

As he was turning his thoughts to evening and dinner, a knock sounded in his doorway, followed by the entrance of a colleague who handed him a large, sealed manila envelope with his name and the hand-stamped message: CONFIDENTIAL.

There was no missing its source: Tennyson & Associates. Kip ran a finger along the flap until it opened. Scanning the cover letter, he abruptly flung the entire contents across his desk and stomped out of the building.

TWENTY

"It could only have been Melvin," Kip said. "He's been behind nearly everything that has gone wrong at the *Beacon*."

"Such as what?" Cass asked.

They were sitting at the time-worn pine farmer's table in Kip's kitchen, and for the last thirty minutes the twins had been dissecting Miles Tennyson's recommendations to sell the *Beacon*.

Upon returning home from school, Cass had found her manila folder with its imploring stamp of confidentiality wedged into her mail slot. She, too, never made it past the cover letter and its synopsis of the following contents. Calling her brother in advance wasn't necessary, since she knew he'd be waiting for her. Both had had trouble absorbing the full impact and meaning of Tennyson's report. To Kip it felt like a surprise slap in the face: Hey, what was that for?

"Such as Melvin feeding *Beacon* information to the *Mirror*," he said. "Such as leading the never-ending pushback on every capital improvement I've requested for the paper. And, more than anything, such as Melvin's obnoxious support of P2. You'd think he wants the paper all to himself."

Having chewed the few details of the report to pieces, they had arrived at the heart of the matter. It was well-traversed territory. Setting down her mug of tea, Cass prepared to revisit the ongoing issues of their cousins' motives.

"You know as well as I do that Melvin is too easy a target on this," she said. "He's probably in on all the things you say he is, but Melvin doesn't have the wattage to actually pull off anything of significance. At least singlehandedly. The poor guy can't even go to the bathroom without asking the board's permission. So don't rule out Stephen and Dorothy."

Kip had heard all this before from Cass. He and his sister may have gone in different directions professionally after college, but she had never lost her love for the *Beacon* and its heritage of family publishing. Even from a distance she remained a serious student of the entire enterprise. The older they got, the more Kip understood and appreciated his sister's approach to family and life.

Where Kip was reserved and given to introspection, Cass hewed to everything outgoing – teaching, community organizing, and embracing a raucous family. When she and Hank learned that having children would not be medically possible, they adopted three in quick succession. Kip envied how easily such things came for his sister, cheerfully messy as they were. He figured her arm's length distance from daily life at the *Beacon* must have given her a clearer picture of *Beacon* board of directors than he ever had. Ultimately, it didn't differ much from Kip's assessment.

"I still say their animosity and trouble-making come from having so little direct participation in the running of the paper," she said. "Mom and Dad may have given us direct responsibility for the paper, but that didn't make it an easier pill for the three of them to swallow."

"Yeah, well, I seem to recall Mom and Dad repeatedly extending them the offer to work at the *Beacon*," Kip said. "They either would have none of it or, when they did get involved, made a hash of it."

"Maybe you should cut them some slack on that count," Cass said. "Remember you only came kicking and screaming back to the *Beacon* – and newspapering is your profession."

They were now in uncharted waters of Kip's unceremonious return to the *Beacon*. He almost snapped back at Cass that at least until today he had been running the paper just fine. Taking a deep breath, he allowed for the harsher truth in Cass's comment. Running the paper in the black didn't necessarily equate to popular acclaim in wider Alexander circles. Perhaps it was because they enjoyed the magical connection common to twins, but Cass was the only person who could make her brother listen.

Kip could have pursued that one down the street and back any number of times but instead opted to wrap up the evening.

"Okay, Sis, I'll grant you that point," he said. "But I believe we can both take some comfort in the fact that nothing can happen until our next board meeting. In the meantime, we might actually stumble onto a way out of this."

"I'm sure as hell they will be doing their best to prevent that," she said.

"No doubt, but what worries me are the alliances they might strike before then: Melvin and Miles Tennyson, Melvin and Ambrose Ralston, and Melvin and who knows who the hell else," he said.

Cass pushed her chair back and learned over to scratch Ike behind his ears. A new thought must have occurred to her, and she settled back into her seat.

"I sometimes wonder if we'd even be having this conversation if Anders Martin had not drowned," she said.

That got Kip's attention.

"Huh?" He figured they had analyzed the recent fortunes of the *Beacon* from every possible angle, and even in all his searching into Martin's death, this never occurred to him. "Why do you think that?"

"It's a thought I had," she said. "Maybe it's nothing. You and Anders were the two faces of opposition to P2 in this town, and now with Martin gone, you're it. And you could say that the other side has doubled down on you, starting with our cousins."

"Geez, Cass, that's all I need."

"Maybe I'm wrong."

"You can bet I'll be thinking about that."

Kip had already thought it through. Rising from the table, he stared out the window above the sink into the dark of the evening. If Cass was correct, then Kip was the target not only of his family's wrath but also someone on the outside. Murderously so.

She stood and joined him at the sink and took his hands into hers and turned him so she could look him hard in his eyes.

"I know this is hard on you," she said. "It's not the end of the world and sooner or later it will blow over. And, as I've always said, I will fully understand if running the *Beacon* gets to be too much for you. I'll always support you in whatever decision you make."

Kip gently pulled his hands back from Cass and returned to gazing into the darkness. "Thanks, but I'm in this one for the long haul. No going halfway," he answered.

"I knew you'd say that," she said. "That's one of the things I like about you best – you never give up."

Cass paused, and her brother knew more was coming, though from which direction he had no idea.

"So, Brother," she continued, "tell me more about Erin Powers."

When Cass changed the conversation in that direction, he laughed so suddenly he almost sprayed the soda he was sipping. Where had that question come from?

"Don't look so surprised," she said. "I do get around, you know."

"Let me guess, you've been around Helen Martin."

"You are smarter than Melvin," she said. "Helen very much approves of your interest in Erin, although she refers to it as infatuation.

Cass paused, and Kip knew from experience that she had shifted gears.

"You need to find someone. For good, Kip," she said. "Both Helen and I agree: You should bring Erin to the Garden Ball."

My, that was blunt, Kip thought, reflecting on what he deemed the antiquated and sexist notion of women as schemers and connivers when it came to marrying off their relatives and friends. He determined it to be an accurate if misnamed characteristic. "Strategic" fit the current social rubric a whole lot better. Those two had shown him how much more strategic they were than he was.

"You are both too kind by half, though you are only half right," he said. "That's one chicken you shouldn't have counted before it hatched. I already have asked Erin out – for a much simpler venue than your grand fundraiser. She shot me down for dinner."

"Yeah, yeah, but as long as we're throwing out clichés, how about, try, try, and try until you succeed? It fits your never-give up personality," Cass said. "Besides, a little birdie tells me your second try might be a whole lot more successful."

"Yeah, yeah, and yeah – and there's no help for those who won't help themselves," Kip answered. "But in the case of Erin Powers, I will stoop to take any help I can get, no matter where it comes from and no matter how much it seems like high school all over again. Thanks, Cass, I'll take you up on that advice."

TWENTY-ONE

The last time Kip had been to J.D. Bushrod & Son, he had ridden his bike. The extra time it took him to get around on two wheels and the occasional sweaty results seemed a small price to pay for a bit more fitness and a greener world. When he absolutely needed four wheels, there was always the *Beacon*'s van. This day, however, called for sturdier transportation.

Having heard Kip's description of Liza Bushrod's auto halfway house and the nearly inaccessible location of Anders's dig, Erin had insisted on driving. Kip readily assented, since a broken axel or missing exhaust system was something he didn't want to explain to Willie Carter. Erin's truck it was.

Sitting on the curb at the end of his half-alley, he heard her well before her coal-black Ford F-150 rounded the corner. Do they sell trucks that loud or do you have pay to make them that way? Kip wondered. Whatever, there was definitely something he liked about a fiery redhead high up behind the wheel of a pickup. It was so un-Port City, with all its BMWs and SUVs that he had to give her ride multiple style points.

The drive to Strawberry Flats went quickly, and there was barely enough time for small talk. Erin seemed more reserved than Kip expected, particularly in light of Cass's loaded reference to little birdies. When she wasn't adjusting the height of the driver's side window, Erin fiddled needlessly with her CD player, never finding the right song. Something was on her mind, and Kip had begun to suspect the topic lay beyond him.

As they waited for a traffic light to change, she turned off the CD player and turned to him. "Sorry – but this whole foray into Martin's life is getting very uncomfortable," she said. Underneath, the Ford's exhaust system rumbled and then growled as she accelerated through the intersection. "I feel like a trespasser into his life. Not his work at Strawberry Flats. Something else."

"What would that be?" Kip asked.

"It's hard to explain, but doing what we're doing today is like peering into his personal life. Particularly the last couple of days of his life."

"Well, it is," he said. "But I think I know what you mean. Even though I don't do stuff like this every day in my job, it still happens more than I like. And I never get used to it.

"A good chunk of our news stories require prying and nosing around for information, even though it doesn't all get used," he said. "Besides, I'd have been run out of town by now if I used half of the stuff we found. The important thing is to be able to pull together as many facts of a story from the biggest pool of information that we can. That way, we don't get scooped later on by a competitor or burned by someone's attorney."

"And you believe today is similar?" Erin asked.

"I do. Very much. We can both agree that Anders Martin was quite a piece of work in his own right. But, his longest suit was honesty, and I believe he'd approve of what we're doing, no matter where it led."

Erin exhaled softly and, without taking her eyes off the road, laid her hand on Kip's. "Thank you. That's what I needed to hear." Her faced brightened into a smile and she goosed the accelerator. "Let's go have fun."

J.D. Bushrod & Son was easing nicely into spring when they arrived. Daffodils, tulips, and hyacinths were in full bloom along the perimeter of the stockade-style fence that shielded the rows of cars and trucks that the city considered unsightly. Two chubby black Labradors accompanied Liza on her way out to greet them. One went to Erin's window, putting his paws on her window, while the other did the same with Kip.

"Say good morning to Eli and Peyton," Liza said. "They're lousy as junkyard dogs, but the boys are good company and they always let me know when customers pull up."

Erin was barely out of the truck before Liza approached her. Kip could have sworn Liza was sizing her up for height, age, looks. What's going on? He asked himself. Don't tell me Liza is in league with Helen and Cass? Her next comment confirmed this.

"So, you are Erin Powers," she said, extending her hand. They shook hands, and Liza continued, "Both Kip's sister and Helen Martin speak highly of you. I'm sorry for the circumstances of your promotion, but I'm sure the city will do well by you."

His sister evidently wasn't the only one who got around.

"I wouldn't call it a promotion yet," Erin said. "I'm only the acting director. But thanks. Kip told me a lot about you on the ride over. I'm glad to meet you."

To be continued, Kip figured. He declined Liza's offer of coffee so they could get on with the day and was glad when Erin agreed. Liza joined them in the truck's cab for the bumpy ride to the creek bed and what now came to be referred to among them as Anders's Dig.

Peyton and Eli raced ahead, circling back and forth alongside the jostling truck until it came to a halt twenty-five feet from Martin's hillside enterprise.

Little had changed, only the beginnings of honeysuckle and other undergrowth. Nothing about the embankment suggested secrets worth dying for. To Kip's eye, it was as he'd left it, riddle and all.

"So, what do you make of it, Dr. Dig?" he asked Erin.

"Not much at the moment," Erin said. She turned to Liza and added, "Not to worry, we'll clean up."

"Go for it. That's what you're here for. But if you strike gold, oil, or winning lottery tickets, remember me. I've got a bank payment coming up, and I doubt the customers coming this morning will be spending enough to cover it. Call me on my cell if you need anything."

And with that, Liza and her two quarterbacks headed back to her office on foot.

She was gone no more than a few seconds when Erin turned

all business. After opening the truck's tailgate to an array of tools, she outlined their approach.

"We'll work from left to right, picking up the larger debris by hand and using spades to place the finer material aside. After that, whisks will get us closer. Just make sure you go slow and concentrate on what you're doing. Pile your dirt in the order in which you took it out."

"That's it?" Kip asked, wondering what other way there was to pile dirt. "I thought we'd be working with tweezers and microscopes."

"Soon enough. First, we've got to see what's here."

If Kip hadn't seen a dozen archaeology shows on PBS, he might have felt impatient. But he knew enough about the process to accept its painstakingly slow pace. Which would be fine, if they had had all the time in the world.

He diligently picked away at the soil and clay, taking his cue from Erin's polished approach. In about an hour's time, Kip began to notice a change in its consistency.

"What do you think?" he asked.

"Definitely something. This could be it. I didn't expect anything so soon. We've got to be careful from here on. If this is what Anders was after, we could botch it all if we get sloppy. You better let me take over from here."

"It's all yours, Boss."

Meticulous before, she was now surgeon-like in her picking and sweeping. Another thirty minutes passed and they were nearly a foot and a half below the surface. Erin had a three-by-two foot section smoothed out.

"This is odd," she said. "It feels like we've hit rock."

"Here, let me see," Kip said, reaching over and rapping the dirt with his knuckles. "This is plywood."

And so it was. Home Depot's finest.

"What a dork I am," Erin laughed. "All that by-the-book scraping and sweeping and our only reward is a pile of fill dirt. I guess I was a little full of myself."

"Welcome to my world," Kip said. "But look at it this way – we found what we're looking for on the first try. If we'd been off by a foot or two, who knows how long we'd be at this. Now, we may be able to see what Anders was after."

Clearing away the dirt from plywood went quickly, since nothing risky was involved other than Erin's pride, which came with a healthy dose of humor. They could only guess at the amount of time Anders had spent unearthing the hillside and then covering it again. After pulling aside the two sheets of plywood, Kip stared at the raw patch of ground.

"This doesn't make sense," he said. "There's nothing here. Why would he go to such trouble to cover up a dud?"

Erin backed up fifteen feet to study the scene, then shifted to her right, then left, and finally up close where, kneeling, she considered it further. Smiling, she said, "Don't be so quick to assume that Anders didn't find anything. He must have stopped digging at this point for a reason and so will we, but not why you may think."

Kip's eyebrows arched as he folded his arms in wait of further explanation. It came fast and animated.

Pacing off the perimeter, Erin pointed to its edges. "I've scraped down and wide enough on this side to know this is no tree or its branch. Look at the difference in color. It's darker along here, here, all the way to the end."

Kip felt like he was listening to Willie Carter expound on the inner workings of the *Beacon*'s printing press. This time, though, he was looking forward to hearing more. "Tell me more."

"Just because you don't see anything spectacularly obvious doesn't mean we don't have something. I see enough now to know Anders was on to something. We won't be doing much more, but I do have to document everything we're doing. Then we're going to rush the process with more probing. God forgive me."

Kip's interest jumped several levels as he realized Erin was climbing out on a professional limb. "Are you sure you want to do this?"

"As sure as I am about anything. We're not going to walk away from Anders at this point."

"Of course not," he said, doing his best not to sound

defensive at the suggestion of cutting and running. "It's just that we, particularly you, are at a go/no-go point and that this is a good time to re-assess our approach."

"Thanks for the thought, but I know what I'm doing," she said, reaching into her bag and retrieving a black digital camera with a fast-looking zoom lens that Kip could only dream about for the *Beacon*.

"Ahem. City property?"

"Nope, all mine. Now step back."

Over the next several minutes, Erin photographed the site from a variety of distances and angles. "We have to do this – because if Anders found anything of significance, we'd be horribly negligent in not recording every step of what we're doing. But now we can move on to the next step."

And with that pronouncement, Erin took a long handled auger from the bed of the truck. "With this guy we can get core samples to take back with us. Just don't tell a soul what I'm about to do, since I'm jumping the process by six months while running the risk of corrupting the site."

"But . . ."

"You got any alternatives at this point?"

"Nope. Fresh out."

Erin spent the next half an hour pulling core samples from various parts of the site with the cork-screw shaped device and then storing them in canisters, which she methodically labeled. When she had enough samples, she declared the only work remaining was to return the site back in its original appearance. Kip felt exhausted, and Erin had done the bulk of the work.

"We'll need to review the photos," she said. "How does four o'clock this afternoon work for you?"

"Fine. I've got catching up to do at the office. Then I'll be free."

"It's a deal," she said. "Let's get out of here."

Silence filled the Ford on the ride back into town. Had he not been awash in conflicting thoughts, Kip might have found the lull in conversation satisfying, even comforting. But even the simplest matters seemed complicated lately, particularly a growing sense of impending danger entwined with the exhilaration he felt for the woman sitting next to him. If it had to be a package deal – dread and romance – so be it.

He was so lost in thought that Erin's question barely registered.

"I'm sorry, what did you say?"

"I said you're mighty quiet. Too much archaeology for one day?"

Kip didn't have to think long for a reply. Maybe she'd declined his invitation to dinner, but the playful tone of her question lifted his spirits. "Far from it. I could get used to your line of work."

"Oh, how so?"

"Well, for starters, you get to work outdoors, and probably only when the weather is accommodating. You can play in the dirt and sand all day and not get in trouble when you get home at the end of the day. Plus, you get to make great discoveries that advance our knowledge of mankind."

Erin laughed heartily and said, "Were it that simple. I'll have to tell you the many downsides another time. In the meantime, we've got a low-tech picture show to attend. It won't tell us much, but we've got to begin somewhere."

Were it only that simple, Kip thought.

TWENTY-TWO

Instead of the *Beacon*, Kip went to the boathouse. His boat needed work in preparation for the spring season and paperwork at the office could wait.

Like many group rowers, he owned a sculling shell for solo weekend rows. He welcomed the diversion from the complexities and competitiveness of engaging with seven other rowers, each with his or her own set of expectations and temperaments. On a wide expanse of the Potomac, a rower could start, stop, and turn at will. The freedom to experiment with technique also paid dividends on future race days.

The door to the sculling shed was already open when he arrived. Stacked four high on racks were some thirty shells of various brands, lengths, and colors. At roughly $5,000 a boat, Kip figured the shed contained an inventory worth nearly $150,000. Stolen boats were never a problem. Vandalism by bored teenagers could be another matter, and Kip was glad of PCRC's good security.

Back in the parking lot, he exchanged greetings with several other rowers and began working on his boat which he had placed on two canvas slings. A relatively new racing shell, his twenty-four foot Hudson needed only minor touches. After washing it inside and out, he greased the runners on which the sliding seat moved. The riggers holding the oars in place looked fine. The hard rubber ball on the bow protecting the composite hull from accidental bumps with the dock and other boats needed re-gluing. Half an hour had passed and he was able to pronounce his boat ready for another season.

Another ninety minutes remained before he would rejoin Erin, which was enough time to check out the *Madison* and still grab a sandwich at home.

The Vespoli racing shell rested upside down at waist level on its rack. Three seasons old, the sleek racer could compete with any boat and it still had many good years ahead of it as well.

Nothing about the 4 seat where Phil Gardner sat on the ill-fated race with Algonquian Boat Club the past Saturday seemed amiss. The oar locks were in good shape, with no difference between it and the other seven sets. Kneeling on the floor to look into the upside-down boat, Kip was able to shake the shoes in their stretchers. Nothing wrong there. Same with the sliding seat. An eerie but unexplainable accident, Kip concluded.

With a start, Kip reeled around at the sound of husky voice behind him.

"Can't leave well enough alone, Alexander?"

Paul Schultz stood an arm's length away, hands on hips, feet apart in a familiar stance.

Something about referring to someone by their last name in this day and age irked Kip. Maybe they spoke that way in isolated pockets of New England boarding schools, but in the cultural and social melting pot of Northern Virginia the effect of being called Alexander was pure insult. It further confirmed the animosity in his voice.

"Not exactly, Paul. Do you know something we don't?"

"You wish. Don't you think people would find it highly odd to know you were seen snooping around a boat that had – how should we put it – an unfortunate event. Kind of like returning to the scene of the . . ." Schultz let his sentence trail off to set the hook.

That was a conclusion Kip would not have expected people to read from his actions. That is, unless a well-worked rumor were to take flight at Schultz's instigation.

"The same could be said for you," Kip replied. "How do explain your presence here? In fact, given your lovely penchant for violence, you shouldn't even be talking."

Kip hadn't directly insulted Schultz's integrity, but he might as well have. This time nobody would be standing between him and the pit bull. The few other rowers present were outdoors and would never hear the resulting fracas.

"Don't worry, Alexander, no thrashing for you today. I know you're snooping around in my business. If you and your sidekick think you can derail my work on P2, you're in for a very expensive lesson. My lawyers are prepared to file a restraint of business suit that will toast your shitty little paper to a fare-thee-well. Got that?"

Not waiting for an answer, Schultz turned and walked out of the boathouse.

TWENTY-THREE

"You look like you got audited by the IRS," Erin said when Kip arrived at her office. "What gives?"

When he finished his short tale of woe with Paul Schultz, Erin was suitably impressed. After a pause of several seconds, she let loose with soft laughter.

"That was funny?"

"No, but the thought of you with another black eye would be a bit much. You had a shiner when I met you, and were you to have acquired another, I will have known you longer with a black eye than without."

"Yeah, well, think how hard it would be for me – I could fill a black hole with the sunglasses I lose."

Crooking her index finger, she motioned for Kip to follow her into the conference room. Like the other quarters in the building, that room had a high, track-lighted ceiling and walls with posters of historic scenes of long-ago life in Port City. Mantled shelves displayed artifacts culled from sites from around town – pottery, glassware, clay pipes. They sat at a table made from the remains of stable door that could accommodate at least eight people. Kip figured many presentations for grants and funding had been delivered in this comfortably authoritative room.

Reaching into his backpack, he produced a bottle of wine, a baguette, and cheese. "Before you begin the feature presentation, here's some sustenance. I hope you like Pinot Noir."

"If you had brought Merlot, I'd have to throw you out," she said.

"Good thing, then," Kip said.

He filled two plastic glasses and set out a plate of bread and sliced cheese. "Now let's get on with the show."

As she worked the keyboard of a Mac laptop, Erin grumbled, "It would have been swell if we had had GPR this morning."

"GPR?"

"Ground penetrating radar."

"Radar?"

"Yep. Engineers, geologists, and the military use that kind of radar for all sorts of purposes," Erin said. "Archaeologists use it to locate grave shafts, walls, and metal artifact deposits. That's how they found that new Super Stonehenge in England. Trouble is, it's expensive, complicated technology and it would take more training than I have to make sense of whatever it might find."

"In the meantime, we've got your Nikon," Kip said.

"That we do. But we'll only be looking at images of what we saw earlier today. Maybe seeing the site on the overhead projection will jar an idea loose. Dim the lights, and I'll show you what little we have."

The clarity and perspective of the first photo beamed on to the wall screen did look impressive. Maybe it was the fancy annotated marker stakes positioned around the plot or her choice of lens angle that made the photos look so authoritative. But, so what? Kip thought. There was still nothing to see but a clearly defined rectangle.

Erin anticipated his doubts. "Yeah, I agree – we don't know what we are looking at," she said. "We can only go on the notion that Anders was after something big and hope for any number of things below the surface – a grave site, a structure, a cook site. Just because we don't have something obvious isn't all bad, since we can carbon date the auger samples we took today."

"You can do all that here?"

"I wish. No. I will need to send samples to a lab."

"How long will that take?"

"It depends on who does it and how much red tape comes into play."

"Could Owen Draper help?"

"N*ooo*. We don't want to go that route. They are too by-the-book at his museum. It would take forever. Besides, I can guarantee you the publicity would be more than we'd want at this point, even if Anders found something minor."

"Isn't that what we want?"

"In due time and on our terms, we do. No, I'd rather use a back channel with friends who can do the job faster and more discretely."

Kip had a good notion of the answer, but he asked anyway. "And that would be who?"

"Randy can fit us in anytime and run the preliminary test. We'll know what to do from there."

"Are you sure you want that?"

"We're good friends, after all. And Randy won't demand the back story."

"Fair enough," Kip said. Not burning bridges has its merits.

Erin continued, "If Randy isn't swamped, he should have something to us by later in the week."

Kip said he would tie down loose ends on tasks he had started, none of which he had control over. Katherine Tisdale could only work so fast and his research into archaeology for the *Beacon* series couldn't afford shortcuts.

As they were gathering up their plates and glasses, Kip asked, "How are you with costume parties?"

"It depends."

"Depends on what?"

"On the costume, of course. And when and where?"

"Garden Ball launches Garden Week and the annual homes tour," Kip said. "It's a big deal – proceeds benefit the acquisition of open space in Port City. My sister Cass is chair, and the *Beacon* is a platinum sponsor, meaning we provide publicity and PR. We'll have our very own table for staff and friends. Mark your calendar in ink for Saturday after next at the Masonic Temple."

"And the dress code?"

"Easy. Pick any era from Port City's history and match it.

"In that case, I wouldn't miss it for all the open space in Port City.

TWENTY-FOUR

While it was no Champs-Élysées, King Street held its own for appeal, especially on a warm spring evening. Italian lights strung in the trees illuminated the twenty blocks connecting the bustling waterfront with the Metro station at the foot of the towering George Washington Masonic Temple.

Kip and Erin decided to walk rather than take a cab or the trolley. Their trip up King Street took them past antique shops, galleries, restaurants, and small offices, many with second- and third-story apartments, giving the area the quality urban planners praise as livability.

The cityscape along the narrow two-lane avenue was no overnight sensation. Rather, upper King Street evolved from wig and gun shops, used-car lots, and dive diners, townhouse offices, and vacant structures awaiting better times. Better times never came in the 1960s, or '70s, or '80s, which was probably the best thing that could have happened. When the boom arrived in the '90s, the bulk of the building stock was still intact and protected by preservation laws. King Street and the streets paralleling it got a plush and toney makeover without the loss of its eclectic architecture and neighborhood feel.

The few remaining empty lots sprouted ambitious structures housing trade associations and technology start-up companies. Architects and ad agencies found the townhouses suitably hip for office space. Throughout the blossoming of King Street, brick remained the material of choice for its sidewalks. Best of all, Kip explained, King Street's evolution was organic – no need for instant mixed-use projects.

"You're preaching to the choir," she said. "I didn't choose Port City for concrete and steel. But the brick sidewalks are murder. I hope people don't stare at my feet."

"You'll be a hit tonight – the only Civil War nurse in running shoes," Kip said. "Besides, that place is going to be so packed, nobody will be able to see your feet."

Kip struggled every year with his costume, despite the twenty-four-hour half-life of a badly conceived outfit. In past years, he'd been a prosperous merchant, a ship's captain, and a colonial fireman. This year he went somewhat in character – a printer and publisher – in knee britches and flouncy tunic-style shirt. With a wig borrowed from the local theater company, he achieved a good working version of Ben Franklin.

After fifteen minutes of "Yo, Ben" and "Hey, Clara" from passersby, they arrived at the foot of the granite behemoth where the Garden Ball was getting underway.

The nine-story, 330-foot high George Washington Masonic Temple tended to be more visited by out-of-towners than by locals, who knew the structure as an everyday sight. Kip was only slightly better informed about the Masons' pride and joy.

Entering the cavernous entrance hall was always a jolt. Memorial Hall on the third level extended back 100 feet under a fifty-one-foot high ceiling supported by eight green granite columns. Giant murals depicted scenes from Washington's life and, as a further reminder of his greatness, a seventeen-foot bronze statue of the Founding Father anchored the west end of the room.

"I feel like a tourist in New York City," Erin said, craning her neck upward at the ceiling before taking in all the granite, bronze, and artwork. "Don't tell me you come here so often it's old hat for you."

"I'll make my confession later, but let's keep moving. There's a line forming."

A queue of Revolutionary soldiers, farmers, merchants, and schoolmarms patiently waited behind them, also staring wide-eyed. It confirmed Kip's notion that people overlook the good stuff right in front of them every day.

After availing themselves of wine from a proffered tray, they wandered to the far end of the hall where a contra dance troupe performed to the accompaniment of fiddler and guitarist. Only a smattering of guests paid them any attention. This crowd was in full social mode. Their chatter rose like steam, creating a dull roar amplified by a quarry's worth of marble and granite. Kip was wondering about the success of this year's turnout when his twin materialized in the form of a grand colonial dame.

"Well, well, it's good to see you, Mrs. Washington," Kip said. "And where might George be this evening? Does he know you're out and about looking so marvelous?"

"Not to worry, Ben, he's fetching drinks," Cass said. "So, Kip, when did you plan on introducing Erin? Folks were considerably better mannered 200 years ago."

He considered the richness of this opening line from the woman who seemed to know as much about Erin as he did and let it pass.

"Erin, meet Cass. Cass, Erin."

He was chagrined by the intensity of Erin's assessment of his sister. Then, again, he was used to this reaction when people first met Cass. Though identical in their twinship, Cass differed from her brother in ways that always drew attention. They both shared strong jawlines, prominent aquiline noses, and barely tamable hair. The difference lay in the crinkle of Cass's eyes that conveyed warmth and mischief. Yes, Kip mentally told Erin, she is seriously beautiful.

"Kip has told me a lot about you. I'm glad to finally meet you," Erin said.

"Kip, as usual, has told me very little about you," Cass laughed. "You and I will have to take care of that on our own."

Before anyone could comment further, a tall figure looking as though he had walked off a dollar bill approached them with a goblet of wine in each hand.

Handing them to Cass, Hank Merrill bowed and kissed Erin on the hand. To Kip he gave a hearty, most un-Washington bear hug.

"It's good to see you, too, Hank," Kip wheezed in mock

discomfort. "You look so, uh, presidential, at least when you can restrain yourself."

"Yep, like that will happen," Hank said.

"How did my ever reserved brother-in-law find such a comely nurse?" Hank asked.

When Erin blushed, Kip remembered how easily Hank charmed, flattered, and disarmed his students.

"Back off, George. You'll have to wait until Erin and I have had lunch," Cass interceded.

"By the way, Kip, have you seen your adoring admirer tonight?" Hank asked. "Paul Schultz is here with his comrades-in-development. You'll love their costumes."

Following Hank's eyes across the hall to Table 23, Kip understood at once. Schultz had bought a double-sized table that was beginning to fill with guests. The theme of the attire of Schultz's staff was blindingly obvious. Dressed in canvas trousers held up with bright red suspenders over plaid shirts, they made for hearty Turn-of-the-Century construction workers. Even the boots and jaunty caps worked well. Irony or hypocrisy, Kip frowned at the sight of the city's less-than-loyal friend of open space.

"I get the message," he said. "Though it's a bit lame for my tastes. Do they really think people will swallow their shtick about building this city?"

"Enough do. You know that." There was nothing light in Hank's assessment. "There are always people who fall for that polemical slop. But, look on the bright side. It must have irked Schultz to pay retail for such a huge table."

"Money's money, and we'll take his as fast as anybody's," Cass added. "But, Kip, do tell me you'll stay out of trouble tonight."

"Surely you remember, I'm a lover, not a fighter," he replied, draping an arm over Erin's shoulder.

In the corner, a classical quartet had replaced the dancers, and despite their most muscular efforts to render Mozart and Haydn audible, the cacophony of 175 escapees from Madame

Toussaint's easily won out.

Kip and Erin spent the next thirty minutes circulating among the guests and were more than ready for the next stage when the long, quavering sound of a gong rang out. The noise level jumped another ten decibel points with the call to dinner. Turning to move on to the Grand Chamber where their table waited, a lone apparition blocked their way. It took Kip a moment to appreciate the sight – a rugged motorcyclist in knickers, brown leather jacket and cap, with goggles perched on her forehead.

"Yeesh, Helen. You win First Prize for Costume and Fright Factor. I didn't even see you there."

"No small wonder in this mob," Helen shouted. "I've been trying to catch up with you two for the last ten minutes. Every time I got close, you moved on."

"We were only going with the flow – and the food trays," Kip said. "Where are you sitting? Need a table?"

"I'm good," she said. "I'm with friends from school. But thanks."

Helen looked around the room and then reached into her messenger bag, from which she retrieved a simple spiral-bound notebook. Her smile was gone as she handed it to Erin. "Put this in your bag," she said.

"What is it?" Kip asked.

"It's Anders's notebook – his last one. I found it going through more of his stuff and I wanted to give it to you in person. It may explain a lot – you'll be able to tell, Erin. I can't. I do know it's interesting."

"How so?"

"You'll see soon enough. I'll be moving on now." Pausing for a second, she looked Kip straight in the eyes and added, "Kip, remember what I told you the other night." And with a peck on his cheek, Helen Martin turned and receded into the salmon run.

"Now, that was not your everyday cocktail party conversation," Erin whispered in Kip's ear, even though Helen was well out of ear shot. "Why here, do you suppose?"

"I guess here was the easiest place to give it to us. But there's nothing like a mysterious thirty-second exchange in a crowded party to make things interesting."

"And what did she mean to remember what she told you the other night?"

"Beats me. She told me a lot of things the other night," he lied whitely. For a moment it looked like she wasn't buying Kip's fudging over Helen's admonition to be careful with her. But Erin moved on.

"Well, I can hardly wait to see what that notebook is all about," she said.

"All in due time. Right now, we've got rubber chicken to confront. Care to join me, Miss Barton?"

"Lead the way, Mr. Franklin."

By the time they got to their table, *Beacon* staff and their favorite advertisers were hard at work on their salads. Thanks to Cass, their table was front and nearly center, a coveted place in the Garden Ball pecking order designed to impress wavering advertisers. The only drawback lay in its advantage – no early exits without a hundred witnesses.

Had his table been situated any differently, Kip might not have noticed the disturbing incongruity of Paul Schultz's table and its guests. Waves of revulsion rolled over him as he took in the sight of Melvin, Stephen, Dorothy, and their spouses.

"I'll be right back," Kip said mildly.

Willie followed Kip's gaze toward the far side of the room and grabbed his arm. Whispering, he said, "Don't do it, Kip. Save it for later. Don't ruin it for Cass."

"Sorry, Willie. I've got no choice. But, don't worry, I'll behave myself."

"It's not you I'm worried about misbehaving," Willie said.

By the time Willie had finished his sentence, Kip was well across the ballroom. Wedging sideways between the two last remaining tables, he arrived at the hornet's nest of betrayal.

"Good evening, Stephen, Dorothy, Melvin," he announced himself. "Would one of you care to explain this loving seating arrangement?"

All heads snapped in the direction of Kip.

"This is hardly the time or place for your animosity," Stephen said.

"Kip, don't you have more appropriate places to be?" Melvin added.

Since his relatives always seemed to speak in tandem in order to communicate simple thoughts, Kip didn't have to wait long for Dorothy's input.

"Really, Kip. You should return to your table. If you have something to say, try to keep it until our next meeting."

Kip knew he had now promised two people he would behave, but control was slipping. His rage felt unbearable and Schultz could see it, and he piled on.

"Let me explain, Alexander, in terms you should be able to understand," Schultz said. "These are my business associates in my Glebe Road project. Stephen handles legal, Melvin sales, and Dorothy interior design." Schultz gestured wide with both arms to each side. Through gritted teeth, he said, "Now, to second Dorothy's suggestion, why don't you leave."

Rage turned to stone-cold comprehension. Kip now understood the seating arrangement all too well.

"Yes, and now with the backing of your new, dearest business associates, you think you've got yet one more way to whore Port City to the Defense Department," Kip said. "But if you think the *Beacon* will play along, think again."

Turning abruptly, Kip walked away, never hearing Melvin say, "We have thought again."

Blood must have been thicker than water, because the sight at Ambrose Ralston's table never bothered Kip. The *Mirror*'s publisher and Miles Tennyson together in conversation paled in comparison with the insulting spectacle at Schultz's table. Kip passed them wordlessly, promising to explore the possibilities inherent in that once improbable alliance at another time.

Kip arrived back at his table as Colonial-garbed servers were distributing plates of dinner.

"You're just in time," Erin said. "Tell us later about your love fest later."

No way would Table 23 ruin the evening for his staff and advertisers. The only thing harder than keeping an advertiser was signing a new one. Tonight needed to go smoothly. "What a bunch of characters," Kip said, taking his place. "Yeah, I love 'em all."

Dinner consisted of fare far better than rubber chicken. The chef at Catesby's Tavern, a 1770 tavern and hotel, oversaw production of rounds of beef and platters of seafood. Other restaurants contributed side dishes found in various periods of Port City's history. A rich rendition of colonial syllabub from the Mount Vernon Ordinary capped off dinner. The Garden Ball clearly bucked the trend of food as a frequent afterthought for fund raisers.

Because this was an event with floral origins, the organizers spared no detail in decorating the room. Pots sprouted shrubbery, wall sconces burst with bouquets of daffodils, and ornate candlelit centerpieces anchored each table.

"This is spectacular," a middle-aged colonial dame told Kip. For Terry Hart, the owner of a newly opened clothing shop, this Garden Ball was her first.

"Don't worry, Terry, you won't get used to it. I never do," Kip said. "That's the beauty of having something like this only once a year. I actually look forward to it."

He was laying it on thick tonight, and even Willie grinned at the sight of his boss in full advertising mode.

"Tell me you don't throw out these center pieces afterward?"

"Hardly," said Carrie Brant. "We have a tradition of drawing lots at the end of the dinner to see who gets to take it home."

"I like that," Hart cooed. "Between Harry and me here, we've got a good chance."

Better than that, Kip thought. Staff was not allowed to win.

As the dessert course was winding down, the speeches began. Over the tinkling of wine glasses and cutlery on plates, Cass stage-managed a series of community figures who gave windy thanks to sponsors and recognized Port City's community pillars. Such formalities greased the workings of fundraisers everywhere.

Hats off to Cass, her brother thought. Now bring on the auction so we can get out of here.

Had he known the outcome of the auction, Kip might have wanted to linger over the syllabub.

Well into the bidding, with the sales of restaurant dinners, vacation condo stays, and spa treatments done, came the bidding for a page of advertising in the Port City *Beacon*.

The cost to the *Beacon* was minimal and the civic payback substantial. Since the winning bid was always below retail value, lesser endowed community organizations competed vigorously each year for the ads while larger businesses left them alone. Kip was piqued to see that *Mirror* hadn't donated to the ball. Bad form, Kip thought, since Ralston got his table gratis for publicizing the ball.

At the *Beacon*'s table they politely followed the modest $50 bumps and raises emanating from around ballroom. Mercifully, Garden Ball appeared to be winding down.

"Looks like we'll be seeing an ad next week from the animal shelter," Willie said with knowing nonchalance, as the pauses between bids grew longer, despite the best efforts of auctioneer Jake Johnson.

"Nah, the high school band booster club will come through," Carrie said. "You watch."

"Are you sure? I don't like what I'm seeing," Erin said.

Following her gaze to the other end of the room, the group saw Paul Schultz rise to bid. They couldn't hear him, but Johnson's miffed look said it all. Schultz's bid clearly had exceeded the other bids.

"If Mr. Shultz is sure of the wisdom of his bid," Johnson announced, "then it's going, going, gone! Sold to Schultz Development and Construction."

The sale produced only a smattering of applause and none of the friendly banter that accompanied the conclusion of other auction items. Johnson thanked everybody and extended his best wishes for a safe and beautiful spring. Dancing would begin momentarily.

Schultz and his entourage stood and then proceeded to file

one at a time silently by the *Beacon*'s table.

It felt like being left in the swirl of dust and debris of a passing truck, a dump truck at that. Kip wanted to spit, and might have had not the entire table been watching him. He knew exactly what would become of Schultz's gesture. He would parlay his bargain ad into a screed in favor of P2 and the benefits sure to shower down on Port City.

"Boss, you know you don't have to take the ad," Willie said.

"That wouldn't be a good precedent," Kip said. "Don't worry, we'll figure something out."

"Suit yourself," Willie said. "But trust me, no good comes from letting that jerk get his way."

Probably not, thought Kip.

On the dance floor, Kip and Erin worked through a decently rendered version of a Tom Petty song and a Glenn Miller chestnut. Neither was in the spirit of dancing, and they returned to their table where the staff had begun the raffle for the floral centerpiece. They weren't surprised when Terry Hart won.

That was only cue needed for the table to disperse for the evening. Having said their farewells, Kip and Erin headed toward the main hall, where he steered her toward the elevator.

"What are you doing?" she asked.

"You need to see this."

"Do show me, then."

The bronze elevator door yawned open and the operator greeted them.

"Sorry, but we only go to the ninth floor tonight," said a girl in gray slacks, blazer with a brass name plaque, and white blouse. A high school student with one of the more inconveniently timed part-time jobs in Port City. Clearly, this kid was Yale-bound, Kip thought. Who else would give up Saturday night with her friends?

"That's fine. Nine, please," Kip said.

And with that, the girl closed the door and the elevator lurched upward.

"Why does this feel so odd?" Erin asked.

"That's because the elevator travels diagonally – it's the only way we could go up a tapered tower," the girl said.

In less than a minute, the car eased to a stop and the doors opened.

"Looks like you've got the terrace to yourselves tonight," she said. "If I'm not here, buzz me when you need a ride back down."

Stepping through a small, unadorned door onto a narrow walkway, Erin gasped. "This is unbelievable."

It wasn't the panorama of the Washington skyline to the north with its illuminated monuments or the bustling Old Town scene directly below them that took the evening far beyond the extraordinary. Suspended above the river, a massive, orange full moon had announced its arrival with stunning drama. Even Kip was amazed.

"You planned this, didn't you?" Erin said.

"Me?"

"You."

"Guilty as charged."

"Oh, shut up. It's beautiful."

Erin hugged Kip, clinging long enough to convey more than thanks for the world-class view in front of them and Kip pursued the embrace to its logical conclusion. Their kiss went on and on, saying everything that needed to be said but could not be said in words. Minutes passed and they were on the verge of first-class teenage make-out session when behind them came a throaty ahem.

"I'm sorry. But this is my last run," their elevator operator murmured apologetically. "We've got to close."

"Not a problem," Erin said, straightening her clothes and hair. "We were ready to leave."

The emotionally charged ride back to earth seemed to take much longer than it did. Emerging from the empty lobby, they joined a small queue of Garden Ball stragglers waiting for taxis.

"You can drop me off at my place first," Erin said.

Kip's heart lurched with disappointment. Hadn't something special happened a few minutes ago? Then, again, it had been a first date. He was about to assent to Erin's request when she continued.

"By the way, are you any good with breakfast? We can go over the notebook at your place in the morning, if you want."

It wasn't quite like being invited back to her place for coffee, but what the heck? It would do.

"Absolutely."

TWENTY-FIVE

They were like two kids sharing the same textbook. "Slow down." "Wait." "How long are you going to take to read that page?"

For the last hour, they had been sifting through the pages of Anders Martin's notebook that lay open on Kip's kitchen table. The spiral-bound book, which looked as though it came off a shelf at the local Staples, was part diary, part scrapbook. The entries began the previous summer and grimly ended in February. If they thought the notebook would easily yield its secrets, they were mistaken.

Guessing was the best they could do with Martin's maddeningly cryptic annotations. The journal entries mostly noted where the archaeologist had been on any given day in the past several months and what he had accomplished or hoped to accomplish.

"None of this deals with Strawberry Flats," Erin said. "So far, he's mostly put together a scrapbook of pre-European settlement in America – maps, charts, graphs. I don't see anything new here."

Kip stifled a yawn and asked, "How about arrowheads and stone tools? Half the pages are filled with drawings of them."

"You've entered the arcane world of archaeology," Erin said. "Those drawings and photos are perfectly normal – a lot of us stay on top of our games with handiwork like that. But it sure would help if Martin had provided even basic context. By the way, we call them 'projectile points,' not arrowheads. It's more accurate."

"Duly noted," he said. "Then I assume there's nothing to connect with Strawberry Flats. Right?"

"Right," Erin said. "Still, we know from our visit there last weekend that Anders may have found himself an old Indian site. There are countless sites all over the country. It's what you would expect from thousands of years of inhabitation."

"So, you're saying there's not enough to call off the bulldozers?"

"It's looking that way," Erin said.

"Then what would be enough to call them off?"

"That's the question," she said. "Anders would need to have found something monumental in significance, and major finds are in short supply. You can't call them up at will. He of all people knew that."

Figuring there was more to come, Kip called a timeout and retrieved the coffee pot to refill their mugs.

Erin continued, piling up theories on Anders's behavior as she went along.

"He may have been looking for some kind of Paleo-Indian transportation nexus – some site where tribes met halfway to trade exchange food and goods," she said. "The Chesapeake region was notable for that kind of activity."

"How far back?" Kip asked. "Was there a Native American Christopher Columbus?"

Erin thought a moment before replying.

In that pause, Kip realized that mundane, repetitive, and elementary questions didn't faze her. She could easily teach archaeology, he thought, and then remembered her father taught the subject on the college level and she regularly conducted tours and field trips. This part of her job was easy for her. Cracking Anders Martin's world was another matter.

"When you go that far back in history," she said, "the best we can do is give entire peoples credit for such things. It's not for lack of trying. Armies of archaeologists and anthropologists are out there pursuing the origins of humans in our hemisphere. Paleo archaeology is way out of my field, but for someone like

Anders, this is smack in the middle of his comfort zone. His notebook could as well have been off-the-clock recreation."

"Then why did Helen give it to us in the first place?"

"It's the closest thing to a journal or diary she has of his last days. She's as interested in learning why Martin was fooling around at the junkyard as we are. Helen couldn't make sense of it, but she must think we can."

Kip hesitated and then articulated a growing suspicion. "Is it possible that Anders might have been trying to plant phony evidence of a find?"

"Impossible."

"Why?"

"Plenty of reasons. First, you would have to have known Anders – professionally, as I did. He built his life on integrity. Second, you would have to know the profession – those things don't happen in this day and age. Third, any college student could see through something as stupid as that. It would be the artistic equivalent of forging the Mona Lisa – the experts would know the moment they saw it."

Greed, ambition, passion, and obsession in Kip's opinion were all first cousins in the human condition. Any one of them could blind a person teetering on the edge of an ethical precipice. Maybe even Anders Martin. In spite of not knowing Anders professionally as well as Erin had, Kip conceded having never seen anything in him that would indicate such, what? Dishonesty? Or Machiavellian cunning? Ultimately, he knew he would have to leave that option open.

"Fair enough," Kip said. "I see your point. But, then, why would someone go to such lengths to stop Anders? And who is that someone. So far, we've got the shortest possible list of suspects."

"And that would be?"

"My good friend, Paul Schultz. But would he really do such a thing?"

"You're the one who knows him," she said. "But couldn't you say he was playing it safe and hedging his bets – in his eyes, anyway. Judging by his ongoing antagonism with Anders, it's possible he cracked when he suspected Anders turned up something that could stop P2."

Kip rose from the table and walked to the window overlooking his small courtyard. Running his fingers through his hair, he eyed a pair of robins hopping around in the flowerbed. The same question, with variations, kept coming.

"Nothing adds up," he said. "If what you say is true about those luckless armies of archaeologists and anthropologists, then why would Anders have worked so hard at Strawberry Flats, knowing it probably wouldn't amount to anything? I'd say we're nearly at a dead end."

"Hey, don't forget, we've still got the radio carbon test," she said. "It should be ready by Wednesday. Randy says he was having trouble getting lab time for running the test and he had to find another lab. That's not easy, but if anyone could, Randy's the man."

So, thought Kip, it's hurry up and wait. That's too much like work.

Their session with Martin's notebook quickly wound down and an easy casualness filled the kitchen. Erin, in her stocking feet, sat on a thick hooked rug with Ike, who nearly levitated with joy at having his ears scratched.

Kip sat on a worn Windsor chair with his feet propped on its mate and sipped coffee as jazz guitar from a Washington radio station filled room with music. The beam of golden sunlight slanting through the window above the sink so neatly framed Erin, Ike and, now, Samantha, that he thought a Vermeer painting had materialized in his kitchen. On second thought, it began to look like a portal into his future. With considerable planning, he had engineered the romantic interlude high above Port City. And now the sight before him was either the payoff or a down payment for such moments in the future. Or, he wondered, was it a comet of good fortune that visits only once in a lifetime?

"Your omelets need work and in the wrong doses, your coffee could kill a moose," Erin said, looking up at him. "But I do like your world here. It must be heavenly to come home to this after a frightful day in the ring with the town's heavy weights."

Kip's hopes lifted with this confirmation of his assessment. He knew what he had going for him, though no one until this sun-drenched morning had expressed such an appreciation. At this moment, life was feeling like it was meant to be, whereas in the past, his occasional flings always ended with relief. Some women took up too much space, physically and emotionally. Others did little things, like fingering household objects and otherwise sizing him up through his possessions. Then there were Ike and Samantha. Some women had pet allergies and others plain disliked dogs or cats or both. Kip never considered himself a love-me-love-my-pet kind of person. But Ike and Sam were his family and, for better worse, they always ended up being an acid test of acceptance. Something in the way Erin got down on the floor and ruffled old and arthritic Ike won over Kip as much as it did his hound.

He measured his response to extend a moment that might never repeat itself.

"Yes . . . you are right," he said. "Sometimes I think this is the only place that makes sense. I used to believe that anyone who really has their act together doesn't need to depend on domestic pacifiers. Funny, but I almost fell for someone who claimed true security comes with mobility and rootlessness, especially in this transient culture of ours."

"But that wasn't you, was it?"

"Nope. At least I've squashed that particular insecurity."

"You're getting old – I mean, older – Mr. Alexander."

Kip laughed. "Yeah, that, too. And what about you. I know next to nothing about you."

Erin shooed Samantha from her lap and rose from the floor. "Consider that part of the conversation as to be continued," she said. "Not that there's much to tell you."

"Somehow I doubt that. When can we take up the to-be-continued part?"

She slipped on her denim jacket and wound a scarf around

her neck. "Perhaps dinner some evening soon," she said. "We may also have some very interesting radiocarbon results to discuss."

They were now in the doorway, and Erin put her hands on Kip's shoulder in a way all men know to mean: Stay tuned for an announcement. Kip didn't exactly brace himself as go slack with an anticipation that meant: "What now?"

"Let's not set any speed records here," she said. "Maybe you don't have anyone in your life to complicate matters, but I do. And hurting someone is not part of who I am. I hope you understand that, and I really hope that's the way you operate."

Kip made a note to tell her how complicated his life had been off and on for as long as he could remember. Now, however, on this highly portent day in early March in his 38th year, there was only one person in his life with whom he'd like to further complicate it. She was standing right before him, imploring him with impossibly green eyes that nearly lifted him off the ground.

"I do understand," Kip said softly, then more firmly, "As for how I operate, I can tell you this – when I know what I want, I play for keeps."

"Fair enough," Erin said.

No further words were exchanged. They hugged, and she left. As her truck rumbled down the street, Kip wondered how one played for keeps in situations like this.

TWENTY-SIX

With Erin gone, the energy drained from the house. Straightening furniture that didn't need it and putting away dishes only made Kip feel silly and inconsequential.

What else could add to the frustration he felt lately? Kip asked, as he began consolidating papers from their breakfast meeting. If he had walked around the kitchen table instead of a boarding-house reach for Martin's notebook, he wouldn't have knocked over his mug of coffee.

"*Arrgghh,*" he screeched, grabbing a dish towel to swab the brown flood on the notebook, Patel's photograph, and news clippings. Helen probably wouldn't mind much and he certainly wasn't going to return the photograph to Patel. Enough of this – time for something more satisfying, he concluded.

After changing into rowing clothes, he snapped a leash on to Ike's collar and walked the several blocks down to the boathouse. The short distance accommodated the dog's aged joints while allowing him to sniff and whine with every interesting scent. Once there, Ike curled up in a sunny corner.

By mid-March, most of the rowing programs were in full swing Monday through Saturday. Sundays at Port City's boathouse were reserved for independent rowing, usually in singles and doubles. This morning, the boathouse teemed with rowers emerging from winter hibernation to take advantage of the warm weather.

It took him less than ten minutes to get his Hudson on the water and ready to go. With a shove of an oar against the dock, he was away and into a world where he always thought best.

By following Anders Martin's final course, Kip hoped once more to glean sense from his life and death. Within minutes, he passed beneath the massive spans of Wilson Bridge where the Potomac widened. The scenery grew dramatically more expansive and pastoral under a huge sky. With each stroke and glide of the boat Kip found it easier to reconsider his late friend.

Martin clearly was complex and multi-faceted. He was professional at the top of his game and highly moral, to the point of combativeness. That much was borne out in his many community tiffs. Martin's world came with only minimum shades of gray which made it tougher for the more nuanced Kip to accept. With Martin, you either accepted the world as worth discovering, preserving, and protecting or you stood in league with those for whom greed doubled as progress. Kip didn't entirely disagree with that philosophy; but it overlooked the vast middle ground.

Yet, Martin was a family man – wife and two daughters. And he was one of the boys – a committed rower, liked and admired by the club's members. Most of them, anyway.

And, as Erin attested, Martin was a good colleague and mentor. Together, they had built up a nationally respected urban archaeology program.

So, what to make of the secret part of his life of warring with bulldozers? What led him to Liza Bushrod's auto resting grounds? Had he really found something of significance? Why the need for secrecy?

The more he thought about that question, the more Kip began to sense an answer. Martin believed he had something big, and until he could prove it and package the discovery on his terms, he wanted it under wraps. So, where did it go wrong? How had he been found out? Did someone follow Martin until he or she had the needed information? That would be too random and dependent on luck, he concluded.

More likely, Schultz's time spent in Strawberry Flats in his role of advising the Defense Department turned up something. Liza Bushrod had mentioned Schultz's visit to gauge her interest in selling her property.

Like Erin had posited, something must have tipped off Schultz, and at that point, he panicked, with Martin paying the ultimate price. If so, then how did he engineer such a flawless death? Kip couldn't remember exactly where Schultz was on that fateful February morning. He hadn't been aboard the *Madison* with Kip's crew. Probably, he had been working onshore repairing a boat, since he had been at the boathouse when Martin was reported missing. Then did he have an accomplice? If only Jake Johnson had looked deeper into Anders's death at the time. But he wasn't going to tell the chief that he now needed to get involved. He would stick to newspapering.

Fifteen minutes of steady rowing brought him to the broad bay bordered by marshland rich in wildlife. He could see miniature hikers and cyclists on the boardwalk of the nature center half a mile away. He figured this must be where Martin flipped over. Any closer to shore, and there was the slim chance he could have swum to safety.

Barely exerted, Kip nonetheless welcomed the chance to drift and think. Had he been in a full rowing mode, he might not have heard the approach of a speeding boat. Looking over his shoulder, he saw a gleaming black bass boat barreling toward him at 50 mph, giving him only enough time to drop an oar and wave his free arm.

Instead of blasting by and swamping Kip, the boat's driver cut its engine. Had it been a car on pavement, the screech would have been terrific. Idling within twenty feet of Kip's shell, the eighteen-foot vessel was far less ominous than it had seemed seconds before. He didn't know what to expect, but two teenagers, a boy and a girl, out for a spin, was far from it.

"Hey, man! We're sorry – we didn't see you," the boy hollered. "You okay?"

"I'm fine," Kip said, "though you scared the hell out of me."

"We said we're sorry."

"So you did. Thanks. Have a good day."

And with that, the engine on the boat rumbled to life; but the boy politely accelerated slowly away toward the marina on the far side of Heron Bay.

Could this have been how Anders died? Kip thought. Damn, he never got the chance I had a moment ago.

In the suddenness of the last five minutes something clicked. Those kids had shown him that he was on the right track. He now had a fairly solid idea of the mechanics of how Martin had died. In the lucidity of near death, Kip also concluded that he needed to force the hand of Martin's killer. The way to do that was to deceive him into believing Kip knew what Martin had discovered. The *Beacon* would vaguely announce a finding in advance of an additional installment of the archaeology series.

He drank from his water bottle, adjusted himself on his sliding seat, and began rowing back to the boathouse in a much different frame of mind than when he left it.

TWENTY-SEVEN

It had taken Kip no time at all to write a blurb about the bonus article for the archaeology series and considerably longer to justify it to his staff. Ben Bailey raised the first eyebrow.

"A fourth article? Isn't that a bit of overkill?"

That's not the way Kip wanted the Monday morning staff meeting to begin. Usually they breezed through whatever needed attention. He realized he wasn't so good at slipping things by his staff, probably because he did it so seldom. Successful spin and prevarication take practice, and Kip evidently needed plenty of it.

"It's hardly overkill," he replied. "We can't stop without including one of the most important parts of the city's history. Native Americans might take exception with that oversight. Besides, Ben, you were the most gung-ho about the series."

The pause that settled over the group had less to do with the merit of his statement than with Kip's recent interest in all things historical. Town hall shenanigans tended to be more of Kip's style.

"Pardon me, but what Native Americans?" Ben asked.

"In case you didn't know, the Potomac used to be the I-95 of the East Coast before we arrived. A whole lot went on back then that we're beginning to learn."

"This wouldn't have anything to do with that sweet young woman you've been seeing?" Della asked.

"Excuse me?" Kip sputtered.

"Boss, it's hardly a secret that there may be more to it than a new found love of archaeology," Carrie said.

When his ad director waded into the scuffle, Kip knew it was over. Better to let them in on the obvious and keep their gossipy curiosity away from the real reason for the archaeology article. Deeper down, he suspected they were having fun with him anyway. Even Ben would be okay.

"Well, maybe, just maybe," Kip said.

And with that, they raised their coffee and tea mugs in a toast.

"To Kip's discovery," Willie said.

TWENTY-EIGHT

Working at a community newspaper is a lot like Mark Twain's quip about the weather in Boston – if you don't like it, wait a day. The *Beacon* had been too quiet for the past week, and Kip wasn't sure he liked the tranquility.

Like a college student cramming for a final exam, he had plunged into researching Native American life before the arrival of Europeans. A picture was slowly emerging of a robust North American civilization pre-dating Columbus. Kip felt like kicking himself for treating this installment in the archaeology series as an after-thought. But the hint of a possible historic find was duly planted in the current issue of the *Beacon* and whether it would prompt a response from Anders Martin's killer remained to be seen. That issue had hit the streets the day before. In the meantime, he had the makings of a most interesting conclusion to his series – or a collective huh? from his readership.

In the corner of his office a family relic gently chimed. Half past four, according to the grandfather clock, when Owen Draper would be paying Erin a visit in her office. Kip had almost given into her entreaties to join them, but ultimately declined in the face of backed-up administrative chores and researching his article. Otherwise, he would have attended the unveiling of the results of the analysis of their carbon sample, which had traveled a circuitous route to Draper.

"When Randy couldn't secure a time slot at G.W.'s. lab, he fanned out across the region in search of someone else who could analyze the samples," Erin had explained. "I know what you're thinking, and you don't have to worry. Randy knew what he was doing when he handed the samples off to a friend at the National Geologic Survey."

"I'm glad to see our little treasure in the hands of someone we know. For a while I was worried it would end up in a janitor's trash can," he had said. "How did it Owen come by it?"

"Dumb luck," Erin said. "Seems like everybody is backed up with work these days. Owen said he was doing a favor for a friend of a friend who needed a radiocarbon dating. When he saw the Port City archaeology office and my name on the tag, he offered to return the samples on his way back from work."

"And?"

"The results?"

"What else would I be sitting on the edge of my chair for?"

"I don't know yet. We'll find out at 4:30 today."

As soon as Kip looked away from the clock, the first of a string of phone calls came.

"Someone was prowling around my property last night, right around where Anders had his project," Liza said calmly and almost matter-of-fact. "Eli and Peyton set up such a ruckus that I thought they had a deer trapped."

"Somehow I don't think I'm about to hear an urban wildlife story," Kip said.

"You're right. When I went out to check on the boys, I saw the bobbing and weaving of a flashlight. That really set off the dogs. Whoever it was must have heard me shushing the boys, because the light disappeared."

"Are you okay?" Kip asked. "Did you call the police?"

"I'm fine, and no, I didn't call the police," she said. "It's not a big deal to me, but I thought perhaps you would want to know."

"I do, not that I know what to make of it," Kip said. "Thanks, though."

The next phone call came the moment Kip had rung off with Liza. Katherine Tisdale from the *Post*. Tisdale got right to the point.

"Your friend Paul Schultz is in a heap of financial trouble," she said. "He's been playing shell games with his various creditors. Without a lot of searching, it's impossible for one creditor to know the extent of his situation. Do you want to hear more?"

Kip most certainly did.

Tisdale explained how Schultz had been using one company to prop up another. Most of his projects were limited partnerships that financed development of townhouse and shopping center projects. Much of his work was done on "spec," meaning Schultz had undertaken the projects without having buyers in advance of completion. Instead, he was counting on selling them in a rising market. It wasn't an uncommon practice, though risky even in the best of times. Kip had a good idea on which parts of the real estate checkerboard Schultz had his projects.

"So, he's toast," Kip said.

"No, not necessarily," Tisdale said. "If P2 moves forward, Schultz will have enough cash to extend his shell game."

"And if P2 dries up in Port City?"

"He's done for."

"We should be so lucky. Are you going to do a story on Schultz?"

"Not at this time. He hasn't done anything illegal. Dodgy, perhaps. There's nothing newsworthy at this point. Donald Trump, however, could sneeze and the media would be all over him. They could care less for the Paul Schultzes of the world at this point."

"Well, I can tell you Schultz has cancelled all his advertising with the *Beacon*; but that had to do with our own squabble," Kip said. "It grieves me to know that the *Beacon* has reduced his expenses by not having his ads."

When Kip started to thank Tisdale, she cut in. Her tone had none of the newsy manner of the previous five minutes.

"One more thing, Kip," she said. "You need to be careful."

Thinking back to his tussle at Hampton Funeral Home, Kip almost laughed. "I wish you'd told me that a month ago. You could have spared me a shiner."

"No, Kip, I mean you need to be very careful around him," Tisdale said. "I'm not entirely sure of what you are up to, but you are involved with a very mean man. He's got a history of violence. Charges of domestic abuse turned up in his divorce proceedings. He attacked a business partner in Chicago ten years ago – right in a meeting. They settled out of court, and I'm fairly certain that's why he living here and not in Chicago."

When Kip didn't immediately respond, Tisdale asked, "You there, Kip?"

"Yes, I'm here. I knew the man had a temper, but not to that extent. We've had a couple of run-ins that in hindsight scare the hell out of me."

"Sorry, I wanted to caution you."

"And you have. I can't thank you enough."

This time, Tisdale laughed. "Don't worry. The day will come when your city dishes up some big news, and you'll be there to return the favor. Right?"

"Right."

Tisdale's admonition shook Kip. The punch at the funeral home and the near brawl at the boathouse attested to Schultz's ease with violence. How the man kept it in check this long was surprising. Or, perhaps, he hadn't.

For a few peaceful minutes after his call with Tisdale, Kip tried unsuccessfully to concentrate on his research. The implications of her information were too much to slough off until later. He had decided to throw in the towel for the day when phone rang again.

Neil Ford with National Public Radio's All Things Considered had read his series on Port City archaeology. Would Kip be interested in an interview? Ford said he was struck by the notion of a town examining its roots so far back in order to balance public thinking on its future development.

You don't know the half of it, Mister, Kip thought. He readily agreed to the interview, and they set a date to meet at the *Beacon* for Friday afternoon, a little more than twenty-four hours away.

After hanging up from that call, all Kip could think of was the irony of the quasi-manufactured basis of the series in the *Beacon* as well as falling for the subject and its lovely red-haired practitioner, and now he would be the subject of a national radio broadcast.

His reverie did not last. The phone rang, again.

"You son of a bitch!" The voice crackled with menace. The phone could have been three feet underwater and Kip still would have recognized the gravelly voice of Paul Schultz. "That two-bit piece of shit you call reporting is going to cost you. I guarantee it!"

And with that, Schultz hung up. The click on the other end of the line almost echoed in Kip's office.

That was no melodramatic conversation, one-sided as it was. Kip was sure the man was prepared to back up the threat. To think, when the morning began, he was worried that life at the *Beacon* was too quiet.

This time, Kip made the next phone call.

Erin picked up on the first ring. Her meeting with Owen Draper had finished a quarter of an hour ago. And, yes, she'd be glad to meet him at the Lee Street Pub.

TWENTY-NINE

Kip secured the last available booth in the restaurant moments before the working world of Port City unanimously declared it quitting time. In the span of the few minutes he'd settled into the booth at the far end of the pub, the brick-walled watering hole had transformed from a gentle oasis to a thrumming cauldron. If he hadn't felt a sense of propriety from having supported the pub for most of his legal drinking life, Kip might have felt like he was getting too old for the joint. Erin had better show up or he would soon have a bad case of morose self-pity. Waiting did that to him.

What seemed like hours but was only ten minutes yielded to the sight of Erin weaving her way along the three-deep bar area and through the maze of tables. She had changed into jeans and a bright red Washington Nationals baseball sweatshirt and stood out like a cardinal against a snowy landscape. What a sight, thought Kip.

Erin smiled as Kip rose to greet her, and she returned the gesture with a hug that put Kip's hormone level in parity with the rest of the crowd that he'd fretted as being so young.

"My God!" Erin said. "Where did this crowd come from? No need to answer. If your friend Lovely Glynda hadn't told me where to find you, I'd still be wandering around in this noisy desert."

"And it's only Thursday," Kip said.

"Let's make it a point to give this place a pass on weekends."

As if on cue, Glynda Barnes materialized to take their drink and dinner orders. Kip asked for a beer and a burger, Erin a pinot noir and salad.

"No worries about your youthful figure?" Erin asked.

"Yep, the day I stop rowing."

"I should be so lucky."

Kip skipped right over his work on the article and related his series of phone calls – Liza Bushrod, Katherine Tisdale, Neil Ford and, lastly, Paul Schultz.

Erin flinched at his recounting of his call with Schultz. "Holy shit! What set him off?"

"I'm sure the announcement of the next installment in the series and its promise of historic findings threw fat on his fire," Kip said. "Katherine made it clear he's on the financial ropes. Then we come along and threaten his one hope for a way out of ruin."

"Are you worried?"

"Journalists get yelled at and threatened all the time when they step on the wrong toes. I haven't dealt with potential murderers before. And, yes, I'm worried."

"And what might be this historic find be?" she asked.

"Good question," Kip said. "I'm still working on that."

"Promise me you'll run it by me before you tell the whole world."

"Yes, ma'am. You'll be the first to know."

"What do you think will happen next? Or, what do we do next?

"I feel like we're in overtime, and if anything is going to happen, it's going to happen very soon."

"Well, I've got a few things to report, too," Erin said, "and they're interesting, depending on how you look at it."

"Do tell, then."

"Well, Owen is certainly punctual – he arrived exactly at 4:30, straight from testifying at an appropriations meeting on Capitol Hill," Erin said. "He looks like he does on the PBS series, only he was wearing a gorgeous three-button suit that screamed good taste and power."

"Lucky you," Kip said. "I have to see the guy in spandex nearly every morning. But I will grant you, he has presence. But spare me the sartorial details – what did his eminence have to say about our dirt samples?"

"It goes downhill from here," Erin said. "The samples came back inconclusive."

"Inconclusive?" Kip's crestfallen face betrayed his disappointment.

"As Owen explained it, not knowing for sure is the worst of outcomes. It's more common than you'd think in radiocarbon dating."

"Can you retest it?"

"We'd need better samples, and those we don't have. We gave them the best we had."

A torrent of thoughts flooded Kip's mind as he tried to reconcile this news with what he'd learned earlier in the afternoon. For starters, a report back from Draper confirming some kind of find – any kind of find – would be dandy. His gamble with the announcement of the addition to the series in the *Beacon* had lost its safety net. If he failed to flush out the perpetrator, then Kip was going to have to spin his discovery into something much, much softer. Between Tisdale's revelations and Schultz's threating call, he felt like he was nevertheless on the right path.

"Did you and Owen talk any more about Ander's handiwork at Strawberry Flats?"

"Not much," Erin said. "He's still very dismissive of the whole thing. I did mention the notebook Helen gave us at the Garden Ball and that barely registered. He said if we felt strongly enough about it, he'd take a look at it."

"And do we feel strongly about it?" Kip asked.

"You got me there," Erin said. "I told him I'd see what you thought and that Helen should have some input into sharing it and in the meantime it was safe in your office."

Kip drank from his bottle and thought for a moment before replying. "I don't think Helen would mind, but I'd still prefer to keep Anders's notebook out of circulation. The more people who know about the notebook, the more it could come back to bite us. It's back at my house, anyway."

"I'm fine with that – keeping it out of circulation – and I'm pretty sure Owen will be okay with that," she said. "Besides, we could always ask him for help later if we need it.

Erin sipped her wine and continued, "I will say, he does know how to make a person feel like a million dollars."

"How so?"

"Owen offered me a job."

Kip went tense with that news. The ease and wherewithal that came with Draper and his job bothered him, and he thought he knew why: Draper's arrival in his sphere could end up costing him Erin. His face betrayed his alarm.

"Relax," she said. "I told him no, that I wasn't going anywhere. But it was a nice stroke to be told I had the potential to head up one of the museum's field offices.

Right, Kip thought – a field office in, say, Mexico or the Andes or some place so far off that he could forget about a relationship with Erin.

"Well, you made a mighty fine decision, right there on the spot," Kip said with relief in his voice. "I was about to say I hardly knew ye."

He didn't know how hungry he was until Glynda arrived with dinner. But as he was about to devour his burger, his phone vibrated in his pocket. He ignored it. It buzzed again, and this time Kip pulled the phone out. A text message.

"Willie Carter. The Beacon Building is on fire. I've got to go."

"I'm coming, too," Erin said. Throwing an assortment of bills on to the table, she raced after Kip.

Outside the pub, the screaming of sirens from every direction told them that his would be no ordinary evening.

THIRTY

Chaos in the form of a small fleet of emergency vehicles greeted them as they sprinted on to St. Edmunds Street. Their flashing lights and rumbling engines and staccato squawking of two-way radios felt like an assault.

But they paled next to the real source of his shock: Thick gray and black smoke roiled skyward from the rear half of the structure. Gritty, acrid particles floated earthward. Kip knew the smell from the fire would be with him for a very long time.

Sniffing, Erin shouted, "This is unbelievable! What do we do?"

"I wish I knew," Kip said. "There's no way to tell who's in charge. Everyone looks so important and busy, but no one seems to be doing anything."

Then he saw Calvin Perkins emerge from a small group of firefighters. At first he didn't recognize his assistant pressman, whose chipper demeanor was replaced with a gaunt and expressionless look.

"Calvin!" he shouted when it looked as though Calvin was heading in another direction.

When he saw Kip and Erin his face brightened.

"Am I ever glad to see you," he stammered when he joined them on the curb. "They," he said, pointing to helmeted men in thigh-length protective jackets, "almost had more questions about the building than I could answer. But they say it's about over."

"It doesn't look like it to me," Kip said. "I've never seen so much smoke."

"That's from all the water and what-all they've been spraying back there, "Calvin said. "It's a good sign – it means no fire, or at least very little fire."

Staring at the sight before them, Kip replayed in his mind what Calvin had told him.

What would be left of the building without its fire suppression system? Probably a blackened brick shell. Thinking about the system evoked memories of bitter shouting matches with his board of directors. A dozen agencies and his insurance agent required it, and still they balked. Only the threats of a permanent walk-out by Kip and the resignation of Colbert Jenkins turned the tide. The building was still standing, but at what cost?

He returned his attention to his assistant pressman. "Thanks for helping out, Calvin," he said. "I'm sure it would have much more difficult for them without you."

Scanning the crowd, he noted the absence of someone.

"By the way, Calvin, where's Willie?" he asked. "He's the one who called me."

"Me, too," Calvin said. "I was only a block away, at the club, and got here in seconds."

This wasn't like his pressman to call them and then casually go home to dinner. He pulled his phone from his pocket and reversed dialed Willie. No answer. Then he called Willie's home number. No answer there, either.

He continued pacing, running his hands through his hair. He had covered hundreds of gut-wrenching tragedies, from car accidents to homicides, and now he found himself on the receiving end of the news cycle. He hardly knew how to handle it.

Before he could say anything, pandemonium of two-way radio traffic broke out, and a firefighter in the alley shouted, "We've got someone back here."

Kip stiffened with realization.

Calvin began crying. His wail floated over the street: "Willie!"

Kip unfroze and laid a hand on Calvin's shoulder. Erin already had a hand on his arm.

"Calvin, we don't know anything yet," Kip said with no conviction.

The kid didn't even try to shake free of Kip and Erin as he said, "You know and I know. He went in there to save the place."

He was right, and Kip thought he was going to faint. Just as Willie had been a guiding hand in Kip's life, so he had with Calvin – only much more. Willie provided the boy first with a refuge in the joyously busy print bay and then a foundation when his family life fell apart and he came close to succumbing to drugs, gangs, and an otherwise bleak future. Helping Calvin was one of many of the gruff old man's unsung accomplishments.

"We still don't know anything," Kip said even more weakly.

The fire hoses snaking down the alley had been shoved aside and the medics disappeared with a gurney through the haze. Minutes seemed like hours and still no one was coming out of the building. Even the unnerving two-way traffic had subsided as it became clear that everyone on St. Edmunds Street was waiting for word.

Kip was at the end of his patience when the medics appeared, one at each end of the wheeled stretcher, gently rolling it over the alley's uneven brickwork. Strapped to the gurney was the inert figure of Willie Carter.

"Look!" Erin said. "There's an oxygen mask on him."

The reason for the mask quickly sank in. They would only give oxygen to a living person.

Kip dashed across the street to intercept the procession before it reached the waiting ambulance. Whether Willie was conscious or not, Kip could not tell. Words failed him, and all he could say was "Willie" again and again, and finally, "We're with you, Buddy."

Against the dark of early evening the back of the ambulance was so brilliantly illuminated Kip barely noticed the tech waving him back. "Sir, you've got to move, so we can get your friend to help as soon as possible," she said.

Kip retreated a few steps. Then the same tech said, "Sir," but nothing else. The reason became apparent when Willie blinked his eyes and gradually lifted his hand. Slowly his thumb poked up. Willie's Churchillian salute produced a burst of applause from the EMS crew and onlookers behind the yellow tape. Then he balled his hand into a fist in a gesture of determination.

"Yes, Willie, by God we will get through this," Kip told him. "I promise."

As the ambulance pulled away, siren screaming, Calvin raced to his car to join Willie at Port City Hospital. Kip said he would meet them as soon as he could; but in the meantime he would call Alma Carter to let her know about her husband.

The smoke had cleared and all that remained was the bitter stench of the fire. Kip's eyes no longer smarted, though the glare of spotlights mounted on a fire truck was all the reminder he needed that the evening was far from over. The truck and several official city cars occupied the space in front of the building. Kip was told he would be able to check out the building as soon the fire officials declared the building safe to enter.

Kip and Erin were soon joined in waiting by stunned *Beacon* staff members. Kip took up Della on her offer to call Alma Carter.

The group mostly stood silent in the growing chill of the evening, suspending conversation of what-next. As if on cue, the tall and athletic figure of Port City's fire chief approached them.

In a town in the shadow of Washington where people come and go with administrations and the vagaries of military and department assignments, Willard Stefanski had Port City flowing through his veins. A fire department was a city agency where a firefighter could still rise through the ranks to become chief. Even after forty years of service in the city, Stefanski had no plans for retirement. Something about their line of work kept firefighters fit and young. Both competent and well regarded, Stefanski gave the town much needed continuity and character.

"Kip, can we be alone for a few minutes?" he said. With one hand clutching a radio, he gestured with the other to an unpopulated section of the street.

"Let me get straight to it, Kip – you've got problems,"

Stefanski said.

"I can't disagree with you there, Chief."

"It's way too soon to say for sure, but my guys believe you've got a case of arson on your hands. They say it has all the signs of a flammable liquid poured on your pallets of papers and rolls of newsprint. Not very sophisticated, but it could have been bad. Really bad."

"Thank God for sprinkler systems."

"Not really – your system failed," Stefanski continued. "Someone cut off the water to your building. It was plain simple to do. The only thing that saved you was Willie Carter's fool-hardy bravery. He went through three fire extinguishers before the smoke got to him. Our guys barely made it in time. Otherwise, you'd be looking at a much worse situation."

Kip felt like he'd been kicked in the stomach.

"Yes, you are going to feel a lot of shock this evening," Stefanski said. "We see it all the time. You'll be better in the morning."

Kip wasn't so sure about that, and he let Stefanski continue without replying.

"Our investigator will start as soon as he can get in the building," he said. "Probably in an hour or so. Tomorrow, he'll have questions for you and your staff and hopefully he'll get to bottom of this. It could be any number of things – an angry employee, vandals, maybe a pissed-off reader. These things have a way of solving themselves. The whole deal will take about a week. In the meantime your staff is free to work in the front half of your building. When we've wrapped up in the print bay, you can resume work there as well."

Stefanski clamped a hand on Kip's shoulder. "I'm truly sorry about this," he said. "But, trust me, you'll be up and running before you know it." And with that, the chief left to rejoin his colleagues.

Kip thought he was dealing well with the steady stream of well-wishers until the only thing worse than a rubbernecker walked up to him.

"Well, Kip, it looks like you're really got a problem on your hands this time," Dorothy Alexander said with no preambles of sympathy. "Some good your fancy sprinkler system did you. I'm sure the fire department . . ."

"Dorothy, shut up," Kip interrupted. "If you want to have a conversation, step over here and spare my staff your pieties."

Kip moved away several paces and waited for his cousin. As little as he could tolerate Melvin and Stephen, Dorothy's ability to get under his skin so effortlessly went well beyond them. There she stood, all scarves, bangles, and jewelry, scolding him in front of friends and staff. He hadn't told them yet about the failed sprinkler system, and he wasn't about to prematurely give his cousin the satisfaction of a we-told-you-so. Sarcasm was the best he could throw back at Dorothy and it felt worse than name calling.

"Dorothy, thank you for your concern," he said through clenched teeth. "If you were a little less worried about yourself, you might want to know we nearly lost an employee in the fire. They've taken Willie Carter to the hospital."

His cousin didn't at first seem fazed by the news, and she continued. "We have every right to be . . . What did you say?"

Kip didn't think it possible, but Dorothy retreated.

"I'm sorry," she said. "Maybe you should start from the beginning."

He explained what he knew so far and what to expect in the next week.

Evidently it was fine for the cousins Alexander to beat up on Kip, but not so Willie; and from that Kip took some relief. How long this thaw would continue was anyone's guess. Not very long, he found out.

Cass and Hank Merrill arrived, and before Kip could say anything, Dorothy reverted to form.

"I'm glad you are here, Cass, so I can tell you both at the same time," she said. "Melvin said something like this was going to happen sooner or later. He was right to make us take a good hard look at the *Beacon*. And this fire proves it."

"What this fire proves is absolutely nothing," Kip said. "We're still here, we're still in business, and we will remain in business. And to borrow from your charming words at the Garden Ball – really, Dorothy, you should leave. If you have something to say to us, try to keep it until our next meeting."

"I'll do that, though it will be sooner than you think," she sputtered. Turning abruptly, she left before anyone could reply.

"Wow," Cass said. "And I didn't even get a word in edgewise."

"Believe me, Cass, after what I have to say, you'll be as glad you held off."

It took less than five minutes to relate his conversation with Will Stefanski. Kip wasn't worried about how this was coming across to Erin, who stood quietly absorbing the discussion. She was deeply in this already.

As he feared, his account raised more questions than it answered. Unlike Dorothy, his sister knew the right questions to ask.

"I can't help but think there's a lot more going on than you're letting on to. Am I right?"

Kip hesitated, and he quickly regretted how the pause created the sense that he was hiding something. "It's complicated and I'm doing the best I can to make sense of it," he answered. Guilt and remorse were already setting in at the thought of how destructive that fire could have been. "Give me some time, and I'll be able to explain the whole mess."

Cass looked hard and long into his eyes. Terrified at the possibility of a rupture in his relationship with sister, he started to explain. But Cass placed her index finger across his lips and gently said, "Later. Hank and I will be off now. Call me tomorrow with an update."

As he watched them walking away, Kip became aware of a fireman waiting to talk to him.

"You're cleared to go in for a few minutes," he told Kip. "We'll accompany you and anyone you want to bring along. You can only observe from the doorway."

Kip, Erin, Ben, and Carrie followed him up the ally.

THIRTY-ONE

Tired and drained from the night before, Kip nonetheless found relief in Friday morning's rowing practice. In its walled-off world of camaraderie and competition, the travails of everyday life were checked at the boathouse door. He knew his problems were far from the everyday variety, as demonstrated by his conversation with Will Stefanski and the subsequent five-minute inspection of the *Beacon*'s print bay.

As he went through his pre-practice warmup routine, Kip mentally revisited the scene of their tour. Electrical power hadn't yet been restored in the rear portion of the building and what they could see looked depressing in the brilliant beam of the firefighter's flashlight.

Thick, black soot coated every possible surface and pools of water remained from the soaking intervention of fire hoses. They gasped when the beam of light settled on the charred stubble of what had formerly been gleaming white rolls of newsprint. On the floor in front lay the three discarded fire extinguishers Willie emptied in his effort to contain the blaze. Kip now realized how close the fire had come to igniting the rafters overhead and then who knew what else.

As hard as he found it to believe, Willie's hospital room had been upbeat, at least compared with what he'd left at the Beacon Building. Alma and Willie, their daughter, Annie, and the inseparable Calvin Perkins were cheerfully gabbing at Willie's bedside. Apparently a cleansing round of oxygen for the patient and the thought of escaping death had a lightening effect on the group.

While they were glad to see him, Kip thought Alma's greeting clipped and terse.

"Kip. It's good of you to come," was all she said before turning back to Willie.

Before Kip could wedge into the conversation, a nurse had declared the end of visiting hours. Details from Willie would have to wait until later.

As Kip and his seven boat mates made their ways down to the dock with the white Vespoli shell on their shoulders, the darkness of 5:30 could not hide the promise of a warm and fragrant spring day ahead. The ever-moody Potomac was flat as glass, with the reflection of the Washington skyline etched on the northern horizon.

Most Fridays, the men's and women's competitive 8s and 4s scrimmaged against each other. Both sets of rowers looked forward to these sprints for the same reason – serious competition that didn't count for much more than bragging rights that never lasted beyond the return to the dock.

More importantly, the informal races gave the coaches the opportunity to experiment with new seating combinations and racing strategies. Often, when a boat lacked a full crew, Hansen would recruit a rower from another other group to fill the vacant seat. Today, Toby Aaronson filled in the 3 seat for the missing Paul Schultz in the men's 8, an absence most keenly noted by Kip.

As they pushed away from the dock, river and sky were already brightening with hues of violet. By 6 a.m. the horizon would erupt in flaming shades of red and orange. It could be the Ganges, for all the rowers cared. Water that smooth had only one purpose, racing. And with the thermometer already registering in the 60s, the rowers were down to t-shirts and spandex.

The racing went well enough for Kip to lose himself in the series of 1,000-meter sprints.

As usual, the women's boats gave the men all they could

handle. Technique trumped power, once again, and Bo Hansen was having none of it. Pulling alongside them in his launch, he succinctly assessed their performance: "Let's hope that was not your best effort – our first regatta is only weeks away and you will be blown out of the water if you don't get your acts together. So show me that you're not beginners."

With Hansen, less was more when it came to coaching. Still, by the time all four boats had finished their last run, the men's boats had only slightly improved their performance. The sun was above the horizon and normally it would have been a fine way for Kip to end a work week. But the thought of dealing with fire and police investigators, insurance agents, family members, and Paul Schultz. weighed him down again.

THIRTY-TWO

The note on Kip's desk explained the presence of vases stuffed with daffodils on each staff member's desk. Della had arrived early, applied her floral touch, and departed in search of pastries and bagels. He doubted her efforts would soften the shock the staff would be feeling in their upcoming meeting.

Kip settled at his desk where he failed to shake feelings of fear and remorse over the fire. Fear that someone could have been killed and, equally bad, that it might happen again. Remorse, because the fire might have never occurred had he not so clumsily pursued his suspicions over the death of Anders Martin. He did not regret, however, his personal and professional stance against the development of yet another federal facility in Port City. But, dammit, why did it have to collide with Anders Martin's campaign against P2?

That was a question on the mind of Police Chief Jake Johnson. Johnson's presence in the doorway to Kip's office startled him out of his dreary reverie.

"Sorry, Kip, I knocked twice. You obviously have a lot on your mind."

"You could say that. To what do I owe the pleasure of a visit from Port City's finest."

"Several things. Ink-stained wretches with fire-happy enemies, for starters. I wanted to see the damage in person and then have a few words with you. Care to give me a tour?"

Johnson allowed that he had never been all the way through a newspaper before and he was suitably impressed in spite of the charred aftermath.

"I'm glad I got to see this," Johnson said. "I hear real honest-to-God newspapers are a dying breed."

"They are, indeed. I just don't want mine to go any sooner than it has to," Kip said, gesturing to the print bay. "We came close last night."

"Yep, and that's why we need to talk," Johnson said. "What's going on, Kip? Arson doesn't happen on its own. Will Stefanski tells me someone kicked in your backdoor and nearly set fire to the entire block. I suppose you know I've got a serious interest in this now."

"There's nothing I can tell you."

"Pardon my French, but: bullshit."

"How so? You tell me."

"How so about this, then?" And Johnson recapped the past month as he viewed it from the outside: the escalating crusade against the Defense Department installation, the violent rivalry between Kip and Schultz, his romance with Anders Martin's assistant, the subsequent archaeology series in the *Beacon*, and then the announcement of a significant archaeological finding which anybody with a third-grade education could read between the lines as an arrow intended for P2.

"Oh, and then for good measure, someone tries to burn down your building," Johnson continued. "I'd say that's a pretty good summation of a mess that seems to be getting messier by the day. Would you agree with me on that?"

"It's interesting, yes," Kip said, "but so what?"

Kip could see Johnson's good cop/bad cop approach faltering. Johnson altered course.

"Are you in trouble, Kip?" he asked. "Is there anything you can say? It's obvious you are in some kind of bind."

"No, I'm fine. I'm working out a few situations. That's all. I appreciate your concern and, as always, if I needed help, you'd be the first person I would ask. Give me some time."

"I don't see that I have much of a choice," Johnson said. "But, let me tell you this – Will Stefanski will have a preliminary report to me to me by late this afternoon, and we all know what that conclusion will be.

"If it's arson," Johnson continued, "we will have to act. A police investigation will pile another layer of trouble on you. You know as well as I do that we have very little to go on. It would help me and the course of justice, if you could shed a little light on the situation."

Kip declined, and they rose, the elder scowling and the younger pale with worry.

"Listen, keep the lines of communications open," Johnson said. "And thank Della for the coffee. Your operation does have good points in its favor. I'll let myself out."

Kip could almost hear the door slamming shut on his last chance to come clean with Johnson. But nothing had changed. Investigating Anders Martin's death was still based on a suspicion barely supported by thin circumstantial evidence. Even if Strawberry Flats had yielded a historic find, it didn't connect dots to anybody.

Kip also considered the notion that his own professional ambition might be blinding him from seeing the situation for what it was. That may have been his biggest mistake: chasing this story for so long, all the while having it escalate into a personal rivalry with Schultz, whom he would soon have to confront.

An unscheduled all-staff meeting always made a day at the *Beacon* interesting. Usually they dealt with personnel comings and goings or explanations of changes in employee benefits. Today's meeting needed no announcement. After Johnson had left, Kip found everybody gathered in the meeting room tearing into donuts and bagels. This morning called for his best game face.

With the exception of Willie, all were present and accounted for, and Kip began his review of events with the staff. He started with Willie's status.

"We all owe Willie a huge thanks for all he did for the *Beacon* last night," Kip said. "Me, most of all."

Their murmurings of assent might have lasted longer had they not been interrupted.

"Then you could start right now be getting me a glass of water." The voice was hoarse and phlegmy, but there was no mistaking it. Willie stood in the doorway, grinning at the surprised faces of his colleagues.

Before he could say anything else, the entire staff had surrounded him.

"Enough. Enough!" he said. "If I can't get some water, how about a seat at the table so we can get this meeting started?"

A seat and water were quickly procured. Kip noted Willie's attire – corduroy trousers and a plaid shirt, not his standard blue pressman's uniform.

"Please tell me you didn't come straight from the hospital," Kip said.

"Sort of," Willie replied. "Alma dropped me off here with orders for you to kick me out at noon."

"We'll be all too glad to do that, William," Della said. "You old cuss, you shouldn't even be here."

"Yeah, well so what?" he said. "Let's talk about how we're going to print next week's edition. Boss, you still on good terms with Metro?"

Metropolitan Press was a major operation nearby where it printed the regional edition of a national newspaper. Rather than have its big-ticket presses idle the rest of the time, the plant took on outside jobs from nearby publishers. Metro's presses seemed to produce brighter colors on white paper than any printer Kip knew. He'd had used them when the *Beacon*'s press underwent periodic inspections and refurbishment, and it pleased him that Willie had suggested Metro.

"We are, indeed," Kip said. "The *Beacon* is paid up and ready to go. Good idea."

Ben Bailey then raised the topic that still shook him.

"Kip, talk to us about arson," he said.

"Right. Arson," Kip said. "I can see word travels fast when you work for a newspaper, especially when it's the subject of the story.

"I can tell you what I know. Will Stefanski's crew ruled out accidental causes right off. Whoever did it, came in through the back door without knocking. We will be replacing that door as soon as possible with something more secure. They poured a flammable liquid on the newsprint rolls and a pallet of newspapers. The only reason we're able to meet in this room today is thanks to Mr. Carter here. By the way, Willie, what brought you back to the building last night?"

"I forgot to bring the press rags home for washing, so I came back for them," Willie said. "Call me picky, but I like to start off the week with a clean set."

"We're mighty glad you do," Carrie said, handing him another glass of water.

As Willie drank, Kip continued with his accounting.

"You may have heard that whoever did this was smart enough to turn off the water supply for the sprinkler system. Yes, we will be moving the on/off valve to inside the building.

"As to who would do this, let me right here and now rule out one of Chief Stefanski's scenarios – an angry employee. All of you will be interviewed by law enforcement today and I want you to know I stand by each of you."

With that statement, spontaneous clapping broke out. It might have gone on longer, but Willie cut them short. "Enough. You'll have the big guy blubbering, and let me tell you, that's not a sight you want to see."

"I'll raise a donut to that," Carrie Brant said. "For a second, I thought you were going to say Kip was giving us the rest of the day off."

Back in his office, Kip wasn't surprised by the blinking light on his phone that indicated a backlog of voice-mail messages. Erin. His insurance agent. Travis Nelson, the fire investigator. Colbert Jenkins letting him know the board wanted a meeting at the earliest possible time. And Paul Schultz. Holy crap, What does he want?

Kip hit the pause button to get his breath before proceeding with the message.

"Listen, Kip, we need to talk . . .

[*That we do, asshole. And what's with calling me by my first name?*]

". . . We've had our disagreements—hell, we still do . . ."

[*No shit, creep.*]

". . . but my dislike for you does not extend to burning down your effing newspaper. Let me say it plainer: I had nothing to do with your fire. You can believe it or not. That's your call . . ."

[*You're right. I'm having trouble believing you.*]

". . . I want to meet with you as soon as possible. Make it on neutral ground. Lee Street at 6:30. Unless I hear from you, I'll assume we're on. We do need to talk."

The message ended there and Kip's emotional roller coaster picked up speed.

As much as he wanted to meet Erin for lunch, he couldn't leave the *Beacon* while Travis Nelson was interviewing the staff for his investigation. She understood, and they agreed to meet at Kip's house after the "meeting" with Paul Schultz.

It had the feel of anything but a meeting.

THIRTY-THREE

Kip knew better than to expect to walk in cold and get a booth at the Lee Street Pub on a Friday evening at the height of tourist season, even as early as 6:30. Tonight's crowd came wholesale, courtesy of two busses that deposited sixty energetic tourists. Hungry and thirsty from a day of scouring museums and monuments and shopping at Pentagon City Mall, they swarmed the main dining area. His call to the pub two hours earlier again secured him and Erin a booth in a far corner.

He arrived straight from the *Beacon* with a backpack of workout clothes and, as an afterthought, his laptop. Schultz was late, and Kip used the time to catch up online with the day's headlines and a quick call with Erin.

"From what you've told me, I can't picture the two of you sitting at the same table," she said. "What brought about the civility?"

"He probably knew that he would be considered an arson suspect," Kip said. "Preempting me with a peace talk might take the heat off of him. He intimated interesting things to tell me."

"And I'm sure they weren't sweet nothings," Erin said.

"The thing is, Schultz is the only one I can think of who would want to get at the *Beacon*," Kip said.

Silence filled the air as Kip waited for Erin's response.

"You there, Erin?"

"Yes, I was thinking."

"And?"

"Would it be possible that someone in your family wants the *Beacon* gone sooner than later? And maybe the fire had nothing to do with Paul Schultz or Anders Martin."

Another pause ensued as Kip thought through the implications of that scenario.

"Are you there, Kip?"

"Aye. That's an interesting supposition. But, I really don't believe any of those loons would choose that route."

"So, you don't think an insurance payout for the loss of the building and business wouldn't be enough incentive?"

"I know crazy and criminal aren't mutually exclusive traits, but I can only go on gut instinct on that one. And I don't buy it."

"I hope you don't mind my suggesting that," she told him. "It was only a notion."

"Not at all," Kip said. "Believe me, I've had worse thoughts about them in the past. But their danger is purely verbal, and that's bad enough."

"Do you think you should let the police know about your meeting?"

"Not yet," Kip said. "I'll know more soon enough, and then we can consider a conversation with Jake Johnson. I'll fill you in when I see you later tonight."

They rang off, and Kip continued waiting. Schultz was half an hour late and Kip was growing frustrated. Two calls to Schultz's cell phone went to voice mail. A career of meetings with interview subjects had hardened Kip to tardy arrivals. No-shows were rarer, and tonight he had no qualms about ordering a second beer.

As he finally began to relax, Erin's observation came back to him. Call it insular family loyalty, but he didn't want Erin to know that he didn't fully dismiss Melvin as only harmless and loony. It was Dorothy's snarky comment about Melvin's warning that something like the fire was bound to happen with Kip in charge and that it was a good thing he made them take a good hard look at the *Beacon*.

Erin had heard her say it and she, too, took similar meaning from it. Melvin must be working Dorothy and Stephen hard to convince them they might be better off without the paper.

A rational person would opt to sell an enterprise instead of burning it to the ground. But how rational was Melvin? Kip wondered. Very, very rational, he concluded from having been around his cousin for an entire lifetime. At the same time, he was a weasel and selfish to the bone. If he calculated the *Beacon* to be more lucrative as an insurance settlement, then who knows what he might do. Having two malefactors to reckon seemed too much for Kip. Right now, he would focus on Paul Schultz and circle back to his cousin later.

By the end of a third beer Kip finally wrote off Schultz as no-show. An hour of waiting in the noisy and congested pub was enough. He knew who would pick up the tab, and he signaled Glynda Barnes for the check.

The four-block walk to his house helped clear the beer buzz. It was going on 8 o' clock but enough daylight remained to fire up his grill to fix an easy dinner in time for Erin's arrival.

Even though they had slipped into a comfortable relationship, Kip still thrilled to the prospect of being together with her. Hanging out didn't quite qualify as a date or night on the town. But the easy way they settled into in an evening of dinner and a movie or board game felt like good dry runs for the real thing.

Several hours later, as Erin was putting on her coat to leave, angry and relentless chirping issued from the kitchen. Kip did his best to ignore it.

"Is that your phone or are you raising crickets?" Erin asked.

Even at 11:30 on a Friday evening, Kip knew not to be surprised by phone calls. They go with the job. Annoyance long ago gave way to simple inconvenience.

"Yep, that would be my phone."

The ID on his cell phone read PCPD. Never a good sign.

"Yes, this is Kip Alexander. You're kidding, aren't you? Would I what? At this hour?. Maybe you could tell me a bit more."

The voice on the other end of the phone told him more. Kip listened and hung up.

Turning to face Erin, he said, "Bad news. We now know why Paul Schultz never showed up tonight. He's dead. Suicide. That was the police department – they want me to come to their headquarters. Now."

"What? Now? Why?"

"The guy told me that anytime they have a death that isn't the result of natural causes they fast track their work. Schultz's cell phone calendar had our appointment listed plus my calls to him, and they think I can help.

"A squad car is coming by in five minutes to pick me up. Apparently, they didn't want to wait for me to trek over to the *Beacon* to get the van and then drive to the station. Gotta like the curb service."

"Did they give you any details on how he died?"

"He hanged himself sometime this evening, obviously after we spoke but before our supposed meeting at the Lee Street. It happened at one of his construction sites. That's all he would tell me."

Kip was in jeans and a sweatshirt and had no desire to make a fashion statement at the Port City Safety and Security Center by changing into fancier clothes. They slipped past the sleeping bodies of Samantha and Ike and walked out into the night. Erin went to her truck, Kip to the curb.

Officer Eric Sullivan arrived moments later in a white, city-decaled Crown Victoria. He gestured to the front seat, and Kip was glad not to be riding in prisoner style.

"Sorry about the hour, but maybe this will help," Sullivan said, handing Kip a paper 7-Eleven cup of coffee. "Cream and sugar are in the bag."

"Black's good. Thanks. You know how to make a guy feel wanted."

"Actually," Sullivan said, "they want you as awake as they can get you. You won't be kept long. But they do want to nail down as much information as possible for a preliminary statement to the press in a few hours. Too bad your paper only comes out once a week. You'd have a good scoop."

Something about the twenty-four-hour nature of hospitals and police stations always made Kip envious. Even though both existed to deal with life's eternal problems of health and safety, they served as stable sanctuaries of orderliness and routine, at least on the surface. Everybody knew everybody, and they casually came and went in well-lighted corridors and office areas. And no matter how often they visited police stations and hospitals, outsiders would always be that – outsiders.

Kip had visited the gleaming new police facility numerous times but had never arrived in such efficient fashion. Sullivan deposited him in a sparsely appointed conference room where two men and a woman awaited him. The unmistakable aroma of stale institutional coffee drifted from a coffee machine in a corner of the room. Obligatory framed photographs of Port City adorned the walls. Most Wanted posters would have been a more effective touch, Kip thought.

Detective Bernard Washington introduced himself along with Ronald Summers, the patrolman who had found Schultz, and Theresa Perez, from the department's communications and media section. None betrayed the stereotype of frumpy, frazzled police types depicted in hundreds of cop shows. Washington and Summers were middle-aged African Americans, pushing 50, while Perez, a Hispanic couldn't have been yet 30. All three looked so fit that Kip figured a gym must be operating around the clock somewhere in the building. Summers and Perez did their crisp blue uniforms justice. Washington looked sharp in pressed wool slacks and open-collared white shirt.

"I'll tell you what we know so far, and then we hope you can add to it," Washington said. "Sound okay?"

At this hour, getting in and out of that building quickly was all Kip wanted. "Sure, okay."

"Our patrol cars observed Paul Schultz's company pickup truck outside his Glebe Street townhouse project around 9:30. Vehicles are never there at night and Officer Summers and his partner noticed the gate to the premises was open. They found Mr. Schultz hanging from a rafter. The forensics unit will be finished in another hour or so and we may know more then.

"There's not much to go on," Washington continued. His voice, deep and controlled, was so matter-of-fact that he could have been reciting a recipe. "His briefcase and cell phone were there. As we mentioned earlier, his phone calendar noted your 6 o'clock meeting and three calls to him between 6:30 and 7:30. We assume your meeting never came off."

"That's right. He never showed," Kip said.

"Do you mind telling us why you were supposed to meet?"

"I don't know how much you know about Schultz and me and the *Beacon*, but we've always been on the opposite side of whatever fence that came along."

"We're aware of that," Washington said. "Your tiff at Hampton Funeral Home was famous here for twenty-four hours."

"Yeah, well, that pretty much summed it up," Kip said. "Then, when the *Beacon* caught fire yesterday, things must have changed for Schultz. He called me around noon today to set up the meeting at the Lee Street Pub. Neutral ground, he said."

"Did he say why?"

"It sounded like he wanted to patch things up. He said our differences did not extend to his setting buildings on fire. I got the impression that he knew we wouldn't walk away good friends, but that at least he could set the record straight. So, I agreed to meet with him. And he never showed. End of story."

"Did he mention anything else that he wanted to talk about?" Washington asked.

For the second time in forty-eight hours Kip felt caught in an ethical vice. He figured Johnson knew he was holding back information. But Kip wasn't about to go out of his way to let Washington know that.

"Nope. As I said, it sounded like he wanted to clear the air. The conversation didn't last more than thirty seconds. If he had more to talk about, he must have been saving it for the meeting."

"Do you know anything about Mr. Schultz that would shed any light on his death?" Washington continued.

Do you know anything about? was beginning to sound like interrogation protocol phrasing. Even in his lamest newspaper interviews Kip mixed up his questioning better than that. Then, again, maybe that's how Washington managed to lull his suspects before hitting them with the knock-out questions.

"Not really," Kip said. "I don't know much about his personal life. I only knew him socially from rowing, and even then we were far from communicative. He was divorced. Professionally, he owned and managed a fairly large development and construction company. He had projects all over Northern Virginia.

"Do you know why Mr. Schultz would feel driven to suicide?" Washington asked.

"What do you mean, driven to suicide?"

"We found a note at the scene," Washington said. "I can't tell you anything beyond that."

"I can tell you that does not sound like the Paul Schultz I know," Kip said. "Schultz was too tough and too proud to give up, especially if someone was pushing him – as you say. I'd bet on the opposite, that Schultz would dig in harder."

"We don't know that," Washington said. "In our line of work we consider every possible scenario. You cannot tell from outward appearances how someone will deal with personal problems. It could be something to do with his banker, a business partner, or he could even be talking about you, if you think about it."

When Kip didn't respond, Washington continued. "We'll work that part out. But Theresa here needs to work up a statement, and we don't want to overlook any loose threads. You know a lot – from your paper, your rowing club, and apparently, how should I phrase it, perhaps, your differences."

This was getting a bit too close for Kip. Play it right up the middle, he thought.

"You could say that," he said.

"And that's why we wanted to talk to you as soon as possible. You may hear back from us," Washington said. "But for now, we're all set. We do appreciate your coming in at this hour. Officer Sullivan will take you back."

THIRTY-FOUR

When he awoke Saturday, it was noon and rain was pounding his metal roof and splattering against the windows.

Over a belated breakfast he read the morning paper. Page three of the Metro section of the *Post* carried a brief article on the death of prominent developer and construction executive Paul Schultz. Even though it was a few paragraphs, the article did a good job squeezing in such late-breaking news. It mirrored what Detective Washington had told Kip. But the enterprising reporter had found a small treasure trove on Schultz – personal detail and education, professional career, and his membership in the Port City Rowing Club. She touched on Schultz's major projects, annual revenue, and current work on behalf of the Defense Department.

But the reporter missed the big one – Schultz's ailing finances. Katherine Tisdale would probably fill in the missing parts in the follow-up article that was sure to appear on Monday. He doubted that Tisdale would contribute information on Schultz's violent tendencies.

A good head-clearing row on the Potomac was tempting but out of the question, thanks to the heavy spring deluge. Instead, he opted for plunging back into work at the *Beacon*.

Several staff members were already at their desks when Kip arrived. He could only attribute their rare appearance on a Saturday morning to the near loss of their place of employment. He knew them too well to believe they'd needlessly sacrifice their free time for more work. Carrie Brant insisted she had to tend to the Garden Week supplement. The always-on Ben Bailey kidded him for providing a job in a town where there was more reporting and writing than could be done in a regular work week. "I never thought I'd have a job in a place that stinks and like it," Bailey said. "How long before they get that smell out of here?"

"Willie and I are meeting with the recovery crew in a few minutes. Hopefully they will get started this afternoon. Mostly vacuuming and wiping down every possible surface with the exception of the presses. They won't touch them, which is fine with Willie. He and Calvin will know what to do.

"I suppose you saw the article on Paul Schultz in the *Post* this morning," Kip continued.

"What little there was of it," Bailey said. "Still, I've got to hand it to someone there – the reporter must have scribbled it onto the moving presses."

Bailey pushed his chair back. His playfulness was gone.

"What more could be happening in the crazy town for us to write about?" he asked. "First that archaeologist dies, then the fire, and now the guy you had the rivalry with. Come to think of it, aren't you worried people will be jumping to conclusions when they realize you're connected with all of this?"

Kip allowed that the thought had crossed his mind. He then recounted his early morning chauffeured visit to Port City's police station and his interview with the detective and his colleagues.

"I wish I could answer that for you," Kip said. "In the meantime, I'd greatly appreciate your writing the article on Schultz. I can help you with sources and background. Write it as you would any other story, knowing the *Post* will also have run a follow-up early next week. I can help you with other stories."

The crew from West End Disaster Recovery Services was already in mid-tour with Willie and Calvin when Kip entered the bay. He thanked them for coming so quickly and told Willie he'd bow out of the process unless needed. A locksmith and plumber were due any minute, the first to install an intruder-proof door in the rear and the other to relocate the water cut-off valve to inside the building. Water could still be shut off from the street, but that would involve removing a manhole cover and being observed by a good portion of the city.

Who would have thought? Kip reflected.

THIRTY-FIVE

If Kip thought the death of Paul Schultz put the entire affair of Anders Martin behind them, he was badly mistaken. From the moment he got to the boathouse Monday morning, problems queued up like planes on a runway.

The loss of a second rower was acutely felt throughout the boathouse. In a departure from jolly exchanges, conversations were muted and confined to small clusters of people. No way could they know more about Schultz's death than Kip; but they weren't far behind in their speculation.

"Things obviously weren't going his way," Norman Grodsky said. "The recession in commercial real estate hasn't let up, so he had to be hurting."

Kip silently congratulated Grodsky for his supposition, hoping it would be the last of the morning. It wasn't.

"He wasn't getting too far in rounding up land for the Defense Department," Rick Porter said. Kip wondered how he knew that, until he realized Porter's position on city planning advisory committee gave him access to that gem. He wasn't ready for Porter's follow-up, though. "You could probably talk to that one, Kip."

There was an insinuation in that comment that irked Kip. Most likely, Porter was hinting that his part of the rivalry was the straw that broke the camel's back.

"No more than anyone here," Kip replied tartly. "The *Beacon* has always maintained the same position on P2. So what? If Paul chose to be a jerk about it, that was his problem. You couldn't possibly believe he was entitled to a free ride for working on behalf of the most controversial development in the history of the city. Or do you mean something different?"

Kip's response was met with stony silence. In their normal bonhomie, someone was always cutting into the conversation to squeeze in a point or a wise crack. This pause was painful.

Owen Draper broke the silence. "No, nobody's talking about anything else. But you've got to admit, you've got an empty seat in the *Madison* under the worst possible circumstances. Everybody feels it. That's all."

"Well, I sure feel it, too. But if anyone thinks the *Beacon* had anything to do with his unfortunate decision, send a letter to the editor – we're fair, we'll publish it," Kip said, thinking that they might want to, should Schultz's note ever see the light of public day. "In the meantime, it would be swell if we could keep this place a politics-free zone."

Whether or not the group agreed was moot. Bo Hansen waved them over to issue a brief set of instructions for the day's practice. Thanks to the patchy fog and intermittent rain showers, rowing on the water was out of the question. But that didn't preclude working out in the nearby park. Groans and light-hearted sarcasm greeted Hansen's news that they would form four relay teams. Each person would flip a heavy five-foot-wide truck tire end-over-end for thirty yards, then jog around the perimeter of the park, and conclude the circuit with five pushups and five sit-ups. After five sets, the teams next squared off for two-man wheelbarrow relay races in the volleyball pit where one person held the ankles of his partner who used his hands as feet to scurry across the thick, wet sand. All in the cold drizzle. They would be stiff and sore for days to come. If only the boot camp torture would trim their times in next week's May Day Regatta, Kip wished.

At the *Beacon* ninety minutes later, Kip got an acid preview of the week to come. Porter had known something after all – about public perception, at least.

Email and phone messages that began with a trickle on Sunday were in flood proportion by Monday. Many readers who had previously straddled the intellectual divide of development issues in Port City turned on the *Beacon*. Enough was enough, went the general consensus. Upstanding community leaders should not be hounded to their death for their heart-felt beliefs. Those who had doubts about the wisdom of a massive federal presence in Port City ditched them.

"Maybe Port City could do with more jobs and less snobbery," wrote one reader.

"Are you happy now?" wrote another.

How did so many normal people become so fickle? Kip wondered. Snobbery? Am I happy? All newspapers, at least the real ones, take heat for their articles. But the swiftness and sharpness of this response surprised Kip. On the one hand, the *Beacon*'s stance on the city's future and his archaeology series got the desired attention. But to backfire like this?

Colbert Jenkins, the *Beacon*'s long-time attorney delivered the crowning blow in the phone call Kip dreaded but knew would be coming sooner or later.

"The board wants to hold an emergency meeting this afternoon." Kip could picture the courtly old attorney in a natty blue-and-white seersucker suit pacing the floor of his Old Town office, puffing on a pipe that was sometimes actually lit. "I wish it didn't have to be, but you can guess the topic of discussion."

"I can, and I don't like it one bit," Kip said. "I guess it's asking too much of them to support their own newspaper in times like this."

"That's never been their style, has it?" Colbert answered. "They see a financial threat in all this. I'm pretty sure there will be a vote of confidence, and I don't have high hopes for you this time."

His next phone call amounted to vote of confidence.

"Hey, Kip, it's Jeff. I wanted to see how you're doing. I hear you're in a bit of a shit storm over Paul Schultz."

"That's putting it mildly," Kip said. "My board wants a vote of confidence – immediately. Advertisers are cancelling. Hell, even some of the rowers this morning were on my case. Tell me you aren't jumping on that bus."

"No way," Benson said. "Sensationalizing and hounding

community members isn't the *Beacon*'s style. You're better at boring them to death with earnest editorials."

"Under the circumstances, I would have to say that's the nicest thing anybody has ever said about me," Kip said. "Thanks. I mean it."

"No sweat," Benson said. "It looks like we won't have to deal with a funeral for Paul. His family has asked to have him sent back to Chicago. As soon as he clears Doc Patel's office, he will be out of Port City for good."

That didn't make Kip feel any better, though it did remind him to check with the medical examiner. This case was sudden, unnatural, and unexpected.

"Yeah, that's one funeral I'd pass on," Kip said.

"By the way, we're due for a poker game," Benson said. "Got any suggestions for our guest?"

Poker could take his mind off his dismal situation but Kip was in no mood for planning something even as light-weight as a card game.

"Check with the other guys," Kip said. "I'll go along with whomever you find."

Board meetings like this one couldn't be prepared for. Charts, graphs, descriptions of revenue flow-through were meaningless in an ideological showdown that would be won or lost on bravado and charm, neither of which Kip had much of at the moment.

By the time his cousins began filing into the *Beacon*, Della had transformed the lunchroom into a good imitation of a conference room. Outside, rain lashed the windows above St. Edmunds Street.

Jenkins arrived first, wearing a dark tan suit. The monsoon evidently didn't foster a Deep South seersucker look. When everyone had settled into their seats, he called the meeting to order and read them the obligatory warnings about price fixing, collusion, and restraint of trade. Then he turned it over to Stephen Alexander.

The elder Alexander performed true to form, playing the

action point person. Kip had seen him in action plenty of times in past board meetings and he liked it less each time.

"I'll be short and sweet about it, Kip," Stephen said. "We believe you did not hear us in our last meeting. Your adversarial approach to publishing a newspaper is not benefiting the paper's bottom line and, furthermore, it's hurting our businesses. Your crusade against Paul Schultz was unacceptable . . ."

"Hold it, right there," Kip interrupted. "The *Beacon* may have taken a position on an issue. That's what papers do. But nowhere, nowhere did we go after Paul Schultz, not even in the obituary coming out on Thursday."

"Be that as it may," Stephen said, "it's one and the same now that Paul Schultz is gone and we hard-working business leaders are picking up your pieces. We believe you've had adequate opportunities to prove yourself and regardless of any reasons you may choose to cite, you've come up short. At this point there's nothing to be done but dispose of the *Beacon*," Stephen said.

Cass jumped to her feet. "Dispose of it? What an odd choice of words," she said. "You talk of the *Beacon* as though it's a cow to be taken to market. The *Beacon* has been in the family for centuries. It's always had challenges and come out well. And because you feel inconvenienced by what every good newspaper goes through, you want to unload it. That would be a tragedy."

Thank you – I couldn't have said it better, and it was better coming from you, Kip thought.

"So you say, Cass. But you are not the one with a business that depends on the health of Port City's economy," Melvin piped in. Here comes the condescension, Kip thought – right on schedule. "Irregardless, I suppose a teacher couldn't appreciate such an obvious nuance."

"Melvin, you're a broken record. An ungrammatical one, too," she said. "We've had this conversation too many times to count: You insult me for not being in business and therefore unable to comprehend your point-of-view and I have to remind you of the burden your ill-conceived, so-called sense of progress places on fire, police, schools, social services, libraries, parks. Should I go on?"

"Now don't work yourself up over something you don't understand, Cass," Dorothy said. "Those things always work themselves out eventually."

"Yeah, eventually, like by the time our kids are grandparents and have to fight the same battles over the same crap, thanks to your misguided sense of progress."

Kip wasn't surprised when Jenkins cleared his throat. He'd heard enough.

"Perhaps it would be best if we got on with the agenda," Jenkins said.

"This *is* the agenda," Dorothy said. "We were discussing why the Port City *Beacon* needs a major attitude adjustment."

Overlooking Dorothy's interpretation of an agenda, Jenkins suggested pursuing more concrete action. "If that's what you think, then does anyone have motion to make?"

"I do," Melvin responded. "I move to have Colbert Jenkins pursue the sale of the Port City *Beacon* at the earliest possible date to the highest bidder. He can work with Miles Tennyson on it."

The wording was so precise and even rational that advance thought, shockingly, must have gone into the motion. Kip figured they had been waiting for the first excuse to spring their plan. So they can't suffice with the modest peanuts coming to them for no expenditure of effort other than attending an occasional board meeting. No, they have to have a windfall, Kip concluded bitterly.

"Seconded!" Stephen said.

Disgust washed over Kip. With raised eyebrows, he signaled to Cass. She nodded back.

They stood, turned, and proceeded to walk out the door.

"I don't believe we've finished," Melvin said. "The motion calls for discussion before a vote can be taken."

"What do you think you've been doing for the past two years?" Cass said. "Go ahead and have your damned discussion and have your vote. We're through with you. Colbert, I'm sure you know how we would have voted. Fill us in later on the predetermined results of that vote."

With that departing comment, the twins retreated to Kip's

office. The sanctuary they anticipated was instead filled by the immense presence of Jake Johnson situated on the sofa.

"You two look like you went the full sixteen rounds with the Family Alexander," Johnson said, rising to his feet.

"Fifteen, actually," Kip said. "Round 16 is underway. They're voting to 'dispose' of the *Beacon*, as Melvin so elegantly phrased it."

"I'm very sorry to hear that," Johnson said. "They invented the phrase 'damn fools' for people like them, if you don't mind my saying. But I'm not surprised. They've been after you from the moment they pulled you away from the *Post*. Go figure."

"Thanks," Kip said. "But somehow I don't think you're here to console us on our choice of family."

"You're right. Mind if I sit down again?"

"Please," Cass said. "You and that couch look like you were made for each other. Can we get you anything?"

Johnson pointed to the cup of coffee provided by Della, and Kip winced.

"You're right, Kip," Johnson began. "I'm still disturbed by all that's gone on this past month. It's got my attention, officially and unofficially. Officially, I'm here unofficially. Cass, you might as well hear what I have to say."

"Go right ahead," she said. "We have no secrets from each other."

"Kip, my offer to you last week is still on the table: If you want to talk about anything, do so. The week is just starting, and already the gossip is getting ugly. Folks didn't particularly care for Paul Schultz, but on the other hand, many think he got a raw deal from the *Beacon*. Call it convenient hindsight, if you want."

"Do you?" Kip asked.

"No, I don't, and that's what bothers me," Johnson said. "Your coverage of P2 has been what anyone would expect of a hometown paper, regardless of the pros or cons."

Kip nodded his appreciation and Johnson continued.

"Detective Washington chalked up Schultz's suicide to mental issues which, when you consider the taking of one's life, sometimes makes sense. But, you and I know that suicide doesn't match up with the Paul Schultz we knew. And what makes even less sense to me today is a fire and the death of two people with very different opinions about the need for a defense installation that may or may not ever get built in Port City. Am I right so far?"

"You're right that not much makes sense," Kip said. "Where are you going with this?"

"Here's what I don't like: your building catching fire last Thursday and two days later your toughest detractor is dead and he leaves a note that, if I were you, I would not want circulating around town."

Kip recalled Bernard Washington's mention of a suicide note. Thinking back more carefully, he remembered Washington's question, "Do you know why Mr. Schultz would feel driven to suicide?" With a shock, Kip understood Johnson's drift.

"Are you going to tell me that note said I caused his death?"

Johnson said nothing, and Kip jumped to his feet.

"This is bullshit and you know it!"

"Do I?"

"Yeah, you do. And if you think for one stinking moment that you can coerce me with that note into telling you what I can't tell you, then you've got more thoughts coming. No way did I have anything to do with his death. Besides, you haven't told me what's in it."

"Kip," Johnson said, "that's exactly what the note says."

Kip tried to cut in, but Johnson waved him off.

"We all know that Paul Schultz could say whatever he wanted in that note, but technically and legally it should mean nothing for you," he continued. "Yet – no matter how I look at that note, it tells me you are still holding back on me. And I don't like it. In my most unofficial capacity, I'm here to advise you the gossip and consequences will only get worse unless there's a way to stop it."

"What are you saying, Chief?" Cass asked.

"I'm sorry you have to hear this, Cass, but it's probably for the better," Johnson said. "Some people are already beginning to think Kip drove Schultz to his death. There's no way they could know about Schultz's note. But that's not stopping anybody from arriving at nutty conclusions. If this gets politicized, the Mayor will be stepping in. At that point, control of the matter will be out of my hands."

"And what can I be doing about that?" Kip asked.

"Like I said the other day – if you know something that I should know, now would be a mighty fine time to tell me."

Kip hesitated, perhaps a moment too long for Johnson's experienced ear. "I can't."

"You mean you won't?" Half question, half statement from Johnson.

"I mean I can't, because there's nothing I can tell you," Kip said, hoping rationale would pass for logic, if not the full truth.

"And I can't say I understand that," Johnson said. "But nothing has changed since we last spoke, only escalated, to say the least. And don't forget, people around here have long memories."

"So?" Kip said.

Johnson scowled. "So, this – if it turns out there's more to what I'm hearing today and you knew about it all along, you could be in a heap of trouble, your journalist shield notwithstanding," Johnson continued. "In the meantime, I suggest getting your legal house in order. That's really all I have to say." Johnson paused and tilted his head. "It sounds like the family menagerie is breaking up. I'll be on my way while I can."

And for a big man, he rose gracefully and made it down the hall un-accosted and out the door.

"Okay, Kip, what was all that about?" Cass asked once Johnson had left.

"I'll tell you in a minute. Colbert will be in here any second to report on the big vote."

As if on cue, Jenkins knocked on the door frame. His pinched look told the story.

"No surprises, Cass, Kip. The vote was unanimous: Sell," he said. "The only surprise was how little time they spent on the discussion period."

"So, what now?" Kip asked.

"I insisted we retain a real publisher's broker and not a crony consultant. We'll see what the appetite is out there for a community newspaper," Jenkins said. "Melvin is confident some city figure will come forward if one of the local chains doesn't bite. One would think you'd have a shot at a nice price tag if the board wasn't so insistent on a quick sale."

Jenkins regarded his pipe, and deeming it empty enough, stuffed it in his coat pocket. "At this point, they are willing for you to stay on," he said. "They aren't completely crazy. So you've got a job for the time being. I'll be back in touch later in the week."

With Jenkins gone, Kip and Cass stared at the wall for what seemed like eternity. Cass broke the impasse.

"So, now, tell me what's going on between you and Chief Johnson."

"It's a long story."

"I've got plenty of time. My teaching assistant is covering for me for the rest of the day."

Kip told her everything. Beginning with his first visit with Erin Powers, the dig at Strawberry Flats, their subsequent finds, and dead ends. It actually felt satisfying to get it all out there.

"I don't know whether to be shocked or amused by this," Cass said. "It doesn't surprise me that you could get sucked so deeply into such a flimsy affair. For your whole life you couldn't leave well enough alone. I guess that goes with newspaper work. But, you've got to admit, Kip, this is simply wild."

Another pause ensued, though not as painful as its predecessor. Kip could see his sister thinking through what he had told her.

"Look at it this way," she said. "Anders died accidentally. A vandal set the fire. And a very disturbed Paul Schultz couldn't handle the prospect of bankruptcy. End of story. Even Chief Johnson would have to conclude that when things settle down. Though I would not tell him everything that you told me."

"And what do you make of Schultz's suicide note?" Kip

asked.

"I think you saw through that right off," Cass said. "Jake was using it for leverage. Think about it, he didn't say what else was in the note – Paul Schultz probably blamed everybody in town for his problems."

Kip should have felt relieved at Cass's assessment. But he had been dealing with the matter long enough to suspect that his problems were far from over. "I really, really hope you are right," was the best he could tell her.

"In the meantime, the best thing to come out of this for you is Erin Powers," she continued. "And you had better not let her slip away."

"I would agree with you there," Kip said. "As far as I can see, I have no choice but to say good bye to the whole sorry mess – along with the *Beacon*. I don't know how Erin will feel about such a fundamental failure."

"It's not a failure and if she thinks otherwise, then you've learned something about her sooner rather than later."

"Thanks, Sis. I'm at a loss for platitudes, so let's wrap it up. I'm sure we'll have more to talk about when Colbert gets back to us at the end of the week."

THIRTY-SIX

His office now quiet, too quiet, Kip decided to throw in the towel on a long and draining day.

Spring had officially sprung and with the sun still up, he chose a long and therapeutic route home. As he walked down King Street staring absently into shop windows, he inhaled the crisp evening air while voices started banging around in his head like the beginning of a nasty earworm: *You could probably talk to that one, Kip. Are you happy now? There's nothing left to do but dispose of the* Beacon, and the most unsettling comment of all, *You had better get your legal house in order.*

Deep into his gallery of haunted voices, Kip didn't hear a real voice calling from a car creeping alongside him. When the driver sounded a diesel-loud horn, Kip jerked back into the present tense.

"Sorry, Kip, I've been trying to get your attention for a least a block, but you evidently are lost in another world."

Kip instantly recognized the car and its driver. How could he not? The massive, burgundy-colored Checker Cab screamed 1970s, disco, and endless gas lines. The deep yet silky voice belonged to Ambrose Ralston, who had slid to the passenger side window, oblivious of the lengthening train of traffic behind him.

"Hop in, old friend," he said. When a look of reluctance and annoyance crossed Kip's face, Ralston persisted. "Come on, we need to talk, and if you don't get in now, that crowd behind us will be getting ugly quickly." He flung the door open, nearly falling out in the process.

Kip relented and he joined Ralston in his cabin cruiser.

As Kip was fastening his seat belt, a muzzle jammed into the back of his neck and he screamed and got a howl of fright in return.

"Rufus, down, damn you!" Ralston yelled, ordering a large, white poodle to sit. "Sorry about that. He's friendly, if not well mannered."

Once he'd regained his dignity, Kip laughed. A dog's affection was the perfect antidote to the crappy shouting matches in his head.

Rufus quickly curled up on a back seat larger than the couch in Kip's office. Ralston said, "He's good company and most people find him a comfort."

"Then your boy back there has his work cut out for him," Kip said. "This has been one of the most uncomfortable days in my life. I'll tell you about it if you tell me what's on your mind."

"I came from your office – all locked up," Ralston said. "I guessed you'd just left and tried to catch up on the street, as I do have a few things to tell you. There's plenty of daylight left, so let's take a spin down the Parkway."

Kip felt like Alice in a mobile wonderland. The tricked-out Checker, all fifteen feet of it, was pristine on the outside. Inside, there wasn't a hint of the vinyl and plastic of its siblings that plied the streets of New York City. The seats were soft, tan leather, and the walnut dashboard sported gauges that looked as though they came from Tiffany's. Even the carpeting felt plush beneath Kip's running shoes. Somewhere in this behemoth exists a bar, Kip thought. Ralston confirmed it.

"There's beer cooling in the drawer beneath your seat," he said. "Help yourself."

Kip offered a can of Heineken to Ralston, who declined. "Thanks, but none for the driver. You, though, look as if you could use a few."

"Ambrose, this is a man cave on wheels," Kip said. "You must own half of Exxon to afford driving this rig."

"Not really. If sallies around Port City and an occasional trip to the Kennedy Center are the only driving you do, then it's not so bad. No doubt you've determined this is about the only car I can drive."

Kip had indeed figured that out. At something close to 300 pounds and beholden to a sturdy cane, mobility and comfort came hard for Ralston. He must be in his early 50s, Kip thought; so at the rate he was gaining weight, he'd soon need a driver for the Checker.

Backtracking up a side street, Ralston maneuvered the car south on to Washington Street and soon transitioned onto the southern portion of the George Washington Parkway. The nine miles of the Depression-era marvel would take them by dense woodlands on the right and expansive vistas of the Potomac and its marshland to the left before culminating at Mount Vernon Estate. In choosing that route, Ralston knew which buttons to push.

"You drive a mean tour mobile, Ambrose," Kip said, "but I don't think gorgeous spring scenery is why we're here."

"Correct. So let's get down to it. You are not going to like most of what I have to say," Ralston began. "You might as well be the first to know: I'm switching sides on the P2 brouhaha."

"What? Why? When?"

"I never felt strongly one way or the other about the issue. Lately, though, I've come to believe that if there is a boost to be had to the local economy, it isn't worth making Port City into a bad episode of 'Dallas.'"

"As I live and breathe, Ambrose, this is news to me," Kip said. "I've got to tell you, though, it's lonely on this side of the ideological fence."

"I realize that," Ralston said. "I've seen the hits your paper has been taking in advertising. I'm prepared for the same, though I don't believe that will happen. This will all pass in time, for you and me. Trust me."

"Then, what's bothering you?" Kip asked.

"I'll tell you. What really has pissed me off is the utter temerity of your cousin Melvin and Miles Tennyson wanting to buy the *Mirror* from me," Ralston said.

The blood drained from Kip's face and betrayal slammed him in the pit of his stomach. He was speechless. So Ralston continued.

"Yes, I know, their offer stunned me, too," he said. "The point is, I have no desire whatsoever to join forces with them, as Melvin phrased it. I never have."

"But why not?" Kip asked.

"Think about it," Ralston answered.

"What do you think I'm thinking about?" Kip snapped, instantly regretting his response. "Sorry. This is a lot to absorb."

"I don't think you will object to my description of those two," Ambrose said. "Miles is a quietly shrewd opportunist and Melvin a lazy dreamer. I've always thought that about him, and he's confirmed it to me with his pathetic leaks. But both Miles and Melvin would like Port City to be a one-paper town – pro-growth, of course. Melvin, I suspect, would also like a free platform for his political aspirations. Neither, evidently, is getting anything from you. So they came to me."

"All I can say at this point, Ambrose, is holy shit," Kip answered.

"The laughable part about it is how quickly their so-called publishing alliance would implode," Ralston said. "Tennyson will devour Melvin as soon as he no longer needed him."

"I don't know about that," Kip said. "I've stopped underestimating Melvin. I'm glad you gave them the boot. How did they take it?"

"As you would expect. Miles was courtly in his dismissiveness. He knew when to quit. Melvin was agitated and got more so when I told him I had no intention of thinking it over. He's selfish, bordering on mean. You have my condolences for having him on your family tree."

They were pulling up to the traffic circle at Mount Vernon at the end of the Parkway. Only a few busses remained at that hour, and Kip realized he hadn't noticed any of the scenery on the drive south. Rufus began to stir, and Kip leaned over the seat and petted his new friend for life.

"I have a question for you, Kip," Ambrose said. "But, first, help yourself to another beer."

Kip took another and said, "What do you need to know?"

"Simply, what in the hell is going on around here? Port City has always had its share of intrigue, affairs, cabals, scandals – you name it. But this one is weirdly off the charts. And you seem – if I am using the right word – connected to it all."

Ben Bailey and Jake Johnson had articulated that exact sentiment hours earlier. Even Rick Porter's barb at the boathouse that kicked off Kip's miserable day had had a whiff of accusation. This time, Kip didn't push back.

"I'm wondering the same thing, Ambrose," Kip sighed. "It's like someone is manipulating reality around here. There was no rivalry between Paul Schultz and me until Anders Martin died, and then suddenly, we're coming to blows over P2 and his legacy. I get subtle and not-so subtle warnings, like arson at the *Beacon*. Schultz commits suicide. My board votes to sell the *Beacon* – though now I know who the likely buyers will be. And then I get a visit from Port City's chief of police telling me to get my legal house in order."

Kip guzzled, wondering if he could finish Ralston's entire stash before they got back to town. "Yeah, you're right," he continued. "It's weird, and the pieces do not fit together whatsoever. And I'm close to going around the bend trying to make sense of it all."

Ralston slowed the Checker to a crawl as several sets of glowing eyes appeared in front of them. After the deer moved on, Ralston accelerated and said, "What you've told me is pretty much what I've observed. And my advice to you is, be careful."

Kip growled a short laugh in response. "Really, Ambrose?"

"Really, Kip. There's a pattern emerging here, one that will snare you if you're not watching out. If another event happens, law enforcement will need to show the good citizens of Port City it's on the job and has matters under control."

"Jake Johnson told me pretty much the same thing ninety minutes ago," Kip said. "Now, let me ask you a question, Ambrose." Taking Ralston's silence for assent, he continued. "If you are able to discern so much intrigue in all this, why would you think me above it and not the cause?"

It was fully dark outside as the Checker pulled into Old Town. Ralston halted at a traffic light and looked at Kip before replying.

"That's a fair question," he said. "It's because I've known you and your late parents for all of my working life in Port City. Sure, I haven't been in publishing all that time, but long enough to get a feel for how difficult it can be."

The traffic light turned green and the Checker accelerated.

"You've always done the right thing, even if it meant suffering for it," he continued. "Unlike me, you're a long-view man, and I respect that. Maybe I've got it easier than you because I don't have the legacy of a 250-year-old paper on my shoulders and a pack of get-rich-quick relatives nipping at my heels."

"Two hundred forty-seven years," Kip corrected. "Although I very much want to be on hand to celebrate 250."

Kip shook his beer can: empty and not enough time for another.

"Look, Ambrose, I know I've been a jerk at times," he said. "It's the competitive side of me. At least I hope so. I know we'll always be competitors, but it will always be on a healthy plane. Especially now that I know the *Mirror* will be staying in your hands. So, thanks for the heads up. Not that I know what to do with it."

Ralston smiled as he pulled up to Kip's alley. "No way I'm driving down that tunnel you call a driveway," he said. "But, you're welcome. I have no worries that you'll know what to do with the information. But you had better step on it. My gut tells me things will be happening faster and faster around here."

That, they are, Kip thought, as he shut the door to Ralston's car and began preparing for his confrontation with Melvin Alexander.

THIRTY-SEVEN

Kip never made it halfway up his alley before turning around. Some things couldn't wait, and Melvin Alexander was one of them.

His cousin lived three blocks away and since it was only 9 o' clock, he would still be awake for a short chat. Whether he wanted to receive irate company was another matter.

Melvin's federal-period townhouse was vintage Port City: narrow, sandwiched by similar homes, and three brick steps leading to a heavy wood door. A window next to the entrance sported black shutters and an attached box of blooming daffodils. Kip knew the floorplan by heart: hallway with a living room and dining room to the left and a kitchen at the rear. Upstairs, three matchbox-sized bedrooms and bath, two baths if the owner were wealthy. Behind the house would be a small, walled-in patio garden.

Modest and tasteful, yes, Kip thought as he hammered a hefty brass doorknocker. Hideously expensive, also. Old Town was full of such structures, many that fetched north of a million dollars. More, if they came with off-street parking. Location, location, location, Kip reminded himself as he gave the knocker an even louder rap.

He was about to leave when the door flung open. Melvin's greeting was cold and terse.

"At this hour, Kip?"

"Yes, at this hour," Kip said, wedging his way through the door into a closet doubling as a foyer. "You've got some serious explaining to do."

"Such as?"

Kip studied Melvin for signs of sanity. In an orange Virginia Tech sweat shirt, faded jeans, and sneakers, he did pass for normal. But Kip didn't give his cousin's appearance another thought – his fury was still peaking.

"Such as betraying the *Beacon*," he said, "or had you forgotten you are a co-owner of the paper when you and Tennyson tried to buy the *Mirror* today?"

Melvin said nothing, and instead, stepped into his living room. Kip followed him in, choosing to stand when Melvin eased into one of two overstuffed wingback chairs facing a fireplace. Waiting for his cousin to reply, he scanned the nautically themed room: oil paintings of nineteenth century sailing ships, old block and tackle pieces on book shelves, and model of a 1960s-era Chris-Craft runabout on the fireplace mantle.

"I see you've been talking to Ralston," Melvin finally said, devoid of the agitation Ralston observed earlier in the evening. "I suppose it was asking too much of that oaf to expect discretion."

"Screw you, Melvin – Ambrose Ralston has you coming and going when it comes to discretion and, for that matter, integrity. Tell me why you did it."

Melvin rose. Kip could see from the tilt of Melvin's head and the way he folded his arms across his chest that he was trying to wait him out. He squared off inches from Melvin. Angry as he was, Kip wondered if he had enough stamina left to knock the smug look off his face so he could get to the bottom of this disaster. Taking a cue from a painting of a British war frigate on the wall, Kip decided to ram.

"So, you really believe you can drive the value of the *Beacon* so far down nobody will want it, so you – or some crony – can swoop in and steal it for pennies on the dollar," Kip said. "Let's see what's left of your standing with the board when they learn about your stunt with Tennyson. They will sue you, and I will be right in there with them."

Melvin never reacted. What's with this guy? Kip wondered. He didn't even deny it. His smarmy attitude wasn't letting up, either.

"Hah! You try that," Melvin said. "Stephen and Dorothy want you out of there so badly that they will listen to anything I tell them.

"Besides, it seems to me you've got problems of your own that are getting bigger by the day," he continued, "and your guardian angel Jake Johnson won't be able to help you, either."

Kip reeled inwardly. All day long he had been hearing this warning, or accusation, depending on who issued it. Melvin even seemed ready for Kip's reaction. Still, he wasn't finished with his cousin.

"Melvin, did you start the fire at the *Beacon*?"

This time Melvin flinched, enough to convince Kip he had hit a nerve. He must have realized that if Kip could ask that question, then anyone in authority might be thinking and asking him the same thing. Still, he was unequivocal.

"Hell, now why would I want to do that?" he said. "We may be so far on the other side of each other's fences that it's laughable, but my disagreements with you don't extend to arson."

With a chill, Kip recalled a similar, less pompous statement – from Paul Schultz hours before he died. It was far from scientific reasoning, but when Melvin uttered the same words, Kip was tempted to let Melvin off the hook for arson.

As Erin had suggested, Melvin had reasons for wanting the *Beacon* gone. The insurance payout would be substantial and had Ralston not rebuffed his offer to buy the *Mirror*, it would have been enough for a nice co-down payment. But that scenario went out the window when Ralston told him to get lost. But Kip wasn't about to let Melvin in on that conclusion. Dear Cousin could have had other motives in mind.

Before he could continue laying into Melvin, the voice of someone coming through the front door interrupted him.

"Melvin, you didn't tell me we would be having company. Well, hello, Kip what brings you around this time of evening?"

It was Liz, Melvin's wife. She was the best thing Kip could find to say about her husband. What this perpetually sunny and outgoing woman saw in Melvin always puzzled him. Where her husband was dour and bean-pole thin, Liz was plump and hearty, always concerned for everybody. Melvin, however, wasn't about to let a friendly conversation get started.

He spoke first. "We were discussing last-minute *Beacon* details, Dear, and Kip was on his way out the door. Weren't you, Kip?"

At another time at another place they could finish this conversation, Kip thought. Liz would find out about her spouse's dubious business dealings soon enough. Right now, he felt momentarily relieved there was still a chance he didn't have an arsonist for a cousin. Kip did his best to put on a friendlier face before replying.

"That's right, Liz," he said. "I'm on my way. It was good to see you, short as it was."

To Melvin he said, "I'm truly looking forward to our next board meeting, Melvin."

THIRTY-EIGHT

From their bench on a sunny knoll overlooking Founder's Park, Kip and Erin could see Port City passing before them: walkers, joggers, cyclists, nannies with prams, a tugboat hauling a gravel-laden barge on the Potomac, and all of nature in its spring glory. Even the lawn sloping down to the shoreline had that green fairytale lushness found in yard and garden ads.

Kip had been anticipating the brown-bag lunch all morning and his spirits lifted as Erin approached in a daffodil yellow sundress and a large hand bag slung across her shoulder. With a blink of a smile and a peck on his cheek, she abruptly sat on the bench. He missed that cue and the next one, when a faraway look came over her face as he recounted the impending sale of the *Beacon*, his car ride with Ambrose Ralston, and Melvin's pompous reaction when accused of perfidy. "And he even called Jake Johnson my guardian angel," Kip said. "If only he knew."

Without changing posture or her gaze out across the river, Erin replied.

"How long have we known each other?" she asked, flatly.

"Four weeks," Kip said, his radar belatedly switching on. "Why?"

Their sandwiches lay untouched and even though the thermometer was bumping 80, a chill set in as Erin straightened. Her gaze lifted from its lock on the Maryland shoreline and wandered over the park, never to Kip's eyes.

"You know, in that time my friend and boss has died and I feel as though I've fallen into a badly made movie where nothing good has happened or will happen."

"How can you say that? What about . . ."

Erin spared Kip the embarrassment of the cliché, What about our relationship? "Please," she said gently, "let me get this out. Then you can talk."

Kip shifted his position on the bench and sighed heavily with acquiescence. "Please do."

"Ever since I met you, four weeks ago, you've been a magnet for trouble," she continued, ticking off the events in Kip's life – and by extension, her recent life. "And in the middle of all this I broke up with Randy."

He knew exactly what she was saying and why, and while empathy wasn't the longest of his suits, Kip felt for her. She had a point and he knew where she was headed. But he also knew he hadn't dreamed the affair – there was, *is* something good between them – and he would do whatever he could to keep it. Even if it meant taking one step back to make it two more forward someday.

"So what are you saying?"

"I want to put space and time between us. If this is what your life is always going to be like, then I need to rethink things, and I need distance to do that. I'm not saying we won't see each other at all."

"And how long do you see this putting of distance between us to last?" Kip asked.

"I really don't know. I think your life needs to settle down. Less intrigue, less drama, less family strife."

Well, she's honest, Kip thought. Usually, it's the breaker-off of relationships who wants time to sort out their problems.

For the first time in their conversation, Erin looked Kip directly in the eyes. "Look, after what I've said, you may find this hard to believe, but in a way this has nothing to do with you personally. You're a wonderful man, and I'm liking you more and more. But you've got too much on your plate, and it's scaring me."

Kip began reassembling the contents of his untouched lunch back into its paper sack.

"I see," he said. "You like me, just not the whole package. Well, I'm not so sure that will ever change. My life certainly hasn't always been quite this mixed up. But I do know that I've always been up to my neck in one thing or another. It's who I am. If quiet and peaceful stability is what you want, then maybe you need to find an accountant."

Kip rose to leave. Then he saw the tears streaming down Erin's face and he sat back down.

Neither said anything for what seemed like eternity. Kip broke the silence.

"Maybe I have been asking a lot," he said in a near whisper that turned into a laugh. "I wish *I* could put some time and distance in my life, too. But we both know that won't be happening any time soon. But here's my promise: I'm not going anywhere or doing anything to ruin the best thing to happen in my life while this all works out. I will take you at your word that we will be seeing each other some in the future. At the moment, that's the best I can hope for."

He stood again, gently laid a hand on her shoulder, and left.

THIRTY-NINE

With anguish closing in from every direction, Kip never knew whether his afternoon went quickly or slowly. Even though it was another Tuesday, production crunch time, the *Beacon* staff sensed his mood and for all but urgent matters left him in peace.

His was the only office without a window and he couldn't let in the spring breezes to relieve the growing stuffiness of the warm afternoon. Not that he'd even noticed. For long stretches at a time, he sat at his desk, staring out in dark contemplation. When he tired of that position, he shifted to one of his leather chairs for more thinking. By evening, when the last of the staff had departed, he'd succeeded in only narrowing his dilemmas to two.

Losing Erin – which was the only way he could look at her decision – felt crushing on its own merits. He had come so close, yet was so far from the one thing he wanted: marriage and a family. Helen Martin's counsel about Erin's fear of commitment came roaring back. Yet, he'd kept his promise to himself: There would never be a lack of commitment on his part. And here he was, good and burned in spite of his best intentions. He also could not shake the conclusion of his usually prescient sister, that Erin was the best thing to ever happen to him.

Kip rose from his chair again and began pacing, trying to fathom the prospects of the other great loss in his life. The signs had been there all along, and lord knew, he was well aware of them. Maybe a newspaper magnate like William Randolph Hearst could have wrestled the Alexander clan to the ground. But Kip knew he himself certainly lacked the cunning needed to break them.

As he walked the hallway and empty offices, he studied the framed front pages of the *Beacon*. How small, slow, and uncomplicated life appeared when seen from the wide end of a telescope. Yet the paper chronicled the home life during the country's major conflicts, from the Revolution through the Civil War, World Wars, Viet Nam, and the Middle East, as well as cultural and societal changes, serious and trivial. Throughout it all, the *Beacon* recorded births, marriages, and deaths in Port City.

The presentation may have leaned to the prosaic at times, especially when compared with the sophistication of the graphic design and photography of current publications. Still, the unbroken tapestry of its content remained. The *Beacon* hadn't always framed life in Port City perfectly and probably it was on the wrong side of history at times; but Kip concluded his ancestors gave it their best. What more could one ask?

And now, the current heirs wanted to sell off the legacy for scrap. How easy it would be to take his portion of the proceeds and light out for the territories, a free man with no obligations. With Erin slipping from the picture, this option came with one less complication.

Yet something far more in his life would be lost if he gave in. For one, he had come to value the rhythm of life provided by the *Beacon*. The weekly news cycle – not too fast (the dailies can have that) and not too slow (the monthly magazines had that down fine) – inhabited Kip body and soul. Granted, he had come to that conclusion kicking and screaming. But here he was.

Kip stopped his pacing when he came to the last of the family portraits – his parents. Unlike their less enlightened ancestors, his parents ran the *Beacon* co-equally as a husband and wife team. Until death took them in the car crash, they had, to Kip's young eyes, functioned happily in their roles as editor and publisher and as parents. Or had they shielded their children from the grittier realities of running an extended family enterprise? If so, they had succeeded in keeping that part of the business out of view. Neither Kip nor Cass had the slightest inkling of discord among their extended family until only recently. Even then, and at an innocent distance, he took their behavior for eccentricity, not bald aggrandizement. In his role as institutional memory keeper, Colbert Jenkins had never hinted at strife in the family.

Realization then hit Kip like a big piece of lumber. His parents enjoyed relative peace in their stint with the *Beacon* because they were in. All the way in. No ambivalence, nothing half-hearted in anything they did. They operated as if everything mattered, with no way out. The *Beacon* was where they chose to be.

That was the difference, Kip realized. The board could smell his ambivalence like sharks to blood. In their neurotic fashion they bit and nibbled at Kip at every opportunity until something had to give. For all his staunch pushback, they never took him seriously, recognizing his splintered loyalties. He wondered if Melvin would ever have turned into such a toxic monster had he approached his role differently. Probably. But, now it was too late: The *Beacon* had a date with the auction block and even if Kip had wanted to do something about it, he would have to get in line.

Which was precisely what he would do – one way or the other. He could borrow the money, mortgage his house, find partners, joint venture with other media outlets. If he had to, he could start from scratch with an online product, provided he could escape the clutches of non-compete clauses that buyers of the *Beacon* would surely insist upon. It would take time to sort out, but he knew it could be done.

First, though, he had to tell the *Beacon* staff of the board's decision. Better for Kip to tell them immediately than to have them learn it in bits and pieces on the street. Their prospects for continued employment hinged on whether Kip or any buyer could keep the paper going, rather than selling off the pieces.

Strange, the staff had been more tolerant of Kip's role at the *Beacon* than he felt they should have been. Willie Carter proved the exception there. He had seen through Kip these past three years and, in his curmudgeonly way, never let him off the hook.

Tomorrow Kip` would tell the staff about the sale. That would test their tolerance.

FORTY

When Jeff Benson and Kip began their monthly poker games eight years ago, their venues rotated among the kitchens of the players. That scheme wasn't always popular with their spouses, and the stinking two-hour visitor parking restrictions in Old Town didn't endear them to Kip's house.

Nobody had thought of Hampton Funeral Home until a tropical storm wiped out power in much of the Washington area for a week. When Benson mentioned his emergency generator backup system, the group sprang at the opportunity. The basement was colder than a supermarket but the operating room-style illumination proved perfect for concentrating light on the makeshift poker table. They learned very quickly which refrigerators held the beer and refreshments and which ones held greater surprises.

All four were seated and dividing chips when Kip arrived through the side door. The local FM country music station provided surround-sound twang. Kip couldn't see who the special guest was until he came around to take his seat.

"Hello, Kip."

There, wearing a long-sleeved black Rolling Stones tour t-shirt with a John Deere baseball cap in rally position sat Joseph Patel.

"Dr. Patel, I presume. I didn't know you played poker," Kip said. With the exception of his cousins, Patel was one of the last people he expected to find. And he looked like he belonged at the table more than Kip.

"It's Joe," Patel said. "I do play poker, and you've got your work cut out for you tonight."

"Ha. I will take that as your first bluff of the evening, and a weak one at that," Kip said, pulling over a heap of faded poker chips. "How did you fall in with this sordid lot?"

"Think about it," Benson said.

Kip thought about it and slapped the side of his head. "I forgot you two are cousins in the same business."

"Yep," Benson said, "though it tends to be a one-way trade."

Four guys groaned.

"Cut the cards," said Dale Keyes, a figure with a shaved head and still in his neat pinstripe suit from work with his K Street lobbying firm. His coat hung from the back of his chair and his starched blue- and white-striped shirt was unbuttoned at the top with the tie pulled open, poker style.

They cut, and the deal went to Kip. He actually liked the funky poker variations his friends came up with – Omaha, Saints & Sinners, Night Baseball – but he preferred to start basic. That might also help to smoke out Patel; though if the M.E. was as good as he talked, he wouldn't show it for another couple of hands. "Straight seven-card stud. Nothing wild, no low cards."

"That's our boy," said Teddy Abrahamson, the owner of Port City's lone independent lumber yard. "Roaring out of the starting gate, slowly."

"That's because I know you all will come up with games so complicated that even an advanced degree wouldn't help," Kip countered. "Play ball."

And so the banter went on for another hour. Kip wondered how long the conversation could go without some mention of Strawberry Flats, Paul Schultz, or the *Beacon*. With Patel sitting across from him, Kip realized that he had not checked in with the M. E. about his report on Schultz. Asking him might open the floodgates to a new conversation, but what the hell. He hadn't had the opportunity until tonight, which was as good a time as any to broach the subject.

"So, Joe, have you released your report on Paul Schultz yet?" he asked.

Patel looked up from his cards with a frown. "Are you trying to throw me off my game or are you on the clock?" he responded.

"On the clock, always," Kip said. "I would never dream of derailing your straight flush."

Four sets of eyes turned on their guest, who smiled confidently.

"We'll see about the flush," Patel said. "The report is out. I suppose you want to know if there's anything special or unusual about his death. If I tell you all, you will have to swear to secrecy."

The stares intensified.

"Nah. Just kidding," he laughed. "Everything is as it looks. Cause of death is suicide, inflicted by hanging. In this era of easy access to firearms, hanging is a bit old fashioned but as shocking to whoever finds the body.

"As for the straight flush, that is mighty suspicious, but you will have to pay to find out," Patel said with an even wider grin.

Four folds followed and Patel raked in a pile of chips. He could indeed play poker.

The M.E.'s succinct summary of his report would have had the effect of further closing the door on Kip's foray into the death of Anders Martin had he not continued.

"By the way, Kip," Patel said, tossing out a chip for the ante of the next hand, "did the printout of that photo from my office ever help you with your work?"

For a moment, Kip had no idea of what Patel meant. Then his face flooded with embarrassment as he realized that Patel had meant all along for him to print the photo of Anders Martin's arm back in early March. He just couldn't officially condone its release.

"I wouldn't exactly call that a poker face," Patel laughed.

"Well, heh," Kip said. "No, I never made anything of it."

"I didn't think you would, but I thought you should have it anyway," Patel said. "We can talk about it later if you want."

Before Kip could tell Patel how much he'd appreciate that discussion, Benson cut in.

"Boys, boys, this is a serious poker game," Benson said. "Take your shop talk elsewhere."

His admonition didn't go very far. Dale Keyes made his ante and said, "You might be interested to know my firm was approached this week by the representative of an anonymous client," Keyes said. "They want us to handle P2's interests at the state and federal levels. Someone evidently thought my Port City connections would help out."

"What did you tell them?" Abrahamson asked.

"Not much, only that we'd think about it," Keyes said. "We seldom do local work. We prefer to flack the pharmaceuticals and make third-world dictators look benevolent."

Amid the chuckles and snorts, Kip considered his friend's response. Keyes's lobbying firm infrequently took on fat-cat clients, preferring to represent nonprofits that by law could not directly lobby Congress – conservation organizations and anti-poverty groups. P2, Kip knew, was out of character for Keyes.

"They would be throwing their money away," Kip said. "The *Beacon* has been doing a dandy job on its own of swaying public opinion toward P2."

Until this point, Teddy Abrahamson had been quiet on the matter. Which side of the P2 fence Abrahamson occupied intrigued Kip.

His family-owned lumber company had been forced by the rise of big-box companies into specializing in high-end wood and fixtures. He, too, stood to gain business with P2. And, like Benson and Kip, he was long-time member of Port City's chamber of commerce. Any of the three would have known quickly if the source of the potential client had been local.

"You should hang in there, Kip," Abrahamson said. "We all know you took some hits this week, but it's way early in the game to read much into it. I wish I could say Port City will wake up to losing paradise to a government parking lot, but I've got my doubts, unless organizations like yours push back."

"Thanks, Teddy," Kip said. "You're right – we took hits this week, and then some."

Nobody said anything, and for a few moments the only sounds in the room were the hum of the refrigerators and Toby Keith on the radio.

"You'll be finding out soon enough," Kip continued. "My family board of directors voted today to sell the *Beacon*. It looks to be the end of an era."

"No shit?" Keyes said. "Can they do that?"

"They can, by outvoting me, which they've done," Kip said.

"What will you be doing?" Abrahamson asked.

"It's too soon to tell, but I'll figure out something," Kip said. "Now maybe on your gracious note of support I could bow out early. I've got a regatta in Georgetown tomorrow and it begins sinfully early."

They relented, but not without a closing round of trash talk.

"Might as well, we're tired of taking your money."

"We hope you can row better than you play poker."

"Come again when you have more money to lose."

The only person not piling on fixed Kip with a look of concern. Joe Patel said, "Be careful."

FORTY-ONE

No matter how badly a work week went, Kip could always count on a rowing regatta for diversion. The annual May Day Regatta in Georgetown was such an event.

The time of year didn't hurt, either. The first Saturday in May seemed always guaranteed of mild and sunny weather. Even if rain did fall, it tended to be mild and seldom interfered with the preparation and racing of the boats.

As he walked into the parking lot off of Rock Creek Parkway all but one piece of the previous week had taken a backseat. Kip's and Erin's grand plans for race day fell apart less than twenty-four hours before when she had declared the cooling-off period. Instead, Erin said she might or might not come to the races; and, anyway, it would not be at the ungodly hour of 8 a.m., when Kip had to be present to help with the boats. If she came, she came, Kip figured. In the meantime, a lovely day of racing beckoned.

His group had entered two masters events: one for four-person boats in the morning and the other for eight-person boats in the afternoon. Anyone with steam left was welcome to race in the informal mixed-8s at the end of the day.

Port City's two 4s raced in separate heats over a course that began below Key Bridge and ended at Thompson's Boathouse upstream from the Kennedy Center. Though shorter, it was much the same course Port City and Algonquian raced a month earlier in their scrimmage. Astonishingly different racing conditions awaited them this time – robin's egg blue sky, temperatures in the 70s, and gloriously smooth water.

Neither of their two 4s fared well in the mid-morning races. No single flaw could explain their performances which made it more difficult to prepare for the afternoon races. Bo Hansen said he wasn't worried, and neither was Kip. The day was still young and he felt good and ready for anything. Until he saw Erin.

As they returned to the trailer area with their boat on their shoulders, Erin rose from a camp chair beneath the team's tent. When Kip caught sight of her in her t-shirt, shorts, and ball cap, he wanted to look away.

"How did it go?" she asked after they had placed their boats on to slings. "I don't see a whole lot of fist-pumping and high fives."

It's funny, Kip thought, when you're on the inside of a relationship, you take the minutia for granted. Now here he was studying the woman as if it were the first time they'd met. And everything that he liked about her came back in a scary rush – the twinkling eyes that always told the truth, the gentle smile that always hinted of more fun in reserve, and the lithesome way in which she carried herself, even among the clusters of impossibly fit female rowers.

"It went well . . . sort of . . . we didn't win, but we had a good time . . . we didn't finish last, either. Well, actually, we rowed horribly," Kip finally answered, wishing he kept his tied tongue to himself.

"Well, Mister Alexander, I hope you're still handy with the printed word," she laughed. "All that work for how many months for how long a race? Three and some minutes?"

With that, he found his footing.

"We didn't come close to that this time," he said. "We needed a good start and didn't get one."

"Couldn't you catch up anyway?"

"Not really – the races are too short. You've got to be at least even with the other boats after the first twenty strokes. After that, it's supposed to be a matter of horse power and sticking to the race plan.

"We got off to an even start but fell off pace as the race went on," he continued. "It happens more than we like to admit. And it's why none of us are quitting our day jobs. If you measured your satisfaction solely against your race times, instead of the joy of months of cold, early morning training, you'd shoot yourself."

Kip was surprised to find himself actually laughing and reviving some of his happy sarcasm.

"But, we race in the 8s at 2 o' clock and can redeem ourselves then. Or not, and then we'll have to shoot ourselves," he said. "In the meantime, would you care to visit our fine vendors and partake of a gourmet hamburger?"

She did. And they spent the next forty-five minutes wandering around, checking out t-shirts and regatta memorabilia. They then returned to the tent that shaded the rowers from the hot afternoon sun.

Kip must have dozed over his book longer than he thought. Erin's chair was empty when he awoke. Mingling with other rowers and their significant others, he figured. How can she not be enthralled with our fine culture here?

After ten minutes, Kip grew more curious than restless and stood to scan the area accommodating the thirty or so boat trailers. He almost sat down to return to his book when he saw Erin and Owen Draper sitting under a tree, deep in what Kip figured was intense archaeology conversation. The way Erin threw her head back for a hearty laugh irked Kip. When Draper laid a hand on her knee to press home a particularly humorous point, Kip nearly spit. He could see how most women could be entranced by his rugged, movie-star good looks. But this plain didn't look right.

Whatever, he thought. After yesterday he had no reason not to expect Erin to expand her horizons, only not so quickly. And what was the man doing there anyway? His singles event finished earlier in the morning. Had they actually arranged to meet today? Well, in Draper she's got herself an archaeologist and a rower. Good luck, buddy.

"Fifteen minutes!"

Dana Parsons roused the rowers from their afternoon lethargy. Those who hadn't already stretched and run a few sprints in the nearby park had enough time before the boats would be carried down to the dock for launching. Their pre-race routine would occur during their row upstream for the start of the race.

Kip and Parsons had agreed in advance to run a series of warm-up sprints to eliminate the flaws that afflicted the 4s in the morning races. By launching early enough, they could also practice racing starts. But, first came Bo Hansen's pre-race talk.

An inspirational college-style pep talk delivered to the assorted Port City rowers would only have produced rolled eyeballs. Their ages ranged between 30 and 65 and they had been getting up at zero dark hundred for years to practice with all they had. They didn't need exhortations to effort and heroism.

"After this morning's races, I was thinking about knocking back the starting stroke rate from 36 to 32 to make sure you can keep together," Hansen said. "But in practice this week you did 36 fine. So, I believe you can pull it off today. Remember to focus, and everything else will take care of itself. Good luck."

With the *Madison* perched on their shoulders, the rowers proceeded to the floating dock with Parsons clearing their way with sharp barks at milling rowers and spectators. As they approached the ramp to the river, Parsons called a halt, and they lowered the boat to waist level for a mandatory safety inspection.

A tall square-shouldered man in the regatta judge's "uniform" of blue oxford button-down shirt and light chino trousers worked his way up the boat tugging on each of eight pairs of shoes affixed to the bottom of the boat. The heel of each shoe needed the right amount of wiggle room to allow a rower to exit more easily from an overturned shell. It was a procedure Kip had been through for countless races and he barely paid attention when the official got to his seat.

"Kip," the man said in greeting.

It was Miles Tennyson. Of course, he should have expected to encounter Tennyson, since he worked all the regattas, either on the water as a judge or on land in a variety of capacities. Kip did his best to drill two holes with his eyes through his head.

Not getting a reply, Tennyson said, "Maybe we should have a

talk next week."

"Fuck you," Kip said, turning to face forward toward the wide eyes of Dana Parsons.

Worrying what might come next, she quickly shouted the command to ready the boat for the walk to the dock, "To shoulders!" Walking alongside Kip she half whispered, "Maybe you will tell me later why you told a race official to get fucked, if he's not busying getting us disqualified."

"Don't worry," Kip said. "He won't. It had nothing to do with racing."

Parsons backed away and cleared more bystanders from their path. Right behind them, Port City's B team followed with the *Jefferson* for the second heat.

They laughed as the rowers from Charleston, South Carolina, launched from the dock attired in black pirate outfits – a bit warm but definitely stylish. They looked capable of ramming boats that didn't get out of their way.

Hansen's confidence in his two teams would be sorely tested. Besides the Charleston boat, the *Madison*'s heat included teams from Pittsburgh, Baltimore, and Richmond.

Kip thrilled at the collective power of the start that began with the gradual lengthening of their strokes: half stroke, three-quarter, three-quarter, full, full, and then the all-out sprint for thirty strokes at 36 strokes a minute. The measured start allowed them to add power over those crucial first five strokes and achieve maximum speed in the shortest amount of time.

The reward for their flawless start was a quarter-length deficit behind the Pittsburgh and Charleston. For thirty more grueling strokes, the *Madison* rowers sustained 36 strokes a minute – the high end for club racing. Kip couldn't fathom the 40 strokes a minute used by Olympic rowers. As far as Port City's rowers were concerned, those rowers were from another planet.

The *Madison* soon settled into the 32 strokes-per-minute main body of the race that would last until the 250-meter sprint home.

Over the miniature loud speakers bolted behind the 3 and 5 seats Parsons shouted out a series of commands. Like most coxswains, she seldom referred to a rower in a race by name, only his seat number.

"Five seat! Raise your hands two inches."

"Bow seat! Slow your slide."

"All! Keep your length. You're rowing well, so the only way we're going to win this one is with power. Power 20 in three!

"3-2-1. Power 20! Give it all you've got!"

Here we go, Kip thought, bracing to tap into a deeper reserve to pull even harder when the order for power strokes came. Parsons called out the next twenty strokes one by one, with more commands and reports of their progress.

Races are won and lost with these surges. Many coxswains call for only ten power strokes and Parsons was counting on their competitors to opt for that saner strategy. Kip suspected she might also be preempting his all-or-nothing impulses in order to avoid an on-water clash of wills.

When the *Madison* commenced its power 20, the two lead boats were settling from their 10s. The Port City rowers may have lost a few feet to Pittsburgh and Charleston in the beginning, but they began an exhilarating process of pulling ahead.

"We're even with their bow balls!"

"We're even with their 5 seats!"

"We're clear! I see open water!"

"Five power strokes to go. Do not let up."

"5-4-3-2-1. Well done! No resting. Fifteen strokes until the 250-meter buoy.

"All eyes in the boat! There's nothing to see. They're behind us. Let's keep them there."

Parsons, however, could look out of the boat, and what she now saw alarmed her. Pittsburgh was fading quickly, but the pirates of Charleston were gaining on the *Madison*. Her guys had come off of a power 20 and needed the settle to regroup for the final 250-meter sprint.

"A*rrrr*, Port City!" screamed the Charleston coxswain. "We're coming after you!"

Screw you, save your bravado for the head races, Kip thought. In those autumn 5,000-meter races there are no lanes and passing slower boats could be tricky and the verbal exchanges even saltier. Sprint races, though, have set lanes from which they cannot wander. Kip knew they were well within their prescribed lane and only needed to stick to their game plan. No reply from Parsons was needed.

"Okay, boys, five strokes to the sprint. Do not worry about that boat. Keep pulling long and hard."

Kip always chuckled when he heard the female coxswains in the heat of a race scream the most Freudian of commands. Usually, it was the high school coxswains on loan to the masters programs who issued the doozies. "I want it long and hard! "Deeper! Harder!" "Push! Push!" They learned early on to avoid certain commands.

The boats were even with Roosevelt Island on the Virginia shoreline. In a few more seconds, the *Madison* passed the large, orange buoy marking 250 meters to go.

"36 in three!" Parsons shouted.

"3-2-1.

"36! This is it. Twenty-five strokes to go. Make them count!"

For Kip, the last twenty-five strokes in a race were the most adrenaline filled. Sitting in the stroke seat meant that he had to perfectly set the pace and distance of the oars in the air and through the water. He knew the only thing worse than tiring in the final strokes of a race was to finish a race with gas left in the tank. And so he pulled with a fury.

"We're dead even! Pull, guys. Pull!"

And pull they did. The rowers wheezed and groaned for the last few strokes until the judge's gun sounded. Pop! Pop! The finish was so close that the winner would have to be confirmed by a laser-sighted devise on the shoreline.

"I've got 3:15 on my clock," Parson said. "Not bad, guys. That was one of your best races, and it's only May. Drink some water. We'll paddle to the dock in a minute."

As they got their wits and breath back, they became aware of the Charleston boat easing alongside.

"Arrr! Good race, maties!" their coxswain called out.

"Good race, Charleston!" the *Madison* rowers shouted. No fist bumps – because of their oars, they could get no closer than ten feet, and the best they could do was wave.

Hansen met the *Madison* at the dock. Usually spare with praise, he uncharacteristically slapped the outstretched hand of each rower as they stumbled on to the dock.

"You guys pulled it off. And you didn't even need the age handicap," Hansen said, referring to the seconds a boat can subtract from its raw time to allow for differences in the average ages of the rowers.

As soon as the crew got the *Madison* back in its slings, they scurried to the water's edge to watch the *Jefferson* finish in the second heat. Their B boat consisted of rowers whose test times didn't qualify them for the first 8. But because of the older average age of its rowers, it was conceivable for them to turn in a slower raw time than the *Madison* but win the race based on adjusted times.

Kip could see the *Jefferson* struggling to maintain third place as the 250-meter sprint began. They were clearly outgunned, and the *Madison* retained first place.

Not for the first time that day did Kip wonder if the loss of Paul Schultz had upset the group ecology of the *Jefferson*. Hansen had had to move a B boat rower to the A boat and then recruit a recreation-group rower for the B boat.

Kip quickly dismissed any feelings of guilt. Rowers often moved to other cities. They get injured. Or they get too busy at work and home to finish a season. Sure, the circumstances stank. But that's all there was to it.

"As the cowboy said to his horse, why the long face?"

It was Erin. She stood next to him at the railing overlooking the river. "You just won a race."

Kip found it easier that he expected to slip back into easy conversation with her. Whether that was healthy or not, he'd worry about later.

He told her about his thoughts on Paul Schultz. "I don't think I'll be leaving the emotional part of that chapter behind any time soon," he said.

"By the way, I still have all the food and drink for grilling tonight," he continued. "Are you still interested?"

Erin thought for a moment and said, "Sure."

Eureka, Kip thought.

"But I can't stay late," she added. "I've got early morning tours to do."

He amended his reaction to half a eureka.

Kip and Erin arrived at his house in separate vehicles. To squeeze her truck down the alley was asking too much, so she parked on the street where Kip met her.

At least the lock on this front door works, Kip thought, as he opened it. Depositing his gear in the kitchen, he was turning to join Erin in the living room when she screamed so loud it hurt his ears. Ike took up the cue and began howling. Grabbing the first weapon he could, a sauce pan on the countertop, he raced into the dark living room where a tall figure faced him.

"Hello, Kip. You can put that thing down. I come in peace."

"What the fuck! I should bend it over your head. What the hell are you doing here and how did you get in?"

Erin retreated to Kip's side and Ike quit barking.

"You left a window open, if you really want to know." The man delivering this was tall, deeply tanned with a week-old start on a beard. His hair, pulled back into a pony tail, had yielded much of its darkness to sun streaks of rusty red. The dark blue t-shirt with the Foster's Beer logo easily fit Alfred's Aussie visage. He leaned on a cane elaborately carved into mermaids, dolphins, starfish, and other marine life. "Aren't you going to introduce me to your friend?"

"Yeah, my friend who you scared half to death," Kip uttered through clenched teeth. "You haven't changed at all, have you?"

"That remains to be seen," Alf said.

"Erin, meet my brother Alf. Alf, Erin Powers."

"Glad to meet you Erin," Alf said. "You look like one of Kip's better decisions."

"Cut the crap, Alf," Kip said. "If you think you can cash in on the sale of the *Beacon*, you've got second thoughts coming. And how in God's name did you even know about it?"

"It's a long story," Alf said. "Surely, you've got a beer for a weary traveler."

FORTY-TWO

With the shock of Alf's dramatic return all but faded, they settled onto over-stuffed chairs and a couch in the living room where Kip had deposited a tray of beer and snacks. Samantha was having none of the brittle silence and made a cathartic leap onto Alf's lap and curled up.

"Sammie, old girl," Alf laughed, "You haven't changed a bit. You're as discriminating as ever."

"Tell us about your last three years," Kip said. "Judging from your cane, they must have been eventful."

"That's the truth," Alf said, nearly draining his beer in one tilt of the bottle. "Whew, I needed that. Gracias.

"I'm here to tell you that you can start life all over," he continued. "Just don't expect it to be the one you planned on."

Alf admitted losing it when Jimmy Bushrod perished in Iraq and worse so with the loss of their parents. The series of jobs as chef in upscale Port City restaurants had lost their allure of hipness and freedom and quickly began to feel like a prison.

"I obviously didn't do well with restaurant culture back then – the hours are upside down and the after-work partying was fierce and was taking its toll on me," Alf said. "I was sinking fast, real fast. You may have noticed. Somewhere near the bottom I realized getting as far out of town as possible was my only hope. There was enough of my inheritance left for a one-way ticket to Melbourne. It didn't take me long to find a coastal resort northeast of the city that needed someone to run their surfing concession.

"I wasn't a particularly good surfer, not that it mattered," Alf continued. "As long as I provided guests with boards and access to the surf boys to teach them the basics, things worked out. It was a good life – sun, fun, and enough cash to get by."

Alf rose from the couch and limped into the kitchen. "Twenty-two hours in a plane is my limit, not a minute more," he said.

"Help yourself," Kip said. "How do you like the Port City porter."

"Impressive – your very own brewery in this town," Alf said, returning to the living room. "But, to continue. It was a good life, what I needed at that moment, though I knew it could not last forever. My big mistake was having an affair with the wife of a local businessman. I thought it was love, and he thought otherwise.

"It was a month before they would let me out of the hospital. The husband's thugs broke every bone they could find in my body. Apparently, they meant it as more than a warning. The doctors told me repeatedly how lucky I was to be alive. I didn't feel so lucky at the time."

Kip nodded to the cane at Alf's side. "I guess that would explain your walking aid. Why didn't you call or write? Even from here there must have been something we could have done to help."

"Asking for help wasn't part of my master plan for the ex-pat's life style," Alf answered.

Pausing, he downed a handful of chips and then more porter. "But then I got lucky," he continued. "An envelope arrived at the hospital during the last week of my stay. I'm not positive who sent it, but I can only think it came from a very remorseful woman with whom I'd had the fling."

Erin had been listening from the kitchen and asked, "So what was in the envelope?"

"A cashier's check for enough dough to set me up in any business I wanted. Don't mess with married women, but if you do, make it a rich one."

"Tell me you didn't spend it on another surf shack," Kip

asked.

"Easy there, Brother," Alf responded, nonplussed. "There's more to this highly moral story, and I think you'll like how it turns out."

"Sorry," Kip replied, instantly regretting his bluntness. "I was out of line."

Alf moved on.

"A friend suggested taking over a restaurant in Melbourne that was in foreclosure. The bones were great and the décor was straight out of a 1930s Hollywood night club. I certainly knew the restaurant business from living in Port City.

"The rest was luck and skills I didn't know I had," Alf explained. "Many good people came together to help me pull the restaurant together. It turns out I like people a lot – at least on my terms – and soon it became a hangout for American ex-pats, the arts crowd, and hip businesspeople. Totally under the radar. We're packed every evening."

"What's the name of your restaurant?" Erin asked.

"I struggled with that one. Yankee Grille didn't cut it. Neither did RWB – Red, White, and Blue. By the time it was ready to open, we still didn't have a name. But everybody kept referring to it as 'Alf's.' The name stuck. The food is good, not great. The beer, wine, and liquor selection is okay. We have entertainment when it suits us. Whatever, mates, we're doing very well."

"Why do I think there's more to this," Kip asked, this time more cordially. "And who is the 'we' you're referring to, mate?"

"I forget what a good reporter you were. Are. Sorry."

Erin winced and Kip laughed.

Alf laughed in return. "You're right, there is more. The 'we' is Melissa. We met at the restaurant. She helps undocumented immigrants from Southeast Asia settle in Australia. Immigrants have it tough everywhere, and Australia is no different from other countries. She's a remarkable woman doing remarkable things. Would it surprise you to know you are an uncle, Kip?"

Silence.

"I'm speechless I am so happy for you, Alf," Kip finally responded. "Good lord, tell me more."

"Amy is one year old. She's gorgeous and healthy. Fortunately, she gets her looks from her mother."

"Good thing. I couldn't picture the alternative," Kip said. "But, let me ask you a serious question: Why are you here?"

"Our cousin Melvin is an idiot. That's why."

"Tell me another reason for his idiocy that I don't already know," Kip said.

"He shouldn't be allowed around Face Book," Alf said. "The jerk has been posting about how he and Stephen and Dorothy are finally cleaning up the *Beacon*. When I read they wanted to sell it, I got here as quickly as I could."

Leaning forward in earnestness he said, "You, Cass, and I may not always be in agreement on my life choices. But, they're fucking with the wrong people when they think they can do in God knows how many generations of the *Beacon*. Maybe I'm too late. I hope not. But if there's a battle to be fought, I'd like to be alongside you and Cass."

"Alf, I'm not the teary type," Kip replied. "But let me say, you earned yourself the guestroom for as long as you want. Samantha thinks it's her room, so you've got her, too."

FORTY-THREE

The warning, half alarm and half buzzer, sounded so many times in the last hour that no one paid it any heed. People working around printing presses know the sound when the machines are about to roll. Last chance to back away.

Willie, Calvin, and now Kip on that Tuesday afternoon had been running the recently cleaned King press to catch any remaining soot and debris from the drums that would show up as smudges on the newsprint.

The day before, the crew from West End Disaster Recovery had put the last touches on their restoration of the print bay. A new coat of white paint on the walls and glossy gray on the floor brought the 1870s era annex into the twenty-first century, as did new overhead lighting.

The eagerness with which Willie and Calvin pursued their preparations for the next day's press run tore at Kip, who wondered if all their extra effort to get the press rolling again would be for naught, thanks to the board's decision to sell the paper. Although the massive drums had been wiped with surgical precision, the only way they could know for certain how successful they were meant running off test sheets. Hence an afternoon of blaring alarms.

Smudges appeared sporadically but gradually disappeared with further wiping. After ninety minutes of stop and start, one elusive spot persisted.

"Out, damned spot!" Kip ordered.

"Macbeth," Calvin said.

"You're good," Kip said. "I didn't know you liked Shakespeare."

"Yeah, I do," Calvin replied. "We borrow from the Big Man now and then for our songs."

Kip didn't even know they wrote their own songs. And, to think, he thought he was up on his staff. "Who else do you borrow from?" he asked.

"e.e. Cummings, some Yeats, Robert Service. You name it. But mostly, we write our own stuff."

"Well, we'll miss you guys when you hit the big time," Kip said. "Don't forget to remember us."

A familiar vibration shook Kip's pocket. A text from Erin: "On my way. Don't go ANYWHERE."

Since that meant she was less than five minutes away, he figured no reply was necessary.

"I've got to duck out, guys," Kip said. "Do you think you'll be good to go tomorrow, Willie? Or should I let Metropolitan know we'll need them for another week?"

"We'll be ready," Willie said. "The damned spot will be gone."

Kip had barely enough time to settle into his office and ponder Erin's impromptu visit. Just last week she had decided to put time and distance between them, and other than their watered-down day at the regatta and later, briefly, at his house, their contact had been painfully nil. He felt a huge void, one made worse by the lack of the routine and rhythm he had come to enjoy. All within the span of four weeks, as she had pointed out. And now this.

Erin strode into his office a few minutes later. Breathless with excitement and the exertion of her dash to his office, she jumped right in: "You're not going to believe this!"

"You're right, unless you tell me first."

"Remember the radiocarbon test? Well, Randy kept back a piece of the sample that made its way to the National Museum of

Archaeology so he could run his own test once he got the time. He felt bad about having to outsource a favor, especially when he heard the original results had come back as inconclusive."

"And . . ."

"His results are far more conclusive than our first test. They indicate something really old, in the neighborhood of 20,000 years."

Intriguing as the direction this conversation was taking, Kip felt none of Erin's excitement. That aspect of Strawberry Flats lay far behind him. "So what does that mean for an everyday lunk like me?"

"It means Anders may have found organic evidence pointing to European settlement of North America. It flies in the face of ninety-nine percent of scientists who hold to a view of an Asian migration across the Bering land bridge." Erin paused, as if to further consider the implications of what she was saying. "Look, this is historic. Among other things, Anders may have found the boat."

"The boat?"

"Yes, the boat – well, maybe one of the boats – that some scientists believe were used for crossing the Atlantic during the last great ice age. It's the proof critics have been demanding for years."

"This is starting to sound interesting," Kip said, still divided in his reaction. Should he end this encounter or help her celebrate? As he considered it, he realized he was still in. "First, I think we should toast to your find."

"Our find. None of this would have come about without your skill with hunches and persistence."

"Well, if you insist. I'll be right back."

It took him less than a minute to relieve the office refrigerator of an unclaimed bottle of champagne.

"Do we need to carbon date that bottle to see if it's safe?" Erin said. "I swear, there's a layer of dust caked on it."

"Aged to perfection," he said, popping the cork and filling two coffee mugs. "Now on with the story."

"I've only got a few minutes before I have to be back in the office. So it has to be the short version. But, I've also brought some books for your reading pleasure."

Erin proceeded with an overview of the theory of Solutrean migration, beginning with the prevailing view of the arrival of the continent's first settlers from the seemingly most logical part of the world.

"For the last century or so it was thought the first settlers came through Beringia – the region between Siberia and Alaska. It was land then, not open sea. This has been the basis of what we know of the origins of Paleo Indians in America. Besides archaeologists, anthropologists, geologists, geneticists, linguists, even palynologists have weighed in support of this theory."

"Paly what?"

"Scientists who study pollen and other stuff given off by plants."

"Well, I just learned a new word. We'll have to add it to the *Beacon*'s weekly crossword."

Erin smiled, then gave Kip a sterner, let's stick to business look. Her few minutes of availability were winding down.

"Then, in the 1990s several archaeologists began reassessing the stone tools and projectile points from ancient East Coast sites and they observed similarities with artifacts produced by the Solutreans in what is now southern France and northern Spain.

"Their big moment came when they learned of stone artifacts and a wooly mammoth bone that came up in a haul by commercial fishermen on the Continental Shelf off the Chesapeake Bay in the 1990s."

"That's deep sea," Kip said. "What would they be doing there?"

"Good question. The answer helps explain how the Solutreans could make it to Port City. Proponents of this theory will remind you that what we know as the Continental Shelf was then dry land extending 250 miles from North America."

"So, where does Anders Martin fit in?" Kip asked.

Erin took a deep breath. "Critics of the Solutrean migration – and there are many – fiercely dispute this theory because the projectile points and other artifacts found around the

Chesapeake region can be explained as variations on the tool-making technology of people with Asian roots. Without carbon-based materials to test, Solutrean proponents have had no way of confirming such a dangerous and implausible transatlantic crossing. Their critics say, 'Show me the boat and then maybe we will believe you.'"

"And, I'm guessing no wood or animal skin or human remains have hung around since then for people to date today," Kip said. "That is, until Anders found the traces of a boat embalmed in our wretched marine clay."

"Right," Erin agreed. "Though archaeologists might have more appropriate descriptions than embalming."

Kip didn't want it to sound like a picky press conference question, but he asked anyway. "How do you know what Anders found is a boat and not a hut or some smokehouse?"

"Another good question," she said. "The location of Anders's project on what used to be riverbank and the shape and size of what we took the samples from support this. If there are other artifacts like you mentioned, the experts will find it."

"So, what next?" Kip asked.

"Well, I don't see the Defense Department building at Strawberry Flats any time soon. It could take years to fully investigate the site."

"Just who does all this? Where do you go from here?"

"I am in so far above my head it's laughable," Erin said. "I'm the messenger and will bow out as fast as I can. You are the first person I've told besides Owen Draper. Randy knows only that he analyzed some very old carbon-based samples. This is Owen's specialty, and he will know exactly what to do."

"Do you think he's going to mind being upstaged with the second sample?"

"Hardly. Second opinions happen all the time. Owen knows that. He's a professional and is as pleased by the findings as we are."

"I'm mighty fine with that."

"Why wouldn't you be?"

Kip's face tightened, and he stared blankly to his side as he made sense of his conflicting emotions. He was tiring of being the chipper suitor who got so little in return, especially given their recently decreed limbo of time and distance. He was about to say so when Erin spoke.

"I think I understand, and you don't have to go into it," she said. Again, that gentle demeanor with no traces of defensive snark. But she wasn't yielding any ground, either. "If you must know, this has been painful for me, too. I wouldn't be in your office at this moment unless it was really important, and I believe you'd agree with me on this. If Anders's find at Strawberry Flats is for real, then it's going to be even more difficult for us. I'm sorry."

He understood. Though, in the span of the last five days since she dropped a shoe on him, this understanding continued to hurt. But this show needed to go on, and he wasn't about to ruin it with protestations.

"Then let's move on," he said. "Do what you think needs doing. I'll still be here." He quickly regretted the poor-me wording. But so what?

Before Erin could reply, he turned the topic.

"You probably got an earful the other night from Alf and me about the sale of the *Beacon*," he said. "My life, too, will be changing in lots of ways. Just so you know, I have no intention of giving up on the *Beacon*. One way or another I will be publishing a paper in Port City."

"Well, I will be rooting for you the whole way," she said. "In the meantime, there is something I need to ask of you."

"Ask away."

"It's important that nobody know about the results of the radiocarbon dating just yet. Owen wants to pull together a team tomorrow and secure the site. After that gets done, he can begin the process of informing the outside world. If word gets out before that, there will be no way to protect it from the hordes of people who will descend on Liza's property."

Kip scowled as he parsed the implications of her request. "I'm not so sure why of all the experts on the planet it has to be Owen Draper, but so be it," he said. "But I can just smell how this is going to end."

"How?"

"Owen will go for maximum P.R. He'll hold a press conference as soon as he can put up a fence around the site, or whatever it is they do for things like this. He will want the entire world to hear the news from him. Certainly not the pissant Port City *Beacon*. Once it's out there, there will be absolutely no need for either of us, particularly me."

"You're wrong. Owen would never do that. I'm the one who brought him into this. Besides, he is qualified to deal with this, probably more so than anyone."

"Maybe so, but based on what you just described, you and I are about to become very minor players. The *Beacon* may be small potatoes in his world, but I would still like for it to get its due."

"It's only for a day or so. I'll make sure Owen understands."

Kip had heard enough for one day and his equanimity was fading.

"You do that," he said. "You have no promises from me, other than I will think about it."

FORTY-FOUR

Holy Moly! Kip thought as he plopped back into his office chair. Even though he'd quite bluntly told Erin he would think about it, he knew he would honor her request.

Defaulting to Owen Draper irked him. No way around that. And it wasn't jealousy. It was hard to compete with Draper's global stature and all his books, TV documentaries, and reputation as the go-to source for the media. Someday, someone would portray him in a movie – a real-life version of the proverbial professor-explorer-adventurer. In spite of it all, he found time to help little people. Knock yourself out, Erin.

The current issue of the *Beacon* had closed for advertising and editorial and was almost laid out. Thanks to the efforts of Willie and Calvin, the press would be ready to roll tomorrow. So, with nowhere to be and no demands on his time, Kip decided to read.

The books Erin had left with him easily plugged the gaps in her account of North American settlement. She had done a good job in providing the essential details, and he only glanced at the migration maps, DNA charts, and endless photo galleries of stone artifacts.

Looking across his office, he eyes landed on the still chilled bottle of champagne. Why not? he asked himself, pouring the last of someone's forgotten Moet.

At his desk he began to reflect. Funny, with so much coming to an end, he was thinking more clearly than he had in months. The death of Anders Martin had begun to look like it did a month ago: an accidental drowning. Paul Schultz's demise did, after all, have the earmarks of suicide. And although his romance with Erin Powers had quickly wound down, there was still a trickle of hope. That particular ending had nothing to do with lack of trying. Lousy luck, maybe.

Sipping from the mug with his feet propped on his desk, Kip's mind returned to an aspect of last month's events that still rubbed him: P2.

What began as an exploratory trip to J.D. Bushrod & Son had quickly become an archaeology story layered on to a wild homicide goose chase. P2 wasn't even off the drawing board and already it had split Port City into two camps: those who stood to gain by it and those who saw an affront to the city's heritage and quality of life. Lately, the gains far outweighed the losses.

Thanks to Randy's tenacity with the radiocarbon tests, Anders was about to get the last laugh. It was too bad he went to his grave unaware of the storm that would be unleased on historians.

Then, with a miserable, sinking feeling, Kip remembered another part of the whole shebang that hadn't gone away. Get your legal house in order, Jake Johnson had advised him. His stitching together of two deaths, a fire, and an extended squabble – in the Chief's mind, anyway – had made Kip the nexus. Johnson was basically warning Kip that he was on the verge of becoming a dreaded POI, person of interest.

Even though he knew he was ridiculously in the clear, Kip decided he would consult with Colbert Jenkins in the morning.

From his vantage point on square one, Kip wondered who knew more about what was going on, him or Johnson. Kip was willing to bet he did, or Johnson would have done something by now. It also told Kip that the chief nonetheless had suspicions that he, too, could not get to the next stage.

As an investigative reporter who occasionally got stuck in blind alleys of inquiry, Kip knew he had to think the unthinkable to learn the unknowable. What he did think, if not know for sure, was that Paul Schultz hadn't killed Anders Martin or set fire to the Beacon Building.

Yet, in the grand Port City Venn Diagram, the only people

overlapping with Schultz and Kip were Ambrose Ralston, Melvin Alexander, and Miles Tennyson. Ralston and Melvin he had already cleared. Well, mostly, anyway, for his cousin. But there was Erin which was preposterous.

Shit, shit, shit. Kip barked. It couldn't possibly be her. He never tasted the last of the champagne as he fought back the notion of Erin's involvement in Martin's death. He must eliminate her, one way or another. People knock off their bosses because they can't stand them, not because they covet their position. Besides, how could she pull off a murder on the frigid Potomac River and in the dark, no less. That would require a boat and knowledge of the club's rowing routines. Had she any maritime experience, he would have heard about by now. From all he knew of her, especially from Helen Martin, Erin practically worshipped Anders. Plus, Kip prided himself a good judge of people. You've got to think the unthinkable to eliminate the undoable, he concluded.

That left Miles Tennyson and his labyrinthine business dealings. Kip decided not to go there, not yet. This was all getting too tiring. He would skip calling Colbert Jenkins in the morning and instead contact Chief Johnson. Enough was enough, and in the meantime he would keep on reading.

He was surprised when he checked the time – well past 7 o' clock. He had been so engrossed in Erin's books and parsing reality that Ben Bailey's "Good night, Boss" an hour earlier had only partly registered. The building had that late-night silence where every creak of settling timbers and gurgle of plumbing reverberated throughout the townhouse. Port City nightlife was getting underway, but the building's thick brick and stone walls muffled the cacophony outside. Even after a lifetime spent at the *Beacon*, Kip never fully grew used to the peculiar quiet of after hours.

From his drawer he pulled a manila file folder with all his notes and clippings from the past month and he began sorting them until he came to Joe Patel's coffee-stained photograph. The high-contrast color image of Anders Martin's arm and its bloody triangle still puzzled him.

The phone rang, and Kip yelped with fright.

Nobody had remembered to set the phone system to auto-answer mode for afterhours. Every phone in the building rang simultaneously, echoing throughout the building. It would be a great day for the *Beacon* when it upgraded to dedicated lines, Kip groused as he answered the call.

"Good, you're there." It was Erin.

"And I'm glad it's you and not my maker," Kip said, explaining the mausoleum acoustics of the building. "I must have left my cell phone in the print bay after you texted me this afternoon. What's up?"

"I talked with Owen after I left your office. He understands your concerns and says we can easily work out a way for the *Beacon* to have first crack at the story."

An hour earlier, Kip had figured Draper for a selfish ass. While it didn't entirely please him, Erin's news eased his reluctance to cooperate.

"People sure are hard to read," he said. "How do we go about this?"

"We can meet you at your office in an hour."

"Works for me. Tell the big man to bring the bubbly – I drained the last of ours."

In the sixty minutes remaining, Kip continued with his amateur archaeology studies.

FORTY-FIVE

Erin and Owen arrived at the same time. She had the look of someone coming straight from work – slightly wrinkled blouse hastily tucked into her slacks, a light go of makeup and brush run through her hair. Draper looked ludicrously fresh – as though he'd stepped on to the set of one of his film documentaries. His cargo pants and double-pocketed khaki shirt made about as much sense as a tuxedo at a bluegrass club.

"Thanks for agreeing to see us on such notice," Draper said. "This is an extraordinary moment in time, wouldn't you say?"

Without answering, Kip gestured to the couch and two chairs. Erin and Kip chose the couch and Draper stood.

"You're right, it's like nothing I've ever been through," Kip said. "But, speaking for the *Beacon*, you need to know we are free to pursue this story any way, any time we want. That's the way we've always operated and always will. Our options are open."

Kip felt foolish. Dishing out bravado from the valley of his old couch to the suavely eminent figure standing before him was stupid and off putting. A look of mild annoyance flickered over Draper's face and then faded as he placed his index finger along his nose as if assessing the wisdom of Kip's declaration.

"I see," was all Draper said, as though that put the matter of the news embargo to rest.

"Just what do you see?" Kip asked, wondering if this would be the world-record for the slowest start to an argument.

Draper set his leather-trimmed briefcase at one side of a chair and took a seat. He was the kind of tall that when he sat, his thighs angled down from his knees to his lap. With a hand on each knee, a posture Kip took to signify full engagement, Draper issued a sigh so patient and weary that it made Kip feel as though the man was going far out of his way to deal with such elementary perceptions.

"I see," Draper said, exhaling, "that we need to have an understanding of what it is we want to accomplish today – and, of course, going forward." He delivered that age-old bureaucratic icebreaker with such forbearance that Kip had no doubts about who in his office thought he was most mature and, by extension, in charge.

"Kip . . ."

Before Erin could fully intercede, Draper relented.

"I believe I understand where you are going with this," he said with less condescension. "Would it address your concerns if we accord first-among-equals treatment for the *Beacon*? Say, be a part of the announcement team, knowing you will be well ahead of your competitors in terms of information?"

Whatever, Kip thought. Draper's offer allowed for that while elevating the *Beacon*'s status. So why not?

"Sure, that works for me," he said.

Erin sighed. Draper relaxed back into his chair. Had he not felt so pissy in the hour leading up to this meeting, Kip would have gladly scurried around the corner to the deli for celebratory snacks. Now he was happy the meeting was underway, civilly, and he intended to nudge it to a conclusion as fast as he could. Maybe he had to respect Draper for his conference skills, but he sure didn't have to like the man.

Yet Draper had more earnest bromides to issue.

"I can tell you I only want what's best for the field of archaeology," he said. "You, I assume have your own high standards of journalism."

"I've been accused of worse," Kip said. "And you propose what?"

"Nothing, really. You have been such an integral part of this discovery that you should have a say in the timing of its announcement," Draper said.

"The timing, but not the content. Is that what you mean?"

"How could it be otherwise, Kip?"

Again, that weary air of patience from Draper. Oh, the favors you do for me, Owen, slowing down for pokey old Kip. Kip held his tongue, preferring to let Draper exhaust his supply of arrogance so they could get a real conversation underway. He'd already assented to the embargo, but he wanted Draper to know that steamrolling him at every turn was going to be grueling for all parties. It was an approach that worked about half the time in his stickier interviews. When this tack failed, however, relations tended to get frosty quickly, often ending interviews before they began. Kip was certain Draper wanted to be a part of this discovery so badly that he would eventually ease up on the pomposity. Soon, they could all bow out of each other's lives.

Draper obliged Kip's reliance on experience.

"You've had a rough couple of weeks, haven't you Kip?" he said amiably. "Hopefully you will be able to draw enough favorable publicity from this to put those troubles behind you."

"Not likely for a while, as long as there are loose ends to sort out," Kip said.

"Loose ends? Such as?" Draper asked.

"Not to air all my laundry, but I've got a board of directors on the warpath, an angry chief of police upset with me over Paul Schultz's death, and stuff like this," Kip said, handing him Joe Patel's photograph of Anders Martin's wounded arm.

Draper winced.

"What is this – or rather, who is it?"

"Anders Martin. That's all anyone knows. I'd say it's a mighty unnatural looking wound on his arm."

"Where did you get it?"

"Let's say I liberated it from a city official."

"You naughty boy. No wonder you were so good at investigative reporting."

"Not good enough, evidently."

Until this moment, Erin had been only observing the elastic interplay between the two men. Taking the photo from Draper, she began studying it.

"You know, thanks to your water-color coffee treatment, I'd swear that cut now looks like an arrowhead," she said, tracing the diamond shape with her little finger. "Could Anders have been trying to say something in his last moments?"

Nobody said anything. The trio stared with dawning realization. Pipes may have gurgled behind the building's walls and timbers creaked with the cooling of evening but nobody heard a thing. Erin slowly placed the photo on Kip's conference table. Still, no comments from any of them.

Kip's mind reeled so intently with realization that he barely heard Draper's question.

"You knew about this photograph, Erin?"

His accusatory tone caught Erin off balance, as though she had been withholding important information that she was required to report.

"I, uh, suppose so," she said. "Kip showed it to me when he first got it. Neither of us could make sense of it at the time. Why do you care whether I'd seen it."

Erin seemed to care even less for Draper's question than Kip, who silently cheered her pushback. As the final piece of the puzzle was falling into place, Kip recognized that he would greatly need Erin's support or, at least, not having to fight her on what he was about to do.

"I believe I can answer that for you, Erin," Kip said, hoping he sounded calmer that he felt on the inside.

Draper no longer exuded languid composure and confidence; instead, he sat bolt upright, clasping the arms of the chair. "And what is there to answer?" he asked of neither in particular. "We're supposed to be discussing a press announcement."

"That's what I thought, too," Kip said. "But I'm coming to believe we're now working with an even larger story."

He had the stage and wasn't about to yield it – too much had come into focus to lose it to diversionary conversation.

Up until the last few minutes, Kip had pegged Draper for one among a legion of ruthless bureaucrats in Washington. At a certain level, the town practically ran on the excesses of competence, charm, and ambition. Journalists weren't entirely immune from the Washington syndrome, but they did have good front-row viewing of the spectacle. Kip thought he'd seen it all until Draper came into focus. But where to begin articulating this horror show?

Running his fingers through his hair, Kip plunged on.

"The wound on Anders's arm doesn't say anything new," he said, "but it does put matters back on track. Anders did die for his discovery. In his last moments, he knew the process of elimination was his only hope for justice."

Kip didn't wait for any tell-tale signs of comprehension from Draper. Still, from the corner of his eye he could see his face reddening with fury. Erin, on the other hand, hadn't betrayed any reaction.

"All along I was trying to figure out who stood to gain the most by P2 and from Erin's discovery," he continued. "Anders's bloody last words reverses that to who stands to lose the most."

Erin leaned forward.

"I can understand someone wanting P2, as well as I can see someone wanting the Solutrean site to stop it," she said. "But how does Anders's message figure into this?"

"If I'm right, Anders knew who his killer was and his diagram was an attempt to tell the world why he died," Kip said. "His violent end connects with all the other events since – suicide, arson, the whole nine yards of my month of bad luck."

"So, what should our next move be?" Erin asked.

For the shortest moment Kip considered telling her that'd back her out of the entire matter as fast as he could. Then he realized he didn't need a firestorm similar to the one he caused the first time he'd met her.

"Good question. I'm tired of pounding my head against the wall on this. Jake Johnson can have it."

"You're giving up?" she said. "That's not exactly your style."

"Not really. I'd rather preempt the Chief now with what we know, instead of him coming after his only person of interest. This calls for more competency than I've got. Two heads, so to speak, will be better than one. So, I will be calling him first thing in the morning."

Draper tensed, and Kip knew he'd hit the right nerve. The archaeologist quickly confirmed his observation.

"Now, why would you want to go and do that?" Draper said. "I thought we'd agreed that your problems in all this were unsolvable."

My problems? Kip thought, resenting the accusatory tone.

"No, we had not agreed on anything," he said. "I only told you what was on my plate, and it was looking inscrutable. But Erin's good eye with the photograph puts everything back on track."

"How so?" Draper asked.

"It would be a safe bet that it all begins and ends with paleo archaeology," Kip said. "A money-hungry person from the business community never had anything to do with any of this."

As soon as he said that, Kip knew he had crossed a threshold. He prayed his jangling nerves would not betray him in the minutes to come.

"Well, Owen, maybe you can help with the answer," he asked as evenhandedly as he could. "Who else in the archaeology world even knows a thing about Anders's discovery?"

"You tell me," was all Draper said.

The first pebbles in a landslide were now tumbling down.

"Three," Kip said. "You, Erin, and I. Liza Bushrod only knows Anders had a dig going on at her property. Randy only knows that Erin presented him with a very old carbon sample."

The air in the office had the charged stillness of an approaching thunderstorm. When nobody said anything, Kip proceeded.

"Call me whatever you want, but I can tell you I've got no dog in this hunt," he said. "Erin has been aboveboard and in plain view the entire time. So, unless you can give me a plausible explanation, I've got a phone call to make."

"Kip," Erin said sharply, "What are you saying?"

"Owen can answer that."

"And I have no intention of doing so," Draper said.

"Then let me," Kip said.

FORTY-SIX

Knee-deep in a rhetorical flashflood, Kip waded further in search of some form of confirmation of his suspicions.

"All along, Owen, you've resisted Anders Martin's work," Kip said. "You outright dismissed his project at J.D. Bushrod & Son. You never checked it out. Then Erin's sample accidentally falls into your lap and, coincidentally, the results turn out inconclusive. Then another sample turns up, and it's not just positive, it's historic. You're knocked off balance and it's almost out of your hands. But at least you not only get to orchestrate the response, you can share in the glory – if you choose to do so."

Kip rose from the couch and took a deep breath. He recognized Draper's pissed-off look. In his early days of reporting, it had scared him to see realization wash over a smug and powerful government official as an investigation reached the end stage. For a short while, the denouements even amused him. Eventually, he took them in stride. Watching Draper squirm, however, felt exhilarating, especially after the hell of the last month.

"Ever since this business at Strawberry Flats began, I've been trying to figure out what's in this for you," he said. "Sure, I was the one who suggested Erin seek your advice in the first place. Silly me."

"Do go on," Draper said, spitting out each word one at a time.

"I did my homework this evening before you arrived," Kip said. "Erin kindly lent me some books on North American settlement. Sure, I learned a lot about the Clovis People and the Solutreans. But I learned a whole lot more about the rivalries and feuds in your field. Most of it is healthy. Then there were the hardcore cases."

Erin jumped from her chair, shaking with agitation. "Kip, what do you think you are doing? Owen deserves more respect than this."

Kip had forgotten the professional bonds between Erin and Draper. Maybe he was going to have to fight Erin as well. He would know soon enough.

"That's what I used to think, Erin. Now, I'm not so sure. You see, our good friend Owen Draper has a dark side to his rise through the ranks of archaeology," Kip said. "I should have picked up on it when you said he'd offered you a chance to head a field office somewhere. Yeah, somewhere as far away as possible.

"I normally skip over footnotes. But a doozie in one of your books led me to an online treasure trove at the National Museum of Archaeology. Your would-be benefactor has been at the heart of every recent controversy surrounding archaeological discoveries and developments there. Unpleasantness befell anyone who crossed swords with Owen. Those he couldn't fire or outright ruin, he had transferred, demoted, or whatever it took to preserve his precious programs and their funding. Hell, Owen, *Modern Archaeology* magazine reported that you were even censured for closing down a program that that turned out to be a big deal in advancing the field. And to think, I didn't even know what to make of it all until now."

Erin sat back down, stunned with apprehension.

"And what the fuck does this have to do with anything?" Draper barked. Gone was his charming TV persona.

"Everything," Kip said. "Until this moment, I had figured you for a basic power-hungry Washington type. No more, though. Erin and I couldn't figure out how Anders really died. For a while we even thought Paul Schultz was behind his death. And he thought I was out to finish Anders's work on P2 which, in a strictly professional way, was correct."

Erin rose again and said, "I've heard enough. I'm leaving."

"Sit down, Erin," Draper said. "It appears your boyfriend is too smart by half and it's going to cost you."

"Wh-what do you mean?" she stuttered.

"It's simple," Draper said. "I don't need some lame P.R. scheme for the *Beacon*. Turning to Kip, he said, "You are right, nothing gets in my way, at least for long. Those people you say I dealt with so badly got the obscurity they deserved."

"And then along came Anders Martin," Kip said. "I assume he didn't fit the mold of your hapless, green researchers. Anders had been around the block. But even he made mistakes, and trusting you was his biggest. When he came to you for help, you tried to dismiss him, and when he didn't go away easily, you tried to string him along – probably with hollow promises like you tried on Erin."

"Owen, is this really true?" Erin asked.

"Yes, unfortunately for the both of you," Draper said calmly. "Now, we're going to do something about this. Good thing I came prepared."

Leaning over, Draper reached into his briefcase and pulled out a hard, yellow plastic pistol. Kip lunged at Draper, but not fast enough. The gun roared an awful booming sound and Kip found himself writhing on the floor like a fish hauled onto the deck of a boat. Erin screamed, and got the same treatment. The blow from the electric stun gun sent her reeling out of her chair and onto the floor.

They regained their senses after a few moments to find that Draper had slipped handcuffs on their wrists. Rope held their feet fast.

"Fuck you, ass . . ." Kip stopped in mid curse when Draper leveled the gun between his eyes.

"You learn fast. In case you are wondering, you got an easy dose. I can do much more with a higher setting. You have to wonder why everybody doesn't have one."

Kip knew stun guns well enough in principle. They had been part of his editorials on gun control. Everyone should not have one. Imagine if every traffic dispute and barroom conflict got solved like this.

Erin pleaded, "Owen, tell me this is some kind of mistake. Surely you know we never meant any of this to happen."

"Not a chance," Draper snapped. "You two could have thrown the towel in at any time instead of interfering in matters where you could really get hurt. This is no misunderstanding. Now, not another word."

"Kip, I'm so sorry . . ." Erin cut short her apology when Draper swiveled the gun in front of her face.

"That's better. I'm glad we're in agreement. I must compliment you on the acoustics of your building – nobody will ever hear us. We are going to be here awhile, as long as it takes to figure out what to do with you two," Draper said. Wagging his gun, he continued. "So let's learn to get along, and that means only I can talk and you must listen. One word, one sound – you know what to expect."

Silence again consumed the building. But neither Erin nor Kip could tell. The ringing in their ears was fierce. They had no options in the matter. Bound hand and foot, they sat on the floor, propped up against the office wall. The handcuffs cut into their wrists unless they constantly shifted positions. But shifting their positions put new pressure on the ropes around their ankles.

As painful as the cuffs and ropes were, Draper's endless drivel was worse. Kip lost track of the litany of "undeserving idiots" who had the misfortune to antagonize Draper. The best he could tell, all were good, hard-working professionals done in by this master psychopath.

He had mostly tuned out Draper until he heard him mention Paul Schultz.

"Weren't you wondering about your old nemesis? Don't even open your mouth."

They could only glare.

"Poor Paul. He made a big mistake when he confided in me about his financial troubles. And when he did that, I knew he was mine, since I had the means to help keep his creditors at bay," Draper said. "Once I threw him a bone, Paul Schultz became your very worst enemy. He never knew how Anders Martin really died. But Paul knew Strawberry Flats needed to be paved over which made him my insurance policy. Whenever you two got close, all I had to do was remind him of what a little bad publicity would do to his relationship with his client, and he would go into action."

Draper was sitting on the edge of Kip's desk, with his feet dangling. "When Paul refused to try his hand at arson, I had to step in. It was easy. You really should get better security around this place, Kip. All I had to do was give your back door a hard shove and I was in. It's a shame your cozy little operation didn't completely go up in flames.

"Unfortunately, Paul grew a conscious and made the mistake of telling me about your upcoming meeting the next night. It wasn't hard to get him to meet me to discuss matters. We took a trip to one of his townhouse projects and, well, you know how effective this little device can be."

Kip tried to picture Schultz's last minutes. Dazed from the stun gun, he must have stumbled around his partially completed building until one last blast allowed Draper to fit a noose around his neck and maneuver him on to some kind of platform. No muss, no fuss, and certainly no clues. That's when Kip's public relations nightmare began.

Kip lamented that if he'd only had the smarts an hour ago in his office, he could have notified Jake Johnson or written a note or emailed somebody – just in case. But, no, he had to verify his accusation beyond a doubt, and now he and Erin were about to pay the ultimate price for his stubbornness. There was cruel irony in having pieced together Draper's game plan: It never mattered that Draper hadn't found Anders's dig. All that remained to be seen was how he would dispose of them. Judging from Paul Schultz's demise, it was not going to be pleasant.

Draper lapsed in a long silence where minutes seemed like hours. Kip could hear the gentle ticking of the grandfather clock in the corner of the room. Somewhere far off in the building, a faucet intermittently dripped water. When Draper finally stirred from his chair, Kip started.

"I haven't answered your question about Anders Martin," he said. "Yes, you are right. Anders was no pushover. The man would not listen to reason and abandon his quixotic quest. I used my skiff that I keep at the marina to capsize him back in February. The poor creature-of-habit made it so easy. He always was his own man and wouldn't row with the pack. Once he went over, he had two choices. He could climb back onto his swamped shell and risk dying on the freezing trip ashore. Or he could hop aboard my boat. Anders made the wrong decision – he couldn't swim fast enough to catch up with my boat. I'm told hypothermia is painless. Which I suspect will be a better departure from this earthly life than either of you will enjoy.

Draper sat in Kip's desk chair, swiveling to face his computer and keyboard. His fingers quickly tapped away for a minute. Then he waited for the printout. When it slid out, Draper studied it carefully before setting it under a paperweight in the center of Kip's desk.

"That should do the job nicely," he said.

He checked his watch, smiled, and faced Kip and Erin.

"Let's go."

FORTY-SEVEN

"The keys to your van."

Withholding the keys held no chance of success. With the stun gun pointed in his face, Kip quickly ruled out any chances of pleading ignorance. All he could hope for was for something to go wrong with Draper's planning during their drive to wherever they were going.

"Top right drawer," Kip hissed.

"Good man, Kip," he said. "I can see you understand how much easier this will be without creating unnecessary complications."

"Fuck you, asshole."

"Hmmm. The last time I heard that, you were sporting a black-eye for a week," Draper said, kneeling down next to Kip and Erin. The sharp shove of his gun in Kip's ribs sent pain rippling throughout his body. When Kip did not reply, Draper said, "That's better. I'd rather finish this task my way."

He loosened the rope on their ankles and said, "On your feet. Remember, there's enough power in this device to make you wish you had never been born."

Kip regretted the convenience of his coveted off-street parking space behind the *Beacon*. If instead he had to circle three or four blocks each time he wanted to park at the *Beacon*, tonight he and Erin might have a chance of attracting attention.

Draper opened the sliding door of the van and told them to get in. It took him less than a minute to retie their ankles.

Although they could see nothing from the metal floor of the

van, it was easy for Kip to sense their destination from the few turns made by the vehicle. He wasn't surprised to see the boathouse when Draper slid the door open.

Only a rower would know how deserted the boathouse would be late at night. All the members were deep in slumber, alarms set for a few hours from then. Draper punched in the four-digit security code on the entrance door.

"Quickly now," Draper said.

Even if they had wanted to move quickly, Kip and Erin were too stiff and sore. Draper prodded them through the door and past the racks of boats. With one hand on his gun, Draper pulled on the chain of the twenty-foot high door to the dock over the river. Outside, the pungency of the Potomac hung thick in the air. The last flights in and out of Reagan Airport had ended an hour earlier, leaving the area so quiet the lapping water below actually sounded loud. At least as loud as Kip's heartbeat.

He had no idea of what to expect of Erin in such harrowing circumstances. Until now, Erin had only glowered at Draper. Not once did she complain or whimper. There on the dock with all looking hopeless, her body language spoke to defiance and determination. In that instant, Kip knew he could never have really let her go.

Draper sat them down, tying Erin's feet to Kip's so that they faced each other.

He was all business. "Do not try to move."

Kip could not tell if Draper was enjoying this. One thing was for sure, they couldn't move if they had wanted to.

Erin broke the silence when Draper disappeared into the darkness of the boat bay. "I'm so sorry, Kip, I had no idea he was such a monster."

"If anybody should be sorry, it's me. Draper was right – I could have backed off this farce at any time," Kip stammered. He was barely aware of how much his body was shaking. Only speaking seemed to subdue his terror. "I am the one who needs to apologize, and that doesn't make us nearly even."

"Can we do anything?" she whispered.

"So far, no. I don't know about you, but I've been waiting for something to go wrong. Or, maybe that he would change his mind. Yelling seems to be all we can do."

"I wouldn't do that if I were you." Draper stood over them, holding the handle of large metal pull cart.

Kip didn't think his body had any adrenaline left to scare him further, but the sight of red plastic gasoline cans stacked three high, four deep on the wagon jolted him to the core. The coaches used the fuel for their launches. It didn't take much to figure out what Draper had in mind.

"You guessed it," Draper said.

He took the cans from the cart and situated them in a tight circle around Kip and Erin. There were so many that he had to stack several of them.

"There, that should do it," he said. "Now, for some insurance."

Draper took the keys to the handcuffs and placed them on the dock far enough that neither Kip nor Erin could reach them. "Whoever finds you will think you intentionally placed the keys out of reach to make sure your murder-suicide succeeded."

Hands on his hips, Draper continued with his monologue.

"Kip, you couldn't take the pressure of losing the *Beacon*. You callously drove Paul Schultz to his death. And, of course, you could not abide the Defense Department coming into Port City. Worst of all, having Erin spurn your advances pushed you over the top. Your suicide note on your desk back at the office says it all. Brilliant, Kip. If only you had thought of this yourself, you could have saved me all this trouble."

Draper took the cap off of a can and began dousing them with gasoline. The fuel felt cold as it evaporated into the night air. But not fast enough. The stench seared their nostrils, forcing them to cough and gag.

"Your van will be out front of the building when your would-be rescuers arrive. But I will be long gone, Draper said."

He leveled the gun at Erin and dealt her a massive round of volts. No noise this time. He had disabled its audio scare feature. Erin yelped and slumped sideways. He next turned the gun on Kip and fired. Kip felt a trillion suns exploding throughout his entire body. Unlike Erin, he did not immediately lose consciousness. The searing ache and visual fireworks in his eyes told him he was alive, but fading. The last thing he heard before slumping forward was one last BOOM.

FORTY-EIGHT

When his eyes came back into focus, the first thing Kip saw was a soldier dressed in black. He was shooting him, and it felt good.

"Easy, there, buddy. It's all over. You're going to be okay. Can you hear me?"

The soldier, he slowly realized, was a Port City S.W.A.T. member and his gun was a hose and the cold water rinsing the horrid gasoline from him really did feel good. Another had done the same with Erin. He still couldn't talk. Just that damn shaking. Only now he was shaking with relief and not fear. Erin looked in better shape.

"*Ughrrrn . . . ughrr . . . duhhmmm.*"

Erin's gentle laugh was the nicest sound he had ever heard. "You wouldn't be at a loss for words, would you?" Erin said. "Don't worry, a couple more minutes and you'll be chattering away."

Kip doubted that. Yet the woman had been zapped by a power plant, and still she has her sense of humor.

Life, sweet life, gradually returned to Kip. He knew so by the headache. But at least he could look around now, and the sight jolted him. Police and firefighters were everywhere. Kneeling next to him, Patrolman Eric Sullivan gave up waiting for Kip to recognize him and put his hand on Kip's shoulder and welcomed him back to the living.

"Close call, Kip. We didn't think to follow you here until it was almost too late. But it looks like you and your friend are going to be okay. Which is more than we can say for the other guy."

Sullivan nodded with his head to another section of the dock. For a moment Kip stared uncomprehendingly at the shrouded black mound that flickered in the blue-and-white emergency lighting of a harbor patrol boat. Then it dawned on him. It was Owen Draper beneath a tarp.

"What happened?"

"The asshole was one second away from lighting all that gasoline. His big mistake was pointing a gun at an officer of the law. I doubt he ever knew what hit him."

So that was the boom Kip heard. How close to death could he and Erin have come?

"EMS will be taking you to Port City Memorial for evaluation," Sullivan said. "Two healthy young people like you and your friend, it should be routine. Detective Washington will ride with you to the hospital and ask you a few questions. And I imagine you will have a few questions – he can fill you in. Sorry I can't give you a ride this time."

As Sullivan retreated through the bay, two EMS technicians, followed by Bernard Washington and Jake Johnson, approached. Johnson spoke first.

"Are you sure you haven't got anything you'd like to tell me, Kip?"

FORTY-NINE

"There's nothing like dying and living to tell the tale," Kip said.

He and Erin were well into a mountainous buffet breakfast at the Regal Restaurant, trying to make sense of the last twenty-four hours. The few customers remaining from the Regal's morning crush were oblivious to the newsmakers in their midst. Their light banter was shifting into confessional high gear.

"Well, it felt like dying," Kip continued. "I thought I was done for when Draper's gun sent me into the next galaxy."

Erin raised her eyebrows.

"Okay. I didn't see the great white tunnel. But, I will say, coming to on the dock didn't exactly feel like heaven."

"So, what were your last thoughts?"

"Easy one. I wish I had asked the locksmith to fix the front door."

"Oh, come on. Try a little harder."

"If you must know, it was nothing cosmic – I was worried who'd take care of Ike and Samantha."

"Good answer. Not the one I was hoping for, but not bad."

"And you?"

"I was glad Owen didn't hand us final cigarettes."

"Riiight."

"I don't know about you, but I was in a lot of pain from those damned ropes and handcuffs," she said. "The gasoline had me gagging. But when he pointed that gun at me, all I could think about was us."

Kip should have expected such a serious moment in their

breakfast. Having stared death in the face hours earlier, he recognized their initial burst of levity for what it was: a way to diffuse effects being zapped that the emergency room doctor had cautioned them to expect. Erin evidently was back in a more serious mode.

He topped off their mugs with the last drops of coffee in their carafe. "Us?" he asked.

"I was surprised at how much thinking I could get done before I got my first tour of your boathouse," Erin said.

"And . . ."

"Let me finish, Kip. I've made my share of mistakes in life. Who hasn't? Some I could overcome, others not. But when Owen pulled the trigger, I knew I had made my biggest mistake ever last Friday on that park bench."

She wound her hand through a mound of dishes and newspaper until she found Kip's hand. He winced when he saw the scrapes and bruising peeking out from the sleeve of her shirt.

When he started to say something, she put a finger to her lips and said, "Shhh, please.

"I never once stopped liking you. Not once. Not before Friday and not after Friday. It's . . ." she blinked back tears and struggled for the right words. "With so much going on around us, I chickened out, plain and simple. I am so, so, very sorry. It won't happen again, if you will have me back."

The spigot opened, and tears flowed – over the freckled ridgeline of her high cheeks, along the contours of her face, and off the prettiest jawline Kip had ever seen. In all his newspaper interviews, not one crier had gotten to him, not even a sobbing Congressman. In Erin's watery contrition, however, he saw the turning point that he had dreamed of and prayed for since he met her.

His face turned grimly serious and he ran his fingers through his hair.

"You know, I will have to think about this. Okay, I've thought about it," he said with a lopsided grin. "Do you remember when I said I wasn't going anywhere? I meant it. Welcome back, Ms. Powers."

Tears of a happier sort fell, and Kip reached across the table with a napkin to dab at the flow.

"I don't know about you, but it's been a long twenty-four hours for me and I cannot possibly eat another bite of food," he said "May I suggest repairing to my place?"

Erin winked. "But what about Alf?"

"He's gone to a restaurant show in Baltimore till this evening," he said. "Nobody there but us and the two chickens."

"Well, then, big guy, what are you waiting for?" she said.

FIFTY

The earth did not shake when Kip and Erin finally hit the sack. Curtains may have swayed and doors banged. But that would have had more to do with the speed in which they both fell into deep, unstoppable sleep. They were still entwined when Kip's cell phone began ringing.

"Are you going to get that?" Erin asked groggily.

"Why didn't I turn that off?"

"Too late now. Someone really wants to talk to you."

"Okay, okay," Kip mumbled as he chased the phone around on his bedside table. Late afternoon sun streamed through his bedroom window, though he wasn't sure what day it was.

"Yes, this is Kip. Who does? When?" he said, and then unenthusiastically, "Okay, in an hour."

Seeing Erin glower at him, he amended his answer. "Make that two hours."

"Two hours for what?" Erin asked when he rang off.

"That was Jake Johnson's office. He wants to see us. His assistant said something about tying up loose ends. Yeah, I know – poor choice of words."

"Two hours?"

"Yes. Two hours. So, we better get a move on it," he said, taking Erin's face in his hands and began a kiss that lasted longer than their first atop Port City.

The earth shook this time.

FIFTY-ONE

As they signed in at the police department two hours later, Kip had a decidedly different opinion of the place from his last visit. The clustered cliques of uniformed and plain clothes police officers, support staff, and other city workers stopped in mid-conversation to get a look at the cause of all the activity from the previous night.

"Word gets around fast," Erin said.

"Word starts here," Kip said.

The long walk down the fifth floor corridor ended at Johnson's corner office. The big bear in a blue uniform greeted them in the doorway. Kip expected the visit to be a formality or Erin would not have been invited. Nevertheless, he would have been surprised if Johnson didn't wrestle explanations from him about his behavior over the past month.

Rather than having them sit in front of his landfill of a desk, Johnson pointed them to the conference table.

"So, you are Erin Powers," Johnson said, extending his hand to her and then to Kip. "I can't say I've heard a whole lot about you before this, but that ought to be changing soon. First, tell me how did you ever fall in with this guy?"

"Ace reporter here found me," she said with a laugh. "If it hadn't been for Anders Martin, Kip and I would still be going our separate ways."

"It's true," Kip said. "Like they say, even a blind squirrel finds a nut every now and then, no pun intended."

"Speaking of Kip's good fortune and lousy humor, I guess you two know how lucky you are to be here at this moment," Johnson said. "We only increased patrols around the *Beacon* after your fire. We hadn't formally staked it out.

"Eric Sullivan saw the three of you getting into the *Beacon*'s van. The oddness of Draper at the wheel didn't register at first, and Eric drove on. But when he saw the van later on Market Street, he decided to follow you. When he saw you getting out of the van at the boathouse, he definitely did not like what he was seeing and called for backup. If it had taken any longer for him to get the boathouse access code from headquarters, you two would be toast by now. I think you know how things played out after that."

"We do. We do," Kip sighed. "I can't begin to tell you how grateful we are."

"Probably not," Johnson said. "But for starters you could begin by filling me in on the rest of your sorry saga."

Given the chance to tell Johnson about what he had held back the week before, Kip plunged in eagerly. He and Erin took turns recounting the last several weeks. When they'd finished, Johnson whistled. "That explains a lot, but it doesn't explain holding back on me."

"It's not like I wanted to," Kip said. "There was nothing to go on. Only wild guesses. And this did begin as a story for the *Beacon*, after all. And I did write some stories, too."

Johnson did not look particularly impressed with his answer. However, that topic had been exhausted, and Kip was relieved when the chief moved on.

"In the future, let's try to be a little more forthcoming," he said. "You might be interested to know what we've learned about your good friend, Owen Draper. If you haven't already figured it out, Erin, he would have made a lousy employer."

Johnson leaned forward with his elbows on the table. Kip could tell this was going to be interesting.

"As it turns out, he had more of an illustrious past than even Kip was able to uncover. The FBI has been monitoring him for possible involvement in stolen artifacts. Wherever he worked, priceless items had a way of disappearing. They would get signed out for shipment to museums, traveling exhibits, laboratories – you name it – and some invariably failed to arrive or return. The paperwork was precise and flawless which made it nearly impossible to track.

"His modus, as you found, Kip, was to pin the blame on subordinates whenever concerns were raised. The genius of it was, they were never accused of anything shady. Only incompetence. Much grayer and certainly as damning."

"So, what did Draper do with the stolen stuff?" Erin asked.

"There's a ready and willing black market around the world for Indian artifacts," Johnson said. "Unlike a stolen Rembrandt or Renoir, a pot or vase is obscure and untraceable. Not that black-market collectors care about such things."

"That would explain Draper's deluxe lifestyle," Kip said. "He must have meant it when he told Paul Schultz that he could hold back his creditors."

"That and the income from his documentaries. The Feds will be crawling through his bank and financial records this week," Johnson said. "We'll know soon enough how much wealth he accumulated."

"But why would Schultz have gone along with Draper on that scheme?" Erin asked.

"It happens all the time," Johnson answered. "Most likely, Schultz feared the risk of his mega-client getting wind of his financial situation. It probably began innocently enough. They both had their reasons for seeing P2 get built and then one thing led to another, and Schultz was bolted tight to Draper's scheme. Schultz had no idea of the type of person he was dealing with, and when he tried to back out, he found out."

Kip frowned, and Erin asked what was wrong.

"We'll never know how that oar broke during our practice race in March," he said.

"What oar?" Johnson asked. "What are you talking about?"

"Oh, nothing – really," Kip said, regretting that he may have already reignited another fuse. "An oar broke in our race against

Algonquian's boat club and I've been curious ever since."

Johnson looked hard at Kip and then turned to Erin with a wink of his eye.

"I can't possibly see you involved in anything like this again, even if you do choose to hang around this character," he said. His smile disappeared when he looked back at Kip. "You, Kip, are a different matter altogether. Will you spare me from having to spell it out for you why I don't want another conversation like this?"

Rising from the table, Johnson didn't wait for an answer. Their meeting had come to an end.

FIFTY-TWO

Thanks to the spectacle at the boathouse, life in Port City got upended.

In the day following Owen Draper's attempted murders, police of all manner swarmed the boathouse. As soon as one group left the premises, another arrived. A unit from the F.B.I. even got in the act and left probably as bored as their predecessors. As crime scenes went, this one was pretty basic.

At an unscheduled meeting of the boat club, the steering committee accepted Kip's plea to relinquish his duties as communications coordinator. Not only was the crush of media requests for interviews overwhelming, the *Beacon* had to contend with its own coverage of Strawberrygate, as the affair had been nicknamed. Orchestrating the details of the paper's coverage fell to a most willing Ben Bailey. "Holy shit, Boss, you're a goldmine of news," he told Kip.

So many film crews, researchers, academics, archaeologists, and everyday gawkers descended on the city that the police department cordoned off entire blocks to assuage annoyed residents. Kip gladly honored his promise to Katherine Tisdale at the *Post* for first dibs on the story. Neil Ford at NPR was on deck for an interview far more interesting than he would have had a week earlier.

Mouse and Liza decided to donate their land to Port City for use as conservation- and historic-oriented parkland: trails, picnic areas, wildlife viewing stands but no water parks and other facilities that would infringe on the archaeological research soon to begin there. With the tax write-off of so much urban acreage, Mouse was set for life.

Overnight, the former junkyard had the makings of a travel and professional destination. After the chamber of commerce and the convention and visitors bureau got over the shock of the Defense Department's withdrawal, they considered the multiplier effect of so much economic activity and smiled.

So many events in such a short period of time did not come without consequences for Kip or Erin.

Over drinks on the trellised veranda of the Lee Street Pub, they reported on their two most important encounters. The evening was balmy, and the lights in the overhead latticework illuminated yet another overflow crowd. A weeknight, they still had barely gotten a table.

Kip looked up from his menu, and there stood Glynda Barnes resplendent in a tight navy polo shirt and khakis shorts. With her loft of blonde hair piled high on her head, Kip remembered one of the better parts of not being immolated. The soft kick under the table brought him around.

"Kip, Erin – I am so very glad to see you. Whatever you want tonight is on me," Glynda said.

"Thanks, Glynda – just drinks tonight, unfortunately," he said. "I'd love to take you up on your offer another time. How about when the boys come in for happy hour next week."

"In their dreams you can," she said. "What'll it be, hon?"

They ordered their usual, a red wine for Erin and a beer for Kip. Glynda faded into the crowd with their orders, and Erin laughed.

"Did she call you hon?"

"Yep," Kip said. "That's when you know you've arrived in this joint. Now tell me about your meeting with the city manager and the mayor. Was it as bad as you thought it would be?"

"Any time you get called in by Ed Gettys and Ethel Wilson for a talking-to is not good," she said. "I knew that sooner or later I would have explaining to do. I was fully expecting to get the boot for the less than transparent way I'd gone about my work at Liza's."

"I tell you, you need to work in the private sector," Kip said. "There are so many more ways to get roasted – by the public, boards, families, advertisers, you name it."

"Maybe, but not this time," she said. "In her infinite wisdom, Mayor Wilson decided to look the other way. Gettys is my immediate boss, so he didn't have much choice at that point. Apparently, public response to Strawberrygate has been so overwhelmingly positive they declared all my actions as having occurred off-duty with no city employees or assets involved."

"Way to go," Kip said.

Erin beamed and blew on her finger tips in exaggerated confidence.

"So there I was, scared for my job and all along those two were worried about losing me," she said. "When they had fully digested the hurricane of unwanted publicity that Draper brought them, the AMA moved heaven and earth to minimize his damage and maximize the good work of its archaeologists and anthropologists. When they offered me the position of Special Field Director at Strawberry Flats, Gettys and Wilson thought they were out of options. They offered me their best – permanent directorship of the city's archaeology program."

"And?"

"And I leapt at it. Community archaeology is why I came here in the first place."

Glynda arrived with their drinks and a generous tray of unordered hors d' oeuvres that she deposited on their table. She departed quickly before either could protest.

"Who are we to argue with generosity?" Erin said.

They clinked glasses, and Erin asked about Kip's board meeting from earlier in the day. "Did Melvin even show up?"

"Damned right he did," Kip said. "It was the most uncomfortable meeting I've ever attended. It was astounding – after all that's happened, Dorothy and Stephen still wanted to unload the paper. They weren't nearly as miffed with Melvin for maneuvering behind their backs as I thought they would be. In the end, they needed him for the deciding vote."

Erin smiled and motioned for Kip to hurry along his telling of the boardroom drama. "And what did they have to say about Alf?" she asked.

"That was the best part. They didn't know he was coming And when he walked in fifteen minutes late, they went ballistic, screaming every objection under the sun, each one shot down by Colbert Jenkins.

"It never came to a vote," he continued. "But, my God, the air in there was absolutely poisonous with resentment. It was the first time they had walked out before Cass and me."

"And you've still got a job and the return of an adoring readership," Erin said. "So, what does it feel like?"

Kip took a long sip from his beer and thought.

"It's not entirely pleasant. I feel like a rehabilitated Soviet dissident – relieved, ambivalent, and low-grade paranoid," he said. "At least that's the way I feel today. My hunch is my cousins will always be cranky and eccentric, but hopefully in less harmless ways."

"What more could you wish for?" Erin asked.

FIFTY-THREE

Kip liked a party as much as the next person, maybe more. Though in recent years he'd gotten pickier about where he chose to spend several hours in earnest discussion, mindless chatter, and the continuous repetition of what had gone on his life lately. He'd concluded that after a certain age parties came with telling prefixes hinting at watered-down fun – cocktail party or dinner party.

"When somebody says they're having a party party, then that's when I get interested," Kip told Erin.

"I'd say you're either regressing or you're getting mighty nostalgic in your old age," Erin said.

"We'll see in a minute."

They had arrived at J.D. Bushrod & Son, where Liza and Mouse were throwing a party to celebrate the sale of their entire inventory to a buyer in the far Maryland suburbs. Their e-vite did betray a prefix, a Hello/Goodbye Party, which did not dampen Kip's expectations.

It was a classic late-June evening, sweltering and breezeless yet still early enough in the summer for people not to be yearning for the next change of season. Whether a thunderstorm would crash the party remained to be seen, since nearly every day's weather report called for a chance of late-afternoon showers.

Taking in the smell of barbecuing food, the pulse of a nearby band, swarms of people, and the sensuousness of a summer evening, Kip declared the party a party.

"Will you look at that," Erin said. "This can't be Port City."

Mouse must have worn out his forklift rearranging dozens of vehicles at the near end of the lot to create a grassy semi-circle large enough for a small rock concert. On one side of the circle, he'd cleaned out the trunks of three of his finer sedans and crammed them with ice and beverages. On the other side, rowers from the boat club worked a bank of charcoal grills laden with chicken and burgers. From atop a wheel-less flatbed, Calvin Perkins and three other Dizzy Gillespies cranked out a good rendition of the limbo rock.

Kip pointed to the center of the grassy lot and said, "If I didn't know better, I'd say that's Jake Johnson and Jeff Benson working the limbo stick over there."

"I don't know how you can tell without sunglasses," Erin said. "That Hawaiian shirt of Jake's must be battery powered. There's your friend Glynda. She shouldn't be allowed around a limbo dance."

Glynda Barnes, with Joe Patel at her side, was lithely scooting under the bar. Kip appreciated Erin's assessment, not that he agreed with her prescription. Behind them was a wide swatch of Port City society that Kip easily recognized. He also noted who was most not in attendance – his cousins. They'd bitch the whole time, anyway, he thought. Ambrose Ralston may have come, but Kip didn't see the big man in the limbo line or in the line to kids' hillside waterslide. Nor did he see Miles Tennyson, not that a party would have appealed to him.

Kip and Erin fell in behind Willie and Alma Carter for a go at limbo. When their time came, Kip could have sworn Johnson and Benson lowered the bar on him. Erin made it under, but he did not. With an oomph he landed flat on his back, another victim of gravity, for which he got no sympathy from the queue behind him.

After eating, they moved on to another area of the party, where a group of rowers was gathering around Bo Hanson. The men's competitive A and B boats had finished first and second in the Stonewall Regatta that morning, and instead of their regular happy hour, the team agreed to merge it with Liza's bash.

The nervous rec rower who filled in the B boat seat left

vacant by Paul Schultz performed admirably earlier in the day, and for his efforts, the team was offering up a toast. Hansen delivered it.

"On behalf of the drinking club with a rowing problem, we'd like to welcome you to our group," he said. "I assume you know what you're getting into. But should you ever begin to think too highly of your skills, the women's competitive group with us tonight can set you straight. Cheers!"

Manny Vargas redirected the conversation to Erin. "So, newcomer, what do you think after three months of hanging around this motley bunch?"

Erin pursed her lips and feigned bewilderment at the magnitude of such a tough question. Slowly scanning the group, she said, "It's too soon to tell. At first, I thought you were all certifiable – what with your early hours and fanatical training. But, I'm not so sure, now that I'm able to see the better half of this group."

That brought round of cheers from the women.

"So, I will have to hang around and see what the future brings," she said.

More laughing and clapping. Then Dana Parsons held up her hand.

"There's only one way to find out, Erin, and that would be on Monday morning," she said. "I couldn't possibly inflict the men on you, but I would bet the women here would gladly take you out for a row."

Erin immediately consented. "I would like that, really, if you all don't mind my having been volunteered," she said.

"Hell, yeah! You're on," a woman yelled.

From atop the flatbed truck, electronic screeches sounded from the Dizzy Gillespies's speaker system. Once Calvin had the feedback adjusted, he turned the stage over to Liza.

Microphone in one hand and the other on her hip, Liza looked like she belonged in front of a crowd. The sun, which was slipping below the horizon, added to the golden glow cast on her face by the torches and party lights.

After welcoming everybody, she said, "Our little enterprise here at Strawberry Flats is about to enjoy a new life. Nothing pleases Mouse and me more than to see J.D. Bushrod & Son become home to a renowned research center. None of us wants to look back too closely, since what is done is done. But in keeping with the theme of Hello/Goodbye, we need say a few hellos and goodbyes.

"First, we would be horribly remiss if we didn't take this moment to acknowledge the person not here tonight but who fought, single-handedly at times, for the future of Port City. Anders Martin would not tolerate such a show of affection, but thanking him is our prerogative.

"For the last several months we thought we'd be saying goodbye to Helen Martin. Helen, however, has decided that Port City is indeed her home and she will not be moving to Colorado. I know the art department at a certain high school will be grateful to see her this fall. To Helen, we say thank you and hello."

Those who knew Helen, and there were many at the party, cheered heartily. From the edge of the crowd, she and her two daughters waved.

"To Alf Kilpatrick, younger brother to our good friend, Kip, we say both hello and goodbye, since it seems like he just got here. Alf grew up here and was a fine friend to my late husband. He now has a good home and family in Australia and we wish them all the best, though we expect to see the entire family here on his next visit."

Rising from a bus seat he was sharing with Cass and Hank, Alf raised his cane.

"We have neither a hello nor a goodbye for our next person," Liza continued. "But we do owe a big thank-you to Kip Alexander. I guess when you run a small town newspaper right, there are few barriers between you and your readers. We've all been hard on Kip at times, but he would be the first to tell you a thick skin comes with the job. But beneath that thick skin lies a north star of a big heart by which he has always steered. If he didn't, we wouldn't be here this evening, and our town would be a darker place. Thank you, Kip."

Short and sweet, but nowhere near short enough, Kip thought as the crowd applauded and cheered.

"And I am saying goodbye to a way of life I happily married into and swore to myself to maintain as long as necessary. With the handoff of our property to a worthy organization, I can now say hello to my former career at the World Bank. But Port City will always be home for me, and even more, I am sure, for Mouse. Party on!"

Liza hopped off the truck, concluding the only formalities of the evening. With that, the Dizzy Gillespies took to the stage again.

Further into the evening, sitting on a pair of bucket seats removed from an immobile Miata, Liza and Alf sat catching up on the last several years. Seeing them, Kip and Erin located Cass and Hank and brought them along. "Mind if we join you?" Kip asked.

"Not at all," Liza said. "Pull up that limousine seat – it should accommodate you fine.

"Alf has been telling me about his life Down Under," Liza continued. "It's too bad you can't take some of this stuff back with you, Alf."

"Ha, in some parts of Australia, these seats would be considered luxury appointments," Alf laughed."

"What time is your flight tomorrow?" Cass asked.

"6:30. In the morning," he said. "Way too early."

Kip shifted his position on the seat and took a pull from his beer. "I know I said it before, but thanks again for everything, Alf," he said. "The *Beacon* was a goner without you."

"The pleasure was all mine," Alf said. "The look on Melvin's mealy face alone made the trip worthwhile. After that, your Agatha Christie caper was frosting on the cake. But now you and Cass owe me."

"Name it," Cass said.

"Ditto," Kip said.

"I expect to see you all in Melbourne next year," Alf said.

"And that includes you, Erin. As a matter of fact, Kip, don't come without her."

"Deal," they said in unison.

"Will you look at that," Liza said, pointing toward the flatbed truck. "Who would have thought to see the likes of Jake Johnson, Glynda, Benson, and all those crazy rowers in a conga line? The kiddies hardly stand a chance."

Kip set his bottle down and said, "Well, you know what Harry Bellefonte said?"

Silence.

"Jump in de line. Let's go."

In the near distance, lightning flickered brightly.

FIFTY-FOUR

Saturday night's thunderstorm rolled through Port City, rinsing it of accumulated pollen and rendering lawns and trees a brighter shade of green in the morning. The air, clear and cool, sparkled with freshness.

The Potomac appeared to be making the most of its day of rest. Its surface, mirror flat after the storm, rippled every few minutes as a passing boat left a kaleidoscope of colors in its wake.

In a single shell, a rower pulled rhythmically on two oars, sending it pulsing south beneath the arches of Wilson Bridge and into Heron Bay. Pull, slide. Pull, slide. Pull, slide. He savored the zen joy of a solo row on a perfect morning. All that registered was the cobalt blue sky above and the pliant water beneath.

For a brief moment in time, all was right in Kip Alexander's world.

THE END

NOTES ON DEADLY STROKE

In this complicated and messy world I have enjoyed the luxury of being able to live and work where I choose. For close to thirty years, Alexandria, Virginia, has been such a place. Like the Port City of *Deadly Stroke*, this city of 130,000 residents does indeed boast history, architecture, and an increasingly enhanced waterfront. Its six-mile proximity to Washington, D.C., also provides it with an exceptionally diverse and talented population base – just the stuff for any writer. Alexandria is also a growing municipality, and its more caring citizens do have conflicting but valid views on how to accommodate this growth while preserving what has made it so extraordinary. I encourage readers to visit Alexandria online (www.alexandriava.gov) or, better yet, in person.

Depending on your sources, it's possible to trace the origins of Alexandria's oldest continually publishing newspaper, the *Gazette-Packet*, to at least 1784. Unlike the Port City *Beacon*, the *Gazette* had multiple owners before its current life as the *Gazette-Packet*; though, I hope, none as dysfunctional as in the fictional version. To this day, the weekly paper faithfully and competently chronicles life and death in this colonial-era town.

Alexandria definitely enjoys a rich archaeological and anthropological heritage. Most gratifying is the value the residents of Alexandria place on its past and the passion with which the city's archaeology department pursues and preserves it.

Visit www.alexandriava.gov/archaeology for more information.

My fictional foray into the Solutrean thesis of American settlement is not all that farfetched. Researchers in recent years have discovered what they believe is evidence of settlement in North America by inhabitants of northern Spain and southern France thousands of years before the arrival of Asians. If so, then it's possible these settlers could well have made their ways up the Potomac to Alexandria. I recommend two books. *Across Atlantic Ice: The Origins of America's Clovis Culture* by Dennis Stanford of the Smithsonian's Museum of Natural History and Bruce A. Bradley of the University of Exeter make a most readable case for Solutrean settlement. David J. Meltzer of Southern Methodist University in his book, *First Peoples: Colonizing Ice Age America*, offers the more accepted, traditional view of North American settlement as well as a rebuttal of the Solutrean thesis. Fortunately, these two schools of thought have not risen to the level of contention that play out in *Deadly Stroke*. Which is not to say archaeology has never had colorful and bitter rivalries. I suggest looking into the nineteenth century Bone Wars surrounding the discovery of dinosaur fossils in America.

The sport of rowing – from solo shells to the sixty-foot eight-person boats – is all and more in what I have written in *Deadly Stroke*. For fitness, camaraderie, aesthetics, and pure competition, rowing rivals any sport. The club for which I rowed for ten years, Alexandria Community Rowing, is among the best of the East Coast clubs. And like its counterparts across the country, it welcomes newcomers. There's always a seat for anyone interested in trying out the sport. ACR and many other clubs participate in Learn to Row Days which provide a free, on-water introduction to rowing. For a view of the high end of rowing, I recommend the current bestseller, *The Boys in the Boat* by Daniel James Brown and *The Amateurs* by the late David Halberstam. Both books explore Olympic rowing – the pinnacle of this amateur sport. Then take in a regatta for firsthand exposure to these athletes and their boats.

ACKNOWLEGEMENTS

I am deeply indebted to my many friends and colleagues who encouraged and advised me at every step of the way. Any flaws or shortcomings are mine alone.

Numerous members of Alexandria Community Rowing in Alexandria, Virginia, provided essential insight and encouragement. Special thanks to former Olympian, coach, and fellow rower Jaime Rubini and boat mate Russ Bailey for their readings of my manuscript. Archaeologist Heather Hembrey's expertise spared me countless technical embarrassments. With her firm and gracious approach, book editor Alice Rosengard worked wonders on a perfectly raw manuscript. You know you've got good friends when they spare their scarce time to read a work in progress. Thank you, Jennifer Barnett, Elizabeth Beard, Maureen Hannan, Jonathan Hayward, Richard Hayward, Virginia Kulajian, Phyllis Lange, Walter Nicklin, and Kathryn Potter. I'm deeply indebted to my good friend Jeanne Clemente Kelly for her wonderful design of *Deadly Stroke*'s cover. To my toughest but most loving critic I owe my greatest thanks and appreciation throughout this long haul, my wife Polly Lange.

ABOUT THE AUTHOR

Philip Hayward is an editor and writer living in St. Mary's County, Maryland, downstream from Alexandria, Virginia, where he lived for more than thirty years. He has been a staff editor of *Air & Space/Smithsonian*, *Mid-Atlantic Country*, and *Lodging* magazines. As a competitive rower with Alexandria Community Rowing, he medaled numerous times in sweep 8s and 4s and competed in the prestigious Head of the Charles River in Boston (although, unlike his protagonist, he never came close to winning it). He is a member of the Maryland Writers Association. *Deadly Stroke* is the first in the Kip Alexander series. Look for *True Stroke* in the near future.

Contact the author: philiphaywardbooks@gmail.com

Visit his website: http://www.philiphaywardbooks.com